For Chynna

'*Dreams, you know, are what you wake up from.*'
– Raymond Carver, *Cathedral*

Also by Jason Starr

Savage Lane

JASON STARR

NO EXIT PRESS

This edition published in 2015
by No Exit Press,
an imprint of Oldcastle Books
PO Box 394, Harpenden,
Herts, AL5 1XJ, UK

noexit.co.uk
@NoExitPress

A CIP catalogue record for this book is available from the
British Library.

ISBN
978-1-84344-681-1 (print)
978-1-84344-682-8 (epub)
978-1-84344-683-5 (kindle)
978-1-84344-684-2 (pdf)

Typeset in 11pt Palatino
by Avocet Typeset, Somerton, Somerset
Printed in Denmark by Nørhaven

For more information about Crime Fiction go to @CrimeTimeUK

1

AFTER THE DINNER party at the Lerners' new 2.6 million-dollar house in Bedford Hills, Mark Berman knew that his wife, Deb, was pissed off at him about something. He had no idea what he'd done, but after twenty-two years together – seventeen married – he didn't have to ask her if there was a problem. He just knew.

During the car ride home to South Salem, Deb was still acting weird, but Mark knew if he said something it would lead to a whole discussion, even a fight, so why go there? Instead he went on about the Lerners' house – 'Can you believe the size of that backyard? The freakin' Jets could play there. And the pool was sick.' – and then went over the schedule for tomorrow: Deb would take Justin to his swimming practice at nine, and he would drive Riley to her school play rehearsal at ten on his way to play golf at the country club, and then she would pick up Riley at noon on her way back from swimming. As he was talking, Deb nodded, said, 'Okay,' a couple times, but that was it.

A few minutes later they were driving along the dark, twisty Saw Mill River Parkway, and she was staring out the window, not saying anything. Sick of the silence, Mark turned on SiriusXM to the Classic Rewind channel – the chorus of 'Dream On.'

Then, after maybe thirty seconds, Deb, still looking out the window, said, 'I saw you.'

'What?' Mark had heard her; he just wanted to hear her say it again.

'I saw you,' she said.

'You saw me,' he said, not as a question. 'You saw me where?'

Looking out at the window, at the darkness, or maybe at her reflection, she didn't answer.

'I don't know what the hell you're talking about.' Actually Mark did know, but he didn't want to say it himself. If she wanted to say it, make an issue out of it, let her.

'You know what I'm talking about,' Deb said, turning toward him.

Though he was looking at the road, not at her, he knew exactly what expression she had – that one where she squinted and her nostrils flared and she looked like she wanted to rip his head off. Yeah, he'd seen that look a few hundred thousand times.

'No, I don't,' Mark said. 'I have no idea, okay?'

She turned away again.

Steven Tyler was screeching the chorus. Mark lowered the music, and said, 'I don't get this, you know? Everything's cool, we have a good night together, out with friends, and then out of nowhere you have to launch into me.'

'How'm I *launching* into you?'

He didn't like the way she'd said that, like she was mocking him. 'It's weird, okay?' He squinted because the guy driving toward him had his fucking brights on. 'I mean this whole attitude of yours is weird. It's like you're looking for drama, like you *want* drama.'

'*I* want drama?'

'Like right now,' he said. 'Like the way you're repeating everything I say. You know it annoys the hell out of me, but you keep doing it anyway. It's like you get off on it or some shit.'

'I think you're the one causing drama in this marriage.'

'*What*?'

'I saw you, okay? I saw you.'

'Saw me?' He pretended to think about it. 'Saw me where?'

'Outside... in the backyard.'

There was no use denying it anymore. 'Oh, come on. Is that what this is all about?'

'I'm so angry at you right now,' Deb said.

'Nothing happened with Karen, okay?' Mark said. 'I can't believe you're actually accusing me of something. It's so ridiculous.'

Karen was a neighbor, a friend, who'd also been at the Lerners' dinner party.

'You were holding her hand,' Deb said.

'I was not holding her hand,' Mark said.

'You were holding her hand,' Deb said.

Mark let out an annoyed breath, shaking his head. 'I was not holding her hand, okay? Maybe we held hands for like a second, but –'

'It was longer than a second.'

'A few seconds, whatever, but it was totally innocent, okay? We were talking, just talking, and she was upset, you know, she's been having some financial trouble, that investment advisor fucked her over, and I was gonna put her in touch with my guy, *our* guy, Dave Anderson. That was who we were talking about – Dave, Dave Anderson.

Anyway, she was upset, and I was talking to her about it, giving her some advice, that's it, okay? And, yeah, maybe at one point I may have held her hand, just in a like friendly supportive way, but –'

'In a friendly supportive way,' Deb said.

'There an echo in here?' Mark asked.

'Look, I know what I saw, okay, so stop denying it. You were having a moment.'

'*What*?'

'It was what it was.'

'It was a conversation about mutual funds.' Mark made a sharp turn, too fast, around a bend. He had to be careful, there was a deer crossing around here, wasn't there? Then he slowed a little, and said, 'I can't believe I'm even talking about this right now. Karen's a friend, that's it.'

'Friends don't flirt the way you two always flirt.'

'*What*?'

'Can you watch the road?'

'I can't bel... I was helping her with a situation, okay, I wasn't flirting with her. You want to talk flirting, how about you and Tom?'

That was the way – put it on *her*.

'What about me and –'

'You flirt with him all the time.'

'When do I ever –'

'I even saw you hugging him tonight.'

After a pause, Deb said, 'You mean when I was saying *goodnight*?'

'You were hugging tightly,' Mark said, glad they weren't talking about him and Karen.

'Oh come on, that's –'

'Yeah, ridiculous, I know. But what if I tried to make a big production out of it? What if I was like, "How could you flirt with Tom? You were having a moment? How could you do that"?'

'Don't try to deny what you did,' Deb said.

'I'm not –'

Raising her voice to smother his, Deb said, 'I didn't go off with him to a corner of the backyard, okay? If I did, what would you think? Would you think that was normal? Would you think, "Oh, Tom and Deb are just good friends, that's why they slipped away together to be alone"?'

'Are you drunk?' Mark asked.

'What?' Deb sounded shocked, but maybe she was just pretending. 'No, I am not drunk.'

'You sure? 'Cause you're acting drunk right now.'

'I had a couple of drinks.'

'You had more than a couple.'

'Look, I told you how I feel about you, you and that woman, but you don't seem to care. You just rub it in my face.'

'Karen is our *friend*. Since when is she *that woman*?'

'Since she started trying to steal my husband.'

'Oh, for god's sake, Deb, will you stop it? It was just holding hands –'

'So you admit it.'

'For a couple of seconds, for a couple of seconds, for god's sake.'

'It was more than the hand holding, okay? It's everything between you two. It's the way you look at each other, at dinner it was so obvious. And when you were telling that joke and Karen got up to go to the kitchen you waited, you *waited* till she came back to finish it.'

'It's called being polite,' Mark said.

'You wouldn't've waited if *I* left the table, or if anybody else left it. It was because of her. You waited because of her.'

11

'No, I waited because she hadn't heard the joke yet, you had, and she was interested, so I... Listen to you, just listen to you. Attacking me, launching into me 'cause I was polite when I was telling a joke, like I committed some kind of crime or something.'

'You know exactly what I'm talking about, okay?' Deb said. 'You won't stop, you just keep doing it, because you want to do it, because you... I don't know, you want to get a reaction from me or something, and you make it so obvious. I don't think you get how embarrassing this is to me.'

'What do you mean?' Mark looked away from the road, at Deb, for a second. 'Somebody said something?'

'No, nobody said anything, nobody had to say anything,' Deb said. 'But everybody saw it, everybody knows, and I'm sure they suspect something.'

'Suspect what?' Mark raised his voice. 'This is fucking ridiculous. Nothing is going on with me and Karen. Nothing at all!'

'I want you to stay away from her,' Deb said, 'or I'm going to say something to her.'

'*What*?' Mark's hands squeezed the steering wheel as if he were trying to strangle it. 'Can you just cool it, okay? This is getting out of control.'

'Why do you care?' Deb said. 'I mean, if nothing's going on, if it's all my imagination, what difference does it make to you?'

'Because she's a friend, she's our neighbor,' Mark said. 'Our kids are friends with her kids and... and you better not say anything, please don't do that. It'll just create drama. You don't want drama, do you?'

'I don't want to talk about it anymore.'

'Don't say anything to her, Deb. *Please.*'

'I said I'm done,' Deb said.

She said it in a loaded way, as if maybe she wasn't just done with the conversation, she was done with the whole marriage. Mark knew it was just an empty threat, of course. She was always getting melodramatic in arguments, then forgetting about it the next day. This would blow over too – well, it had better blow over. If she said something to Karen, confronted her in some way, Karen would freak, feel uncomfortable, and maybe would want to cut him off. Mark couldn't let that happen. Karen was one of his closest friends, probably his best friend; he didn't know what he'd do without her.

Rush was into 'Tom Sawyer' but Mark, not in the mood for music anymore, shut off the radio. Ah, finally, it was silent in the car. A few minutes later, they veered onto Savage Lane, a narrow road with seven houses along it including the one at the cul-de-sac where Mark, Deb, and their kids lived. Karen and her kids lived in the second house on the left and as Mark drove by he noticed – without actually turning his head to look – that the light on the second floor in Karen's bedroom was on. Karen had left the party about ten minutes before Mark and Deb, so it figured she was home already. Mark wondered what she was doing in her bedroom, if she was getting undressed, watching TV, or if she was on the phone, talking to that new guy she'd been dating. What was his name? Steven? Yeah, Steven. Mark hated the name Steven; it reminded him of Steven Litsky, a cocky kid in his sixth grade class in Dix Hills on Long Island, who had bullied him, making his life hell. Thinking about Karen and Steven, *this* Steven, talking on the phone, Mark felt a pang of nausea, jealous nausea, which was ridiculous, because what did he have to be jealous about? Mark was married – maybe not completely happily married but, yeah, solidly married – and it was true that he and Karen were nothing more than friends. They had a connection, a *special* connection, but it wasn't anything more than that. Still, when he thought about her with Steven, or any other guy, he always felt that pang.

With the remote, Mark opened the garage door, then pulled in and cut the engine. Without a word, Deb got out and slammed the door and went into the house. When Mark got out, Casey, their golden retriever, came over to greet him, jumping up on him, panting excitedly, swiping his chest with his paws.

Thinking, *Well, at least somebody isn't mad at me,* Mark said, 'How ya doin', Casey? How ya doin', boy? How ya doin'?'

Casey, still breathing heavily, trailed Mark into the house.

Karen's kids, Elana and Matthew, were over. Elana, like Mark's daughter Riley, was sixteen, and they were hanging out in the living room watching a movie, something with that teenage girl actress Mark had seen before on TV and on the covers of magazines, but he could never remember her name. Matthew was ten, two years younger than Justin, but they'd always played well together, and they were up in Justin's room playing on the Xbox, Call of Duty; Mark knew because he heard the intermittent machinegun fire and explosions.

'Hey girls,' Mark said.

'Hey,' Elana and Riley said, without looking away from the TV.

Then Elana asked, 'My mom home yet?'

Mark saw Deb, who was looking through a pile of mail on a table in the foyer, give him a look right before she exited into the kitchen.

'Um, should be,' Mark said.

'I better go,' Elana said, getting up from the couch.

'FaceTime you later,' Riley said, still staring at the TV.

'Cool,' Elana said, then called upstairs, 'Matthew, we gotta go!'

'I think it'll take more than that to get him away from that game,' Mark said.

'Yeah, you're right,' Elana said as she went upstairs.

Mark went up too and went into his bedroom and shut the door. Then he texted Karen: **Great seeing you tonight! Hope you got home safe, sweetie.**

Mark texted with Karen all the time, especially since her marriage had ended. He texted with a lot of his friends too, but it was somehow much more fun to text with Karen. Maybe it was because they had the same sense of humor, they *got* each other. When he read some interesting article online, or something funny happened at work, Karen was always the first person he wanted to tell. He usually made sure to delete his texts to her, especially the ones where they called each other 'sweetie' or sometimes 'babe,' knowing that if Deb found them she'd get suspicious.

Mark stripped to his boxers and then washed up and got ready for bed. He knew he looked great for forty-four. He was losing some hair from the top and around the sides, and he probably needed to lose ten, okay fifteen, pounds, but he was definitely aging well, just starting to hit his prime. If he was single now, on those dating sites like Karen, man he would've cleaned up. How many guys his age even had hair? He didn't have a lot of wrinkles and a couple of women at work had complimented his eyes. What had Erica McCarthy, in HR, said? Oh, yeah, that he had 'a dark, brooding Javier Bardem look.' The comment had gone straight to Mark's head even though he had to Google Javier Bardem to make sure he knew who he was.

Mark looked out the bathroom window; too bad it was June and there were so many leaves on the trees. Even though Karen lived a few houses away, in the winter Mark could see part of her house, including one of her bedroom windows – once he'd seen her naked, which was amazing – but now he couldn't see anything.

His phone chimed – a text arrived from Karen: **Yep thanx gnight!!**

He always loved getting texts from Karen, even when they were munutiae. He responded, **Awesome babe xoxox**, then deleted the entire thread.

In bed, he watched TV – a little *Sports Center*, part of a rerun of *The Office*, and then some guy doing standup on Comedy Central. Mark worked his ass off all week as a Systems Analyst for CitiBank, sometimes staying at the office in Manhattan late, not getting home till nine or ten, and his favorite thing to do at night was to sit on the couch or lie in bed and stare at the TV. It didn't really matter what he was watching – sports, talk shows, sitcoms, reality TV – as long as it didn't take up too much brain energy. He used his brain all day, managing trading systems on three continents, so when he was home at night, and especially on weekends, the last thing he wanted to do was think too hard. He just wanted to stare, zone out, disappear. He liked movies, but they had to be funny or have action, no period bullshit. Deb once took him to some Jane Austen movie and it was freakin' painful, and he said to her afterwards, 'No more period movies – period.' And reading, that was the worst. Mark didn't get why people liked reading, why they wanted to spend their free time, concentrating, staring at words in a book. Jesus, why not lie on a bed of nails or get in a bath with a bunch of rattlesnakes while you were at it. Okay, maybe if you're a teacher or you were in school, if you *had* to do it, but in your free time, for *pleasure*? Deb always had a stack of books next to her bed, went to book club meetings – god knows why. Talking about books and having to spend time with those yentas? The only books Mark read were on the stock market or sports, but even those were sometimes painful to get through. He didn't want to feel like an idiot, though, so Mark had read one book about fifteen years ago, *The Firm* by John Grisham, because he'd liked the Tom Cruise movie. The book was worse than the movie but now, whenever he was at parties or at work meetings, when somebody asked him if he'd read any good books lately he said, 'You ever read *The Firm*? That was pretty good,' and it was enough to get by.

Mark had heard a flush from the kids' bathroom and music in Riley's room, so Riley and Justin were probably getting ready for bed. Deb hadn't come upstairs yet, but this wasn't necessarily because she was still angry. She usually hung out downstairs late at night, watching TV or reading, and downing a nightcap or two.

The comedian was talking about his divorce, making fun of his ex, and Mark laughed out loud a couple of times, and then he remembered Deb in the car, saying, 'I'm done.' It had definitely been a fake threat. She'd told him just last month, 'We're stuck with each other, let's face it,' and that was pretty much how he felt. Even when they were fighting, or just not getting along, things weren't *so* bad. There was no violence or major problems. They had a good, comfortable life – a big house, country club membership, two healthy kids, some money put away, no debt. What more could you want? Yeah, maybe the sex wasn't as good as it used to be, but it wasn't bad. At least they still did it a lot – at least a few times a month anyway, which was more than a lot of couples Mark knew. But, most importantly, they were good parents. Riley and Justin were great, happy kids and, as far as Mark was concerned, things with Deb would have to become unbearable before he'd ever seriously consider putting his kids through the pain of a divorce.

But, just for the hell of it, Mark imagined what it would be like if Deb hadn't been joking – if she really did leave. He'd played these 'what if?' games before; it was just harmless fantasizing. If his marriage ended, Mark knew he'd wind up with Karen. He'd move into her house, and the kids could go back and forth, right on the same block, how convenient would that be? It would be an easy divorce, there wouldn't be any bitterness or drama; everyone would get along. It would be even better for the kids because they could be step-brothers and sisters with their best friends. Meanwhile, not only would Mark be with his best friend all the time, he could have sex with his best friend. Karen had looked so amazing at the club last summer wearing bikinis at the pool. How many women her age, forty-two, with two kids could pull off a bikini? She had perfect natural breasts and the sexiest arms and back. Oh, and he loved her lips. What would it feel like to kiss her? He knew she'd be incredible in bed; she had to be. Holding her hand tonight, her skin had felt so warm, so smooth; he bet her whole body felt that way. What if she was in bed with him right now – in that little blue dress she wore tonight; no, in the bikini, yeah, the bikini. They would've just got back from the pool, still wet. He'd kiss her – god, those lips, the way the lower one was thicker than the upper so it seemed like she was permanently pouting – and feel her smooth toned arms, her smooth fatless back, and then he'd undo her bikini top and let it fall off and then cup his hands over her breasts, feel her nipples harden against his palms. Then they would be in bed, he'd be on top of her, untying her bikini bottom, and licking the insides of her thighs, listening to her moan – *Mark, Mark, Oh, Mark…*

'Mark.'

He'd been masturbating under the covers, but it was dark in the room, the only light coming from the TV. Just in case, he shifted onto his side.

'Yeah?' he said.

'Were you sleeping?' Deb asked.

'Um, yeah, just starting to.'

'Can we talk for a sec?'

Maneuvering again, he said, 'Yeah, sure.'

Still in the dress she'd worn to the party, Deb sat at the foot of the bed, and said, 'I just want to say sorry for the way I acted in the car. I had no right to jump down your throat like that.'

Mark could smell rum.

'Never mind,' he said. 'It's no big deal.'

'No, it is a big deal,' she slurred. 'I know we haven't been getting along lately, but I don't really think anything's going on with you and Karen, and I won't talk to her, so you don't have to worry about that. I just… I just don't wanna be like this anymore. Seriously, I don't wanna be like this. D'you wanna be like this?'

Mark imagined licking the insides of Karen's thighs. 'Can we talk about this tomorrow?'

With the remote he flicked off the TV. It was pitch dark in the room now.

'Let's go away somewhere,' Deb said. 'A trip, just the two of us. The kid's're gonna be away at camp in July, let's plan something. We never went to Italy. We said we wanted to go to the Amalfi Coast someday, let's just do it, let's go for two weeks, have a real adventure together.'

Imagining how frustrating it would be to go away for two weeks and be so far from Karen, he said, 'Let's think about it.'

'That's what we always say, but we never go. Why not just do it?'

'We already paid for the country club for the summer,' Mark said.

'We always pay for the country club,' Deb said. 'I'm talking two weeks, just two weeks. Come on, the kids're older now – this is it, this is someday.'

'I've got that big project next week,' Mark said, 'people in from Hong Kong.'

'That's next week,' Deb said. 'I'm talking about *July*. Will you look online with me tomorrow? Can we look *together*?'

Just to end the discussion Mark said, 'Okay, fine, we'll look, we'll look.'

'Thank you.' Deb leaned over Mark and kissed him, and then she felt him through the blanket and said, 'Ooh, I guess you really *are* excited about Italy.' She sat up again, turning her back to Mark and said, 'Undress me.'

More disappointed than excited, Mark unzipped Deb's dress. Then she stood, kicked off her heels and wriggled until she was naked. A few moments later, she was in bed with him.

'Kiss me,' she said.

Mark kissed her, tasting rum. He couldn't stop thinking about Karen in her wet bathing suit. He imagined pulling the knot off the bottom, how it would come right off.

'Kiss me like you want to kiss me,' Deb said.

Mark continued kissing her, using more tongue, tasting more rum. He closed his eyes, imagining he was kissing Karen. His hands would be on her ass – her smooth, firm ass.

Then Deb got on top, but it was Karen. How would it feel to have Karen on top, riding him? He pictured her arching her back, her bikini top off, his hands over her breasts now.

'Never mind,' Deb said and got off him.

Mark had no idea what was wrong. 'What is it?' he asked.

Deb was lying next to him, turned away, and pulled the covers up to cover her head.

Now Mark was getting seriously paranoid. Had he said Karen's name out loud?

His pulse pounding, he asked, 'Come on, what's wrong? What did I do?'

Deb was silent for a while, then he heard sniffling. Shit, she was crying. He must've said the wrong name. Why else would she be acting this way?

'Come on, just tell me,' he said. 'I have no idea what's going on here.'

'Forget it,' she said. 'Everything's so... never mind.'

'Everything's so what? What is it?'

'Nothing,' she said. 'Forget it, okay? Just forget it.'

Frustrated, Mark turned away in the other direction. He was trying to picture Karen naked again, but it was foggy now. He couldn't even imagine what her face looked like. He could see her eyes, her lips, her hair, but he couldn't see *her*.

He kept trying, though, until he finally fell asleep.

2

WHEN DEB WOKE up, at the edge of the bed, turned away from Mark, hung over, exhausted because she'd barely slept, hovering over sleep for most of the night, she thought, *I can't take this anymore.* She had no idea exactly why or how she'd gotten into this situation, but it was wearing her down, mentally and physically. She was stressed out all the time – bitter, edgy, paranoid. She was lucky she'd made it this far, but if she didn't end it soon, find some clean way out, her life would turn into a full-blown nightmare.

She remained in bed, ruminating, till the alarm blared at seven. Mark, facing away, stirred, then fell back asleep. As she stood, wooziness hit. Shit, mixing vodka and rum had definitely been a bad idea. She could mix vodka and whiskey and be okay, but the rum always got her.

She wobbled into the bathroom. A few minutes later, heading downstairs, she almost lost her balance and had to grab onto the banister. She should've made herself throw up last night or at least had some water before she went to sleep. She always forgot the water.

In the kitchen, she filled one of Justin's Sponge Bob cups with water from the Poland Spring tank, but was too nauseated to have more than a couple of sips.

Advil, she thought excitedly, as if she'd just come up with a brilliant idea, and found some in the cabinet. She swallowed two capsules, then, wanting to feel better faster, took one more. She made a cup of coffee in the Keurig machine and then rested at the kitchen table, sipping coffee. She still felt like shit, but it wasn't just the alcohol in her system – it was everything. Sometimes life seemed so exhausting and overwhelming and, worse, she knew she was responsible for making it this way. Seriously, how many forty-four-year-old women would kill for what she had? A four-bedroom house in Westchester, a successful, hard-working husband, two amazing kids. Maybe she was bored, maybe that was her whole problem. She used to work for a market research firm but had quit when Riley was born. She didn't want to go back to her old career, but she'd always wanted to paint. She used to have talent, had taken a couple of art classes in college and loved it. She could go to art school in the city a couple of days a week – she'd already checked out the Art Students League online – and she had plenty of space to make an art studio in the basement. It would be amazing to live a creative lifestyle, meet new, interesting creative-type people in the city. All she had to do was take the first step, register for a class, but she had forgotten how to be proactive, how to do things for herself.

She heard a vibration and then spotted her second cell phone, the one with the prepaid calling plan, on the kitchen table. Shit, she must've taken it out of her purse last night when she was drunk, looking for Advil. She was usually careful not to leave the phone in the open, but what about *him*? How many times had she told him not to text at all unless he was absolutely certain that she was home alone? What was he doing, *trying* to get caught?

She checked and, sure enough, there was a message from Owen Harrison right there on the front of the screen: **Can't wait to fuck the hell out of you today!!!**

'Jesus,' she muttered, deleting the text. Having the second phone was a good precaution, but it didn't protect her entirely. Even if she was careful about deleting every call and text, she wasn't sure how she could explain the phone itself if Mark found it. She could say a friend gave it to her, or she found it, but any explanation would be flimsy. She couldn't take this stress anymore – living on the verge of catastrophe, fearing that Mark or, god forbid, the kids would find the phone or see a text that could ruin the rest of her life, was way too stressful.

Then, hating herself, she responded: **Oooo, you're so naughty!**

This was how it always went with her and Owen – she couldn't stick to what she *wanted*. There were times she tried to end it, but she was weak, impulsive, and made the same stupid decision again and again. The worst decision had been getting involved with him at all, putting her whole marriage, maybe her whole life, in the hands of an eighteen-year-old boy.

An eighteen-year-old boy.

Sometimes the whole situation seemed surreal. Owen had been sixteen when the affair began, which made her an adulterer *and* a rapist. Yep, Deb Berman was a rapist. Not somebody else, not a stranger on the news – *her*. She'd had moments like this before over the past two years.

She'd be having a normal night at home with her family, sitting at the dinner table, or helping her kids with their homework, and she'd think, *I'm a rapist*, and she'd shudder, feel lightheaded and weightless; this couldn't possibly be happening. It was as if she'd been inserted into an alternate reality where she was still Deb Berman, but she was a different Deb Berman, someone in the news she'd look down on: *How could she actually do that? How could she be so sick, so perverted?* She wished she could go back and be the high-and-mighty Deb Berman, that she could be the judger instead of the judged.

Another text from Owen: **I'm so horny right now, I want you so bad**

She knew she should feel repulsed, disgusted – she wasn't so far gone that she'd forgotten how she was *supposed* to feel. She knew this was wrong, that she had to stop being so selfish. This wasn't about her, about filling whatever void it was filling; it was about her family and about his family. Owen was just two years older than Riley, for god's sake, and Riley and Owen had known each other for years, had friends in common. While Deb wasn't friends with Owen's mother, Linda Harrison, they were friend*ly*. For years they'd run into each other around town – at school pickups, at the mall, at soccer games. What if Linda found out? How angry and devastated and vindictive would she be?

Deb had to explain this to Owen, not some other day – *today*. She had to make him understand that they couldn't do this anymore, hurt the people they loved. She'd remind him that they'd already had a couple of close calls, like that time they were in his car in the high school parking lot and those kids walked by and almost saw them. Or the time they were having sex in Owen's bedroom that afternoon, when Linda and her husband Raymond –

Owen's stepfather – were supposed to be at work, and Raymond came home unexpectedly, and Deb had to hide in Owen's closet, like a character in a movie, a slapstick comedy, but this wasn't a movie, and it certainly wasn't a comedy. This was the real world where there were serious consequences so they had to do the smart thing, the right thing, and forget about each other, go on with their lives.

Then Deb sent: **I'm so horny for u 2!**

She hated herself for being so weak, so pathetic. She had to text him again, tell him she wouldn't be able to see him after all, and that they had to end this now, today.

She typed, **Actually I really don't think**, then deleted it, telling herself that breaking up by text was an awful idea. For an eighteen-year-old, Owen was level-headed and mature – if he wasn't that way she wouldn't have been attracted to him at all – but she had to make sure he understood, *really* understand, that this was it, she was ready to move on.

She still felt nauseated and her head was killing her. After making sure she'd deleted all the texts she'd sent and received, she switched the phone to silent mode and put it away in her purse. Then she heard Casey clacking down the stairs and a few moments later he came into the kitchen, panting, and went right toward the sliding screen doors. She let him out and then, watching the happy dog sprint toward the backyard to do his business, she thought, *Dog, hair of the dog, that's it*, and she got a glass, went to the liquor cabinet in the dining room, and poured some vodka – not much, just a half a glass, enough to get *back*.

As she was putting the vodka away she heard, 'Hi, Mom.'

Justin's voice startled her, and she nearly dropped the bottle.

'I didn't know you were up, you scared me,' Deb said.

'I don't feel good,' he said, holding his stomach.

Thinking, *Join the club*, she said, 'You're probably just hungry. Why don't you go into the kitchen and watch some TV, and I'll make you breakfast?'

When he was gone she drank the vodka in one gulp. At first, it made her feel even worse, and she thought she might throw up, but after a few moments she felt better. Well, less sick anyway.

In the kitchen, Justin was at the table, already gripped by Pokémon on TV.

'How about some pancakes for that hungry stomach of yours?' Deb asked.

'Okay,' Justin said, staring at the screen.

As Deb got busy making the pancake batter and greasing up the pan, she felt great – not only because the hair of the dog had had its full effect, but because she was back in her mommy role. *This* was what she had been risking for a fling with a teenager. She was so glad she was ending it, that she'd woken up from this nightmare.

She served Justin the pancakes and after a couple of bites he said his stomach felt better.

Later, when she was clearing the table, Mark came down to the kitchen in boxers and an old T-shirt, grunted, 'Morning,' and went right to the Keurig.

'Good morning,' she said.

He remained with his back to her, waiting for the coffee. Although Mark's behavior wasn't so unusual – they never said much to each other in the morning – today it obviously had to do with the fight in the car and all the tension last night. Deb knew she'd made a mistake, making a big deal about him and Karen. While it was incredibly obvious that they were at least contemplating an affair, Deb knew that confronting him about it and threatening to tell Karen was a bad idea while she was still involved with Owen. The only reason Mark hadn't found out about Owen yet was because he was so preoccupied with Karen and, besides, what right did Deb have to be upset about *anything* that Mark did?

'Can we talk about last night?' Deb asked.

The coffee was spurting into the mug.

'What's there to talk about?'

Typical Mark, preferring to let things stew than deal with an issue head-on.

'About yesterday in the car.' She lowered her voice to make sure Justin couldn't overhear. 'I still feel bad for attacking you. That was wrong of me.'

'Whatever,' Mark said, still staring at the coffeemaker. 'It was no big deal.'

Deb noticed Mark was holding his iPhone. This was normal too – well, normal lately. He seemed to carry his cell around with him all the time and sometimes he'd say he needed to 'get some air' or make excuses to drive to get gas or milk or whatever else he could think of.

'Also about what happened in bed,' Deb said. 'I don't know why I freaked out like that. I guess it's just been a while since we –'

'Do I have to go?'

Justin had just entered the kitchen, still in his pajamas.

'Yes,' Deb said, 'the coach said this practice is mandatory.'

'No, do I have to go to Andrew's sleepover tonight?'

'Yes, and please get dressed.'

'Okay.' Justin left.

'What was I saying?' Deb asked Mark.

Adding milk to the cup of coffee, Mark said, 'I don't know.'

'Oh, last night,' Deb said. 'I was a little drunk, and I'm not sure what happened, but I meant what I said about us going on a trip. I think it would be good for us to get away from all of this, escape. I really think we need this right now.'

Walking by her with the coffee in one hand, iPhone in the other, Mark said, 'Can we talk about this later? I just woke up, I can't focus on this now.'

'I don't want to put this off,' Deb said.

Mark went into the den/office across from the kitchen, and Deb heard the door shut. Deb knew he was going to text Karen, maybe complain about how bitchy Deb had acted in the car and how now she wanted to go away on a trip to Italy. Deb felt angry, violated – *what right did that woman have to know anything*? She wanted to barge into the den/office, demand that he stop texting Karen, and to cut off all contact with her – that was what any wife who wasn't cheating would do – but because of her own situation, she felt powerless.

Deb went to the liquor cabinet. She reached for the handle, then paused, deciding she was probably better off without a second drink of the day at nine in the morning, and returned to the kitchen. Loading the dishwasher, she was proud of herself for resisting the drink; it proved that she wasn't a total victim – she had the ability to take control when she wanted to. Like she'd walked away from the liquor cabinet, she could walk away from Owen Harrison. All she had to do was be strong, focus on the things she couldn't afford to lose, and she could do it.

On her way upstairs she saw that the door to Mark's office was open, and he wasn't there, and then she spotted him in the bedroom, sitting at the foot of the bed in gym shorts and a T-shirt, pulling his socks on. This was very new behavior. For years the only exercise he got was when he played golf, but lately he'd been going running almost every morning, and he'd even dusted off the weight bench in the basement and he'd been bench pressing.

'Going for a run?' Deb asked, opening her dresser to pick out clothes for the day.

'Yeah,' Mark said, not looking at her.

She took out a pair of jeans, and a gray scoop neck T.

With her back to him, she said, 'You have to be careful, running along the road.'

'I am,' he said.

Instead of getting undressed in the bathroom before she showered, the way she did lately when Mark was in the room, she decided to get undressed in the bedroom. Why shouldn't she get undressed in front of her husband?

She took off her T-shirt and sweats and was topless in panties. Mark, tying his running shoes, was still at the edge of the bed, not facing her, but there was a mirror ahead of him, above the other dresser, and if he looked at it he would see her part-naked.

'How far do you go?' Deb asked.

She wanted Mark to look at her, to notice how sexy she was. And she was sexy. She went to the gym four days a week – okay, two days – and swam at the country club. Okay, maybe she wasn't as in shape as exercise-obsessed Karen, but she looked damn good for forty-four years old. She weighed 127, only seven pounds more than when she'd gotten married.

Mark finished tying his sneakers, and now he was standing, texting somebody, probably Karen. Deb felt pathetic, standing there topless, waiting for her aloof husband to finish texting his girlfriend so he could notice her, maybe give her a compliment.

Deb was about to give up, just go into the bathroom, when Mark, still looking at his phone, said, 'Oh not too far. Just a few miles.'

'A few miles is great,' Deb said. 'Maybe we should play tennis together sometime.'

'Tennis?'

Deb wasn't sure he was paying attention.

'Yeah, tennis,' she said. 'We used to play all the time. I want to get back into it.'

'Yeah, maybe.' He put the phone in his shorts' pocket. 'Have you seen my keys?'

He glanced around the room, looking right *past* her, then zeroed in on the dresser, to the immediate left of her.

'There they are,' he said, and he came up right next to her, not even noticing she was naked, and snatched the keys. Then, walking away toward the door he said, 'Can you wake up Riley before you go? If you don't she'll sleep forever. I'll drop her at dance and then I'll text you later from golf. Text me if we need anything from Trader Joe's. See ya later.'

Deb watched him leave the bedroom.

Showering, Deb knew time was running out. Yeah, she and Mark had been distant for a long time, but she'd never seen him so detached. Had she pushed him too far? Would it be impossible to get him back?

Deb got dressed quickly, eager to get to the school and have a talk with Owen. Usually, when she was going to see Owen, she put on one of her nicest lace bras and sexy panties, but today she put on her shabbiest underwear so she wouldn't feel tempted.

Then she went to get Justin and saw he was still in his pajamas, playing a video game.

'What the hell're you doing? You're supposed to be getting dressed.'

She knew she wasn't just blowing up at Justin, she was blowing up at everything, but she couldn't help it.

'Sorry,' Justin said.

31

She grabbed the joystick.

'Hey, give it back,' he said.

'You have five minutes to get dressed, or I'll throw it away.'

Deb went across the hallway into Riley's room. She was curled in a ball, dead asleep, looking more like a twelve-year-old than a sixteen-year-old.

'Come on, time to get up,' Deb said.

Riley's eyes opened. 'What?' She seemed disoriented.

'Dad's going to drive you to dance class,' Deb said. 'I don't know why you can't get up on your own, why I have to be your alarm clock.'

Deb went downstairs, pulse pounding, and put Justin's DS on a high shelf in the hallway closet. Fighting off an image of Karen and Mark, holding hands in the Lerners' backyard last night, she shouted, 'Four minutes, I'm warning you!' and then went into the dining room, right to the liquor cabinet, and took out the bottle of Stoli. She knew this wasn't a good idea, she was being weak, but she needed a drink, one *little* drink, to steady herself. She poured a half a glass, then added a little more, just for a little extra boost, and gulped it down fast.

Okay, that was better, she felt more relaxed now, and that was the most important thing, right? She couldn't put her mistakes behind her and get through this day with so much anxiety.

'Three minutes!' she yelled, then went to her purse and checked her phone. She saw a new message from Owen: **I'm gonna give it to you so good today baby!!!!**

Hating that she was turned on, she deleted the text and did a search on her iPad for 'Amalfi coast vacations.' She scanned the results and went to a site that offered a trip of six days, seven nights, including guided tours, at a spectacular-looking resort. Maybe they could do a week in Italy, then a week in Greece. Besides, going away wasn't a luxury, it was a necessity. They were never going to get their marriage back on track here in Westchester. They had to get away from the routine, the distractions. She loved the kids, but the routine, the sameness of their lives, had ruined them more than anything.

'One more minute!' she called out.

She straightened up in the kitchen and made sure Casey was in the house. She was about to announce that time was up when Justin came down, fully dressed but carrying his sneakers.

'You're lucky, you just made it,' Deb said.

They got in her car, Justin in the back seat, and she pulled out of the garage, feeling very buzzed, but it was okay – she could drive.

'I really, really, really don't wanna go to the sleepover,' Justin said.

Deb heard her phone vibrating in her purse, another text from Owen.

'You're going,' Deb snapped, 'and that's final.'

She steered the car onto Savage Lane, thinking that she definitely didn't want to get into a big discussion with Owen – the shorter, the better. Maybe she'd say, 'I'm sorry, it's over. We can't see each other anymore.' No build up, just be direct. Or, better, 'I'm sorry, it's over, Owen. We can't see each other anymore.' Yeah, saying his name would underline it, put her in control, but why say *sorry*? What was she apologizing for? Maybe just go, 'It's over, Owen.' The other times she'd tried to break up, she'd been wishy-washy, left wriggle room, but this time he'd hear the seriousness in her tone. Maybe she was wrong thinking that breaking up with him would be difficult and there would be drama. Maybe he'd be on the same page, understand that it couldn't go on like this, and he'd agree to move on, and that would be the end of it.

Deb was jarred from her thoughts when, up ahead, she saw Mark and Karen near the road in front of Karen's house. Karen was also dressed to go running in Lycra and a tank top, showing off her perfectly toned Pilates arms.

'Hey, there's Daddy,' Justin said.

Karen was smiling, and Mark was talking in a very animated away – did he ever show so much enthusiasm when he was talking with anyone but Karen? It amazed and disgusted Deb how they were so open about their relationship, how they were flaunting it for everyone to see.

Deb was hoping she could drive by without them noticing, but there wasn't much traffic on Savage Lane and a passing car always got attention. Sure enough as the car approached, Karen's gaze shifted toward Deb and when they made eye contact Karen stopped smiling, just for a moment, and suddenly looked very serious, and then Mark looked over with a similar guilty expression. They were having an actual affair; Deb was certain of it.

As the car passed, Karen's smile returned, but it was obviously a strained, fake smile, trying to cover up for her guilt, and then taking it even further, she waved at Deb. Meanwhile, Deb didn't smile back, just glared at both of them until she had passed by, out of view.

A few minutes later, driving along Old Post Road, Deb still couldn't believe that Karen had actually smiled at her. The bitch was flirting openly with her husband, an obvious home wrecker, and then she *smiles*?

Talk about balls.

Pulling into the lot of Barlow Mountain Elementary School, Deb saw Owen's car – well, the Sentra he always borrowed from his mother – parked in a spot near the entrance. Deb had had sex with him in that car so many times, the latest just last Tuesday evening when she'd told Mark she was going to hang out for a while at a friend's house, but she'd really met Owen at the parking lot behind a hardware store. Deb couldn't help seeing a flash of Owen – his pale, hairless chest, him squeezing a fistful of her hair like he didn't want to ever let go – but refocused quickly and rehearsed what she was going to say to him. *It's over, Owen. We can't see each other anymore.*

She hoped when she pulled out of the lot after swimming practice that would be it, he'd be out of her life for good, and she could work on rebuilding her marriage.

In the school, Justin went to the lockers to get changed, and Deb went to the pool. Most of her buzz had worn off which was annoying because she could've used a little more relaxation. She scanned the bleachers for Owen, but didn't see him at his usual seat, second row, near the aisle, or anywhere else. There were about twenty other people scattered around – mostly moms and dads. Deb wasn't really friends with any of them, but she said 'hi' or waved to the few moms she'd spoken to before and then sat alone a few rows behind Owen's usual seat.

Practice had already started, the kids doing the breaststroke and the coach, Dave, shouting echoing instructions that were impossible to understand from where Deb was at the opposite end of the pool. Owen's brother, Kyle, was swimming in lane four, so Owen had to be there somewhere. Deb looked again and, sure enough, Owen was heading toward the bleachers.

Deb felt the way she always did when Owen walked into a room – excited, horny, and very alive. It wasn't just because she was so attracted to him. Yeah, he was a good-looking guy – six feet tall, dirty blond hair, bright blue eyes

– but he was far from gorgeous. His ears stuck out a little too far and, at eighteen, his hairline was already receding, and he was lanky, a little awkward. Sometimes his arms seemed too long for his body, and he had a tick where he blinked too hard and too often when he was nervous or self-conscious. But there was just something about him that always sharpened Deb's senses, mesmerized her. When he was nearby, even when she wasn't looking at him, she was hyperaware of his presence. To Deb, Owen wasn't a person; he was passion. He made her feel wanted, desired, sexy and, yes, younger.

Owen went to sit in his usual spot on the bleachers, not even looking at Deb. Though sometimes Owen wasn't as careful as he should've been with his texting, the main reason the affair had lasted as long as it had was because they were always discreet in public. Was she imagining it or could she smell his Axe cologne? He was probably too far away to *actually* smell it, but being around him was so intoxicating and arousing in every way.

It's over, Owen, we can't see each other anymore. It's over, Owen, we can't see each other anymore.

After he watched about ten minutes of practice, Owen left the pool area. Deb knew exactly where he was going.

Deb waited about five minutes and then she got up and left as well. A five-minute lag was enough that no one could suspect that her exit had anything to do with Owen's.

Deb went down the first floor hallway to the ladies' room, where she went to the bathroom, washed her hands, and then spent a couple of minutes staring in the mirror, trying to get up the strength to do what she had to do. Then she left the bathroom, but instead of returning to the pool area, she made sure no one was around and went up to the third floor.

Walking along the third floor hallway, Deb's heart rate accelerated. In front of room 314, she paused, gathering more strength, then entered.

Owen was where he always was – sitting at the desk.

'Good morning, Debbie,' he said.

She took a deep breath and tried to slow her heart rate.

'We need to talk,' she said.

That was good – taking control, or trying to. She shut the door, but remained near it.

'I know we do, Debbie, that's why I've been waiting for you.'

She loved when he spoke to her in a commanding tone; it was so goddamn sexy.

'Seriously,' she said. 'We have to.'

'I know, it's very serious,' he said. 'You got an F on your term paper, and you're usually an A student. Was there some sort of problem?'

Ok, this was the time to do it. Right now.

'Yeah, actually there is a problem,' she said.

'Really?' he said. 'Okay, what's your excuse?'

She wanted to say the line she'd rehearsed, tell him it was over, but then she had a vision of Mark and Karen, on the road in front of Karen's house, looking so *together*. What if Mark was planning to leave the marriage? Deb knew she couldn't handle being alone. She'd go crazy.

'I...' she said. 'I... I don't know.'

Owen stood, facing her.

'I'm sure you have a good excuse, Debbie, and I'm sure we can work something out.'

Owen was deep in the fantasy, in his role, and Deb wanted to be in it with him, just one more time.

She approached the desk, swinging her hips back and forth. She stopped, biting down a little on her lower lip, looking like she wanted to devour him, and then, after she got on her knees in front of him, she looked up at his smooth face, and he seemed so tall, so commanding, and she heard a sad, desperate voice that sounded nothing like her own say, 'Well, you know I'd do *anything* for an A, Mr Harrison,' and she couldn't stop it anymore.

The fantasy was back.

3

KAREN DAILY DREADED making the phone call, but she had no choice. Steven was a good guy – funny, honest, sincere – but if she'd learned one thing from her divorce it was that life was too short to spend with the wrong person.

'Hey, I was just thinking about you,' Steven said. 'How was the party?'

Karen had just gotten back from dinner at the Lerners', but the Steven situation had been gnawing at her all evening, and she wanted to get it over with. She'd made the call while standing up, leaning against the wall in the foyer. She hadn't even taken her coat off.

'Pretty good,' Karen said.

'Yeah,' Steven said, 'was the house as fancy as you expected?'

'It was pretty spectacular actually,' Karen said.

'Wow, sounds awesome.'

'It was... Look, Steven, I hate to do this, I really do.

I mean, I think you're a really great guy. You're smart, you're funny, but this just isn't working for me. I'm really sorry.'

Silence. Uh oh, he wasn't going to get angry or start yelling, was he? She'd had to end several relationships since her divorce, and it was always a mystery how the guy would take it. Some were mature, but some begged, and others got angry and threatening.

'Oh okay, I understand.' Steven sounded relaxed, cool with it.

'Thank you.' Karen was relieved.

'No worries,' Steven said. 'I think you're great, and I was looking forward to getting to know you better, but you have to follow your heart in these situations. I get that.'

Relief hit Karen. 'Thank you for being so understanding,' she said. 'I can't tell you how much I appreciate this.'

'No problem, seriously,' Steven said. 'I hope our paths cross again someday. And, hey, we're still Facebook friends. Maybe we can play Words With Friends sometime.'

Karen laughed. 'I'd like that,' she said.

Later, Karen was in her bedroom, getting out of the dress she'd worn to the party, still feeling good about how it had gone with Steven. Why couldn't ending relationships always be so easy? If something was wrong, why couldn't people accept that sometimes things don't work out and happily move on?

She'd changed into PJ bottoms and an old T-shirt and then heard the front door open. She went to the landing and saw Elana and Matthew; they'd spent the evening at the Bermans'.

'Hey, how's it going?' Karen was happy to see them. 'Did you have a fun night?'

'It was pretty good,' Matthew said, running upstairs, past her.

Karen went down and said to Elana, who was texting, 'And how was your night?'

'Okay,' Elana said distractedly.

'Please look at me when we're talking.'

'Sorry.' She stopped staring at the phone, but Karen could tell she was still lost, thinking about whomever she was texting with. Then full consciousness returned and she said, 'Oh, yeah, it was pretty good. Hey, can I go to a party with Riley at Dylan Ross' house tomorrow night?'

'Will Dylan's parents be there?'

'No, but they'll be home by midnight.'

'I want you home by eleven the latest.'

'Eleven-thirty?'

'Eleven.'

'Okay, Mom,' Elana said. Then she kissed Karen on the cheek. 'Goodnight.'

'Goodnight, sweetie,' Karen said.

Elana went upstairs, and Karen made a cup of green tea, then relaxed in the living room with her iPad. As a single mom, there were times when Karen was lonely and missed having a man around – not her ex, a *man*. She missed doing couple things – going on trips together or just out to dinner or into the city for an afternoon. But usually, like right now, she loved the alone time, having her own space, being able to have a relaxing late night at home. Compared to the tension at the end of her marriage this was practically bliss.

After commenting on a few statuses on Facebook, Karen logged on to Match and reactivated her account. She used to be skeptical about online dating – the idea of shopping for men had been a turnoff – but there really was no other way to meet people these days, especially in the suburbs, and over the past three years she'd met some great guys online. Okay, she'd met some creeps too, like Paul the stalker and porn-obsessed Mike, but most of her experiences had been positive. She'd had several relationships that had lasted a few months and several that had petered out. After being in a long marriage, it was fun to have new adventures. Karen was always honest and upfront with guys. She wasn't looking for anything serious from the get-go, but if she stumbled upon the right guy and the right situation she'd happily settle down.

Between the time she'd met Steven, and before she'd deactivated her account, about thirty guys had written to her. The most frustrating thing about online dating was how hard it had been to meet a nice guy around her age; it seemed as if most guys were either looking for Lolita or Mrs Robinson. In this batch of notes, two – 'Richard' and 'Dave' – seemed like possibilities. Richard was a forty-four-year-old dentist from Scarsdale, which was less than a half hour away. Dave, a forty-year-old, never-been-married-before ad exec from Manhattan, had sent her a nice note about a couple of Broadway musicals he'd seen recently because Karen had mentioned in her profile that she likes Broadway musicals.

After reading both profiles again, she decided to write to Richard first because he had kids and because his location was more convenient. She was tapping out a note to him when her phone chimed, and then she glanced at the text from Mark: **Great seeing you tonight! Hope you got home safe, sweetie.** She was going to text back, but got distracted by the main profile photo of Richard the dentist. He was actually really attractive – thick dark hair with streaks of gray, bright blue eyes – and in another photo he was in a lotus position. Hmm, a dentist who was into yoga – Karen liked that. She wrote back to him, thanking him for getting in touch and – because he'd asked her what type of teaching she did – added that she was a speech pathologist, and she loved what she did. Lastly, for a flirty touch she included a PS – *Nice lotus pic. You seem very flexible!* with a smiley face emoticon.

After she texted Mark back a quick thanks, she went upstairs to get ready for bed.

Although she'd gotten used to not having a man around full-time, sleeping alone still felt weird. As usual, when she didn't have a guy over, she piled the extra pillows on Joe's old side to make the bed seem fuller. It didn't really help, but she got under the covers on her side and managed to fall asleep quickly anyway.

It was a perfect morning for a run – sunny and cool and the dense, misty air smelled like spring. As Karen was stretching in front of her house, she saw Mark jogging down the road toward her in sweat-shorts and a T-shirt. This had happened a few times lately – when she was getting ready for a run, Mark would suddenly show up. She liked his company, he was a good guy, but she preferred to run alone, listening to her iPod.

'Hey,' Mark said, smiling.

'Hey,' Karen said, trying to think of a way out of this without being too rude.

'Good timing, huh?' Mark said, stopping in front of her and jogging in place.

'Yeah,' Karen said. 'Great.'

'I was hoping I'd run into you,' he said. 'Beautiful day today, huh?'

'Yep,' she said, leaning against a tree, stretching out her left calf.

'You look nice and rested,' he said. 'Want to hear something funny? I dreamt about you last night.'

'Really?' she asked, still trying to think up an excuse. Maybe she could tell him she wanted to go for a longer-than-usual run today, but she didn't think that would deter him.

'I don't really remember it all,' he said. 'I mean some of the details were fuzzy. But we were in some exotic place – maybe Hawaii. We were on the beach, hanging out. Then I think we were swimming together, scuba diving. The water was really clear. We could see all the fish.'

'Sounds nice,' she said. 'I really need to get away. It's been ages since I've been anywhere.'

Looking beyond Mark, Karen noticed Deb's SUV approaching – Deb was driving with Justin in the back seat. Karen smiled at Deb and then waved as the car passed, but Deb returned her gaze, stone-faced. Now Karen was certain last night hadn't been her imagination – something was going on.

'Deb's not angry at *me*, is she?' Karen asked.

'Who?' Mark said.

'Deb,' Karen said. 'Your wife.'

'Oh. Why would she be angry?'

'I don't know. But last night she barely looked at me and now she just gave me the evil eye. I don't know what I did to piss her off, but I must've done something.'

'Yeah, I know, she's been that way with everybody lately,' Mark said. 'She's moody all the time.'

'I don't know, she didn't seem to be treating anybody else like that,' Karen said.

'I'm telling you,' Mark said. 'It's her own personal shit. Has nothing to do with you.'

Karen stared at Mark – she knew him well and got the sense he was hiding something. She stretched her other calf, feeling a nice pull. 'Well, if it doesn't have to do with me, maybe it has to do with you.'

'Me?' Mark said. 'Why –'

'Is something going on with you two?'

One of the best things about her friendship with Mark was that she was able to speak openly with him, say whatever was on her mind. She hadn't been able to do that in her marriage.

'Just the usual bickering,' he said.

'Bickering or fighting?'

'Okay, fighting.' He took a breath. 'It got pretty bad in the car.'

'She said something about me?'

'No, no, not about you – seriously, this has nothing to do with you. But you saw her drinking last night at the party, right? In the car, she was really drunk, and she started saying all this crazy shit, complaining, yelling at me, and then she threatened me. She said if things didn't change she'd leave me.'

'Oh no.' Karen felt bad, but she didn't want to say *I'm sorry*, knowing how annoying and cliché it was to hear *I'm sorry* from her friends when she was contemplating getting divorced – she didn't need sympathy, she needed support. So she hugged Mark tightly and said, 'Ugh. Don't worry, it'll be fine.'

'Yeah,' Mark said. 'I know it will.'

Karen pulled back and said, 'It was wrong of her to say that to you, though. She shouldn't just be throwing around the D word so casually. Joe used to do that, and it has an effect after awhile, it starts to wear a relationship down.'

'Yeah, I know, you're probably right.'

'You have to work on it with her. Maybe go to counseling, and you have to get her to stop drinking, maybe even get her into AA.'

'Her drinking's not *that* bad,' Mark said.

Karen glared.

'It isn't,' Mark said. 'I mean, it's not like she gets drunk all the time.'

'She has a problem,' Karen said. 'Every time I see her at a party she's drunk. And I've seen her drunk at the country club, in the middle of the afternoon.'

'A lot of people drink at the club,' Mark said.

'Look, I'm just trying to help you,' Karen said. 'I think you're in a little denial about it, but that's okay. I just think you should confront it, for the sake of your kids and for the sake of your marriage. But that's the end of my speech, I won't tell you what to do.'

'Thank you, I appreciate all your help, I really do,' Mark said. 'I guess I'll have to think about how to handle it. Ready to roll?'

While Karen still wished she could run alone, she knew Mark was in a bad way about whatever was going on with Deb, and could probably use the company.

'Yeah, let's do it,' she said.

They went along Karen's usual route – to the end of Savage Lane, then up the road a bit to the path around Truesdale Lake. They were having a nice chat, mainly small talk about the Lerners' party. Karen was convinced that Michelle Lerner had gotten more plastic surgery, and they had fun joking around about it, referring to her by the name they always called her – Plastic Woman.

Later, runner's high kicking in, enjoying the nice cool breeze off the lake, Karen said, 'Oh, so I broke up with Steven last night.'

'Finally,' Mark said.

'Why finally?'

'He was totally wrong for you, and that name is so annoying.'

'Steven? What's annoying about the name Steven?'

'I don't know, it's grating,' Mark said. 'Not Steve or Stevie – *Steven.*'

Karen laughed. 'You're ridiculous.'

'Besides,' Mark said, 'he sounded like a flakey guy. An *actor*?'

'What's wrong with actors?'

'If he was a real actor he'd live in Manhattan, not Dobbs Ferry.'

'How do you know he's from Dobbs Ferry?'

'You told me a couple weeks ago.'

'Oh, I'm surprised you remember that. But his acting wasn't the problem anyway. I liked that he was an actor, that he was different. I'm tired of dating cookie cutter financial guys.'

'Hey,' Mark said.

'You know what I mean,' Karen said. 'I'm talking about the typical guy in finance who's still playing that stupid status game. Going to the best restaurants, wearing the best clothes, driving the best cars.'

'Whatever,' Mark said. 'It didn't seem like you had a real connection with Steven.'

Karen thought about it, then said, 'Yeah, that's true, I guess we didn't.'

They jogged for a while, not saying anything.

Then Mark said, 'Don't you think that's the most important thing? I mean, in a relationship. To have a real connection – to *get* each other, the way best friends get each other?'

'Yeah, of course I do,' Karen said.

'Me too,' Mark said.

Karen was remembering her last date with Steven – dinner in Dobbs Ferry, then a DVD back at his place. The sex that night was kind of mechanical, and she remembered lying in bed afterward, him hugging her from behind, and how his arms had felt like clamps.

'Yeah, you're right, something was missing,' she said. 'Maybe I just wasn't attracted to him enough. Anyway, another guy's been writing to me, so we'll see where that goes.'

Mark was looking straight ahead with a very serious expression. Karen didn't think he'd heard her so she said, 'I said another guy's been writing to me so –'

'What other guy?' Mark asked.

'Just some new guy from Match,' Karen said. 'He's a dentist from Scarsdale.'

'Sounds like a prick,' Mark said.

'Why do you say that?'

'You dated that dentist last year, right? The one who you found out was still having sex with his ex-wife?'

'Yeah, you're right, Carl *was* a prick. But just because one dentist was a prick doesn't mean all dentists are pricks.'

'I didn't say that,' Mark said. 'I just think this guy sounds like a prick.'

'But you don't know anything about him.'

'You said he's from Scarsdale, right? You know how stuck up they are in Scarsdale? And a dentist from Scarsdale? Jesus. What's his name?'

'Richard.'

'Richard what?'

'Gross.'

'Richard Gross? *Dick* Gross? Told you – a prick.'

Karen smiled. While it was a little annoying that Mark was being so oppositional, she knew he was just looking out for her, trying to protect her, the way a brother would try to protect his sister from bullies in a playground.

When they got to the halfway point of Karen's usual run, Mark, asked, 'Should we turn back?'

Thinking about the one-and-a-half pounds she'd gained, Karen said, 'I think I'm gonna keep going, but you can head if you want.'

'No, it's okay,' Mark said. 'I have another gear.'

'Are you sure? 'Cause –'

'Yep, let's keep goin',' he said.

They continued along the lake for about another mile, then headed back. Mark wasn't talking as much, and Karen could tell he was struggling to keep up. She knew he'd never complain, though – men and their silly egos.

When they were back, running along Savage Lane, Karen wanted to finish up strong for a final calorie burn so she sprinted ahead. A few minutes later, she was on her front lawn, stretching her quads, when Mark approached, straining to catch his breath, his T-shirt soaked.

'So, how's the rest of your day look?' Mark asked between gasps.

'I have to take care of stuff around the house and then I'm heading to the country club this afternoon,' she said.

'Me too,' he said. 'I have an eleven forty-five tee time. But maybe we can meet up at the clubhouse afterward for coffee or something.'

Karen was planning to play tennis with her friend Jill, whom she was bringing to the club as a guest. Afterward she wanted to hang out with Jill and chat, but she didn't want to be rude.

'Yeah, maybe,' she said. 'I'm playing tennis with Jill, but we'll probably be gone by the time you're done.'

'Oh.' Mark seemed disappointed. 'Well, you never know, I'll text you from the course and maybe we can work something out.'

'Sounds like a plan.'

Bending down, stretching her hamstrings now, Karen expected Mark to leave but he stood there, watching.

When he noticed she was looking at him, his eyes shifted upward guiltily, and he said, 'This was really a total blast. Thanks for letting me tag along.'

'Oh, it was no problem,' she said.

'We should do it again.'

Karen wanted to be honest – tell him that it was nothing personal but she preferred to run alone – but she figured she'd discuss it with him another time.

'Yeah, we totally should,' she said.

He remained, watching for several seconds while she continued to stretch, then said, 'Well, see you later,' and she said, 'See you,' and he finally headed back toward his house. When he was beyond her driveway he turned back and smiled and raised his hand, so she smiled and raised her hand as well.

Poor Mark. Karen could tell he was suffering inside and she had a feeling things were worse at home than he was letting on. She wished she could help, but there was nothing she could really do – he'd have to work through it on his own.

She went into the house, laid out a yoga mat, and continued with her workout.

4

WHEN DEB RETURNED to the pool area, ahead of Owen, she felt dirty, disgusting, and ashamed. Everything about her classroom fantasy that had excited her just a few minutes ago, now repulsed her. She wanted to be dead, buried or, better yet, burned. The world didn't deserve her miserable, unfaithful body. She wanted to evaporate, combust, disappear forever.

'Hey, Deb.'

Deb glanced to her left, toward the bleachers, at the smiling face of Grace Shapiro, the mom of Aiden who was on Justin's swim team.

Deb had to smile back – talk about being fake – and said, 'Hey, how are you?'

'Great, thanks,' Grace said. 'Are you just getting here?'

'No, I was here before, I just had to take a call.'

'Oh, too bad,' Grace said. 'I love your hair, did you get it cut?'

Fighting off an image of Owen grabbing a fistful of her

hair as he leaned close to her ear, grunting, *You like that, student*? *You like that, right*? she said to Grace, 'Um, no, not recently.'

'Well, I love it,' Grace said.

Deb managed a half smile then went and sat in the same spot in the bleachers she'd sat in before, still feeling filthy. What kind of person was she, sneaking away from her son's swim practice to have sex with a teenager? She could smell Owen's Axe cologne, as strong as if she were wearing it herself, and she wished she could run down there and jump in the pool to rinse off. But washing his scent off her wouldn't be enough, because she could still feel his body on her, *in* her.

She was so absorbed in her self-loathing that she hadn't noticed that Owen had returned to his seat a few rows in front of her. Now the scent of Axe was even stronger, and she wanted to move – maybe go sit next to Grace or, better yet, in the top row of the bleachers, and all the way in the corner, as far away from Owen as she could possibly get – but she couldn't do that as the sane, logical voice was still lurking somewhere in her brain, reminding her the worst thing she could do was draw any attention to her relationship with Owen. The only positive of the whole situation was that the perverted side of herself was a well-kept secret, that she was alone in her suffering.

The boys were doing freestyle. Shit, that meant there was another forty-five minutes of practice. That wasn't enough time to drive somewhere; she had to get outside to get some air, but she didn't want to make a display of leaving right after Owen had returned just in case someone was paying attention. She looked over in Grace's direction and, sure enough, Grace was looking, maybe staring, right at her. This time Deb didn't smile, though; instead maintaining a blank expression and pretending to look beyond Grace, at the wall displaying school championship banners, before shifting her gaze back toward the swimming pool.

While Deb knew that Grace probably just happened to be looking in her direction and that it probably didn't *mean* anything, it was hard not to be paranoid. Maybe Grace had seen Deb returning from the classroom upstairs and Owen returning from the same direction and maybe suspected something was going on. Grace was a gossiper. Deb remembered how a few months ago Grace had told her a story – in confidence – about how the Adlers, a couple they both knew, were in marriage counseling because David Adler had been hitting his wife Marissa. If Grace couldn't keep that to herself, how would she be able to not blab about an affair with a teenager?

Deb was jarred by a blast of Owen's Axe. Was she imagining it or was the scent getting stronger? It seemed like she had her nose in the bottle, and that the bottle was fastened to her face, like a horse's feedbag. He had his head tilted down slightly – looking down at something, probably his cell phone. She hated herself for letting this situation linger on, for not being assertive, for getting sucked in all over again. Now she would have to wait until the next time they were alone, but what if she couldn't go through with it then either? What if the only escape would be everyone finding out, for disaster to ensue?

Her purse vibrated. She opened it and saw she'd gotten a text from Owen: **That was so fuckin' hot!**

The Axe was overwhelming now; she couldn't breathe. Worse, she was getting turned on. She couldn't take this anymore, she was going to lose it, have a breakdown. As she stuffed her phone back into her purse she saw the little bottle of Stoli. She'd forgotten it was there – she'd thought she'd had the last one the other day when she'd been running around, doing errands and had gotten antsy in the car in the parking lot outside Walgreens.

Deciding that enough time had passed since Owen had returned for her to leave again, she walked, trying not to seem like she was rushing, toward the exit. She noticed that Grace was involved in conversation with another mom and didn't seem to see her, and she realized that the whole idea that Grace was suspicious had probably been ridiculous.

In the bathroom, she went into a stall, tore off the seal and gulped down the vodka in one swig, as if she'd been wandering around a desert and it was the first liquid she'd come across in days. It relaxed her a little, but it wasn't enough. She was afraid if she went back in there and had to see the back of Owen's head again and breathe in more of his cologne she'd have a panic attack or, worse, lose control and want to be with him again. She was already fighting off an urge to text him back and keep the fantasy going.

Instead, she went outside. Ah, air. This was what she needed: freshness, clarity. It happened to be turning into a particularly beautiful day – a very blue sky, a light breeze, and it had to be around seventy degrees. She walked around the grounds of the school, along the soccer field and by the building through a woodsy area. It felt good to be outside, to be moving, and maybe the vodka was hitting because she definitely felt more relaxed. But then as she approached the back of the school, her tension suddenly returned. It seemed as if the odor of Owen's cologne was everywhere again, dominating the scents of pine trees and freshly cut grass.

'There you are.'

When she turned she saw him standing several feet away, smiling obliviously. She was surprised to see him there; then she was upset.

'You shouldn't be here,' she said.

'I had a feeling you were out here,' he said. 'You didn't text me back, and I knew something was up because you always text me back, then I looked behind me and, I was right, you were gone. But I knew I'd find you out here. Isn't that so freaky?'

Deb looked around and then said, 'I'm serious, you have to go back inside – right now.'

'Are you mad at me about something?' he asked.

'Yes.' Deb realized she was talking at a normal level, which was too loud, so she continued, stage-whispering, 'We can't be out here together, Owen.'

'We're not doing anything, we're just talking,' he said. 'It would've been a lot worse if somebody came into that classroom.'

'Keep your voice down,' Deb whispered harshly. 'I'm gonna go back inside, but you wait, just wait about ten minutes before you come back in, okay?'

'Why didn't you text me back?'

'We can't talk about this now.' Deb was walking away.

Behind her, Owen said, 'Talk to you later… student.'

Deb, fuming, returned inside. This was bad – very bad. Sending raunchy texts at inappropriate times, like he'd done this morning, was one thing, but this was going too far. Owen was usually discreet, careful; in the past, he never would have followed her out of the building. He probably sensed that something was wrong, that she was having doubts, and he wanted to fix the situation, which made Deb even angrier for not ending it when they were alone in the classroom, when she'd had the chance. As she fought off a flash of herself on her back on the teacher's desk, her legs in the air, Owen clutching her ankles, she thought that the last thing she needed now was for him to become too clingy.

'Another phone call?' Grace asked.

Deb looked up at Grace in the bleachers, noticing her forced smile.

'Yeah,' Deb said. 'I'm getting some work done on the house and the contractor's driving me crazy.'

The kids were already doing the breaststroke, so the practice seemed to be ending early. Owen returned but didn't ignore her the way he normally did. No, he looked right at her, as if trying to get her to look at him, to *notice* him. What the hell? Deb maintained her gaze toward the pool, but saw in her peripheral vision that Owen kept looking back at her. Then when the kids were getting out of the pool, she got up – noticing that Owen wasn't watching her – and left the pool area and went down to intercept Justin on his way to the locker room.

'Change fast, we have to go,' Deb said.

'What?' Justin was distracted, talking to a friend.

'We're in a hurry,' Deb said. 'I'm serious, no dawdling.'

She waited outside the locker room and as soon as Justin came out, she took him by the hand, and led him out to the car.

'Why are we in such a hurry?' Justin asked.

'We have to pick up Riley,' Deb said, noticing that Owen and his brother were just leaving the building. She got in the car quickly, let Justin in, and then backed out of the spot. As she was driving away she checked in the rearview, sensing that Owen was watching, and sure enough he was standing there, hands on his hips, glaring in her direction.

Deb knew he was probably confused, or angry, because she'd never behaved this way before, but maybe this was a good thing. It could cushion the blow, make it less of a shock, when she ended the fling. She'd arrange to meet him someplace public – a Starbucks, a Chipotle – where nothing could happen, and she'd tell him it was over and that would be it, the end.

Driving along the winding two-lane road, Deb suddenly felt empowered. Justin, in the back seat, was playing with his Nintendo DSi, and she went through songs on her iPod, skipping 'Love The Way You Lie.'

'Why do I have to go?' Justin asked.

Deb stopped at 'Believe' by Cher, much better, then said, 'What? Where?'

'Andrew's sleepover,' Justin said. 'Why are you making me go?'

'You're going, and I'm done discussing it with you,' she said, and turned up the volume.

It was about a fifteen-minute drive to the dance studio at a strip mall, where Riley was waiting outside talking to a couple of friends. When Riley looked over and saw the car she seemed annoyed. She said goodbye quickly to her friends then got into the back, next to Justin.

'Am I late?' Deb asked loudly, over the music.

'Just drive,' Riley said.

Deb took out her phone, glanced at a text from Owen – **I don't understand what's going on with you. What did I do wrong?** – and then put the phone back in her purse and pulled away.

'*Mom*,' Riley said.

Shit, had Riley seen the second phone? She was usually careful, never using it when the kids were around.

'I told you not to do that,' Riley said.

'Do what?' Deb asked, panicked.

'Pick me up right in front of the school,' Riley said. 'I told you to like park in the back of the lot and text me and I'd come over and meet you.'

'Sorry, I forgot your instructions were so specific,' Deb said.

She was relieved about the phone, but now was worried about the text. She told herself, *It's okay, he's just upset, but that was a good thing, it would be easier for him to let go.*

'I'm serious.' Riley seemed agitated.

'What, you don't want your friends to know you have a mother?' Deb said. 'You want them to think you were a miracle baby, that you just appeared in the world out of thin air?'

'You just don't get it,' Riley said

'I don't like your attitude right now,' Deb said.

'Whatever,' Riley said.

'No, not whatever. Don't whatever me.'

'Why do I have to go?' Justin asked.

'Will you stop it about that already?' Deb snapped. 'I told you we're not discussing it.'

'Where don't you want to go?' Riley asked Justin.

Deb felt the seat vibrate next to her. Shit, what was he texting her about now?

'Both of you just stop it,' Deb said, glaring in the rearview. The Stoli was doing nothing for her now; she needed another drink badly but would have to wait about fifteen minutes until they got home. She had to get on Expedia and start seriously looking into Italian vacations, because she needed to get away from everything. Ending it with Owen wouldn't be enough; she needed physical distance so she wouldn't feel tempted.

At a red light she looked at her phone in her purse and the text from Owen: **your the one causing the scenes not me why didn't you text me back???**

'Jesus Christ,' Deb said.

'What?' Riley asked.

'Nothing, nothing,' Deb muttered.

Deb wanted to hit back with a scolding text, ordering him to stop texting her, but she resisted, knowing that responding would only lead to more texting and that it was better not to engage.

The light turned green and Deb hit the gas.

Then Riley asked, 'Did you see Owen Harrison today?'

'Who?' Deb was trying not to panic.

'Owen Harrison,' Riley said. 'Was he there today at swim practice?'

Deb's hands were sweaty; her pulse was pounding. Maybe it was a mistake not texting back. She was the adult, after all. Shouldn't she take charge?

'Owen Harrison?' she said, pretending she couldn't quite place the name.

'I saw him,' Justin said. 'He picked up his brother, Kyle.'

'Was he with anybody?' Riley asked.

'I don't know,' Justin said.

The car got quiet again. Deb was confused, paranoid. She knew she should let it go, that it probably didn't mean anything, but she wanted to make sure.

'Why were you asking about Owen?' Deb asked.

'No reason,' Riley said.

She was hiding something; Deb was sure of it. But what? Noticing that her hands were actually shaking the steering wheel, Deb asked, 'Have you even seen Owen recently?'

'Never mind,' Riley said. 'It's not important.'

Then a thought hit – oh god, no, Deb didn't even want to think about this, but she had to because it was possible; it even made *sense*. Riley's sixteen, and sixteen year olds have active hormones and crushes, and Owen was an older, good-looking boy, so why wouldn't she have a crush on him? But a crush wasn't a big deal – teenage crushes were innocent. She probably had crushes on lots of boys.

But what if it was worse than a crush? What if she was actually *involved* with Owen? Owen had told Deb that he wasn't interested in dating girls his age, and she'd believed him, but maybe it had been silly to believe a teenage boy. He could have been dating other girls all along and Deb wouldn't have known. And if he suspected that Deb wanted to end the affair and he was angry about it, why not try to get revenge by seducing her daughter? Riley had been spending more time with her friends lately – going to parties, movies, hanging out at the mall. She could have easily started seeing Owen without Deb knowing about it. Deb didn't think Riley had become sexually active yet, but Riley was good at keeping secrets. Like mother, like daughter.

'Slow down, Mom,' Riley said urgently.

This was all Deb needed – something else to worry about. She needed another drink, or *something* to make this all go away.

'*Mom*,' Riley said.

Approaching a bend, Deb realized she was driving way too fast. Then she hit the brake a little hard, and the car skidded. She was able to get control back quickly, though, and made it the rest of the way home without incident.

On the approach to the seventh hole, Mark knew he had to be aggressive and get to the back of the green or else he'd wind up in the sand trap, and he was already having a rough round, way over his recent average. He tried to swing strong through the ball, get some backspin on it, but he undercut too much and watched it three-bounce right into the trap.

'Didn't eat your Wheaties today, huh?' Stu Zimmerman said.

Stu was a tax attorney, married, in his forties, whom Mark had been playing golf with for years. They also rode into the city together during the workweek sometimes on the 7:08 train from Katonah, when Mark was able to make that train. Stu had two kids, including a son Justin's age, and the kids played on the same Little League team.

'What am I gonna do?' Mark said. 'I guess today just isn't my day.'

After Stu shot his approach, which landed right on the green, maybe ten feet from the cup, he got into a cart with Doug Carlson. Doug was married with kids and owned an office supply business in the city and, like Mark and Stu, was in his forties. Mark put his eight iron back in the bag, wishing he'd used a seven, then got into the cart that Richie Rosen was driving. Richie was a single investment banker, about thirty years old.

'You'll pick 'em up on the back nine,' Richie said, as they bounced along the fairway.

'I'm not counting on it,' Mark said. 'I don't know, I just didn't bring my A game today. I guess I'm just a little tired, that's all.'

'Out clubbing last night?' Richie asked, smiling.

'Not exactly,' Mark said. 'I was at a dinner party last night in Bedford Hills, then I went running this morning and my legs're feeling it. Not that I'm making any excuses.'

''Course not.' Richie, with his very white teeth, was still smiling.

The truth was, though, that the running was definitely having an effect on Mark's game. His legs felt tired and heavy and it was hard to get any strength into his swing, but it had been worth it to spend more time with Karen. It was also hard to focus on his game because he was distracted, looking forward to hopefully bumping into her in the clubhouse later, maybe having coffee or a drink.

At the tee-off to the eighth hole, they were waiting for the group ahead of them to finish up on the next green when Stu said to Mark, 'So, how's everything with your girlfriend?'

Mark knew that Stu meant Karen. The guys often teased him about them spending so much time together.

'Ha ha,' Mark said.

'Seriously,' Doug said. 'Are you tapping that or what?'

'We're just good friends,' Mark said.

'Yeah, friends,' Doug said, pushing his cheek out with his tongue and moving his fist back and forth in front of his mouth, simulating a blowjob.

Stu also looked incredulous. Richie was smiling again, checking his phone.

'It's true,' Mark said.

'He wouldn't tell us if something was going on with them,' Stu said, 'because he'd be afraid we'd blab about it.'

'That's a good point,' Doug said. 'But, seriously, she's looking smoking lately. Did you see what she was wearing the other day in the clubhouse? She had the boots, the short skirt –'

'And her tits looked fucking incredible,' Stu said.

'Her tits *always* look fucking incredible,' Doug said. 'I mean she has that cougar, workout chick body going on, not an ounce of fat anywhere, and then these huge fucking knockers.'

'They're not *that* big,' Stu said. 'They're probably like B-cups.'

'No fuckin' way,' Doug said. 'They're easily C's. And they're firm too. She has two kids and her tits look like that? Jesus.'

'Maybe they're fake,' Stu said.

'They're not fake,' Richie said, putting away his phone.

'Whoa, listen to the tits expert here,' Doug said. 'Mr Single Guy.'

'When they're fake they don't bounce at all,' Richie said

seriously. 'I saw her playing tennis the other day and hers were bouncing up and down every time she hit the ball.'

'I don't know,' Stu said. 'I think when something looks too good to be true it usually is.'

Mark must've made a face, or maybe rolled his eyes, because Doug said, 'Wait, does the *friend* wanna weigh in?'

'They're not fake,' Mark said.

'Whoa, whoa, hold up,' Doug said. 'You're just friends but you know her tits are real?'

'Sounds like a confession to me.' Stu was smirking.

Wishing he'd kept his mouth shut, Mark said, 'She mentioned it to me once.'

'Mentioned it?' Doug laughed. 'How did she just *mention* her tits? Were you like, "How're you doing?" And she said, "Pretty good, oh and, by the way, let's talk about my tits"?'

Stu and Richie were laughing so hard that an old guy, maybe twenty yards away, who'd been in the middle of his backswing, about to tee-off, glared back at them.

'Oh, sorry,' Stu stage-whispered.

'I forgot how it came up,' Mark said. 'I think we were talking about some famous actress who'd gotten a boob job and Karen said she'd never do that, even when she got older.'

'That sounds mildly believable,' Doug said.

'*Mildly*,' Stu said. Then he said to Mark, 'Hey, I have an idea. Why don't you set Richie up with Karen?'

'I love it,' Doug said. 'Then at least somebody we know would be fucking her, and we can find out what it's like, you know, vicariously.'

'She's too old for me,' Richie said.

'Too old?' Doug said. 'You gotta be kidding me.'

'Yeah, she's gotta be what, forty?' Richie said. 'In ten years she'll be fifty. My mother's fifty-three.'

'That makes sense.' Doug rolled his eyes.

'You could be a motherfucker,' Stu said.

Stu and Doug were trying to stifle their laughter, middle-aged guys acting like kids in the back of a classroom.

Mark, getting seriously irritated with the conversation and wanting to change the topic, said to Stu, 'What're you using on this, iron or a wood?'

'I'm using an iron, you're the one using the wood on Karen.'

All the guys, except Mark, laughed.

Then Stu said to Richie, 'Seriously, I'm not talking about *marrying* the broad. Just to fuck around with a few times. I mean *somebody's* gotta motorboat those knobs.'

'Yeah, you gotta check the cougar box before you get married,' Doug said to Richie.

'And you know she knows her way around in the sack,' Stu said. 'Since she and Joe broke up she's been a dating machine. My wife said she's on Match, OkCupid, all that shit.'

'Yeah, I think I've seen her with three different guys in the past month,' Doug said.

This was ridiculous; she'd only been with one guy lately – Steven. Unless there were others Mark didn't know about. This thought made his gut tighten.

'Did you see her with that new guy?' Stu asked. 'I think his name's Steven? Tall guy, long hair, ponytail. I ran into them at the bagel place one morning a couple of weeks ago.'

'Nope, then I guess it's been four guys in the past two months,' Doug said.

'Great, so now you're trying to set me up with a slut,' Richie said.

'Okay, that's enough,' Mark said to Richie.

'Oooh, I think somebody's getting protective over his girlfriend,' Stu said.

'Relax, I'm just kidding around,' Richie said to Mark.

'Take it easy,' Stu said to Mark.

'Yeah,' Doug said. 'And if you're not hitting it yourself why do you give a shit who she's fucking?'

Mark cocked the three iron he was holding over his shoulder like an axe and took a step toward Doug, as if about to whack him over the head with it. He actually started the backswing.

'Hey, whoa, whoa, take it easy, man,' Doug said, backing away.

'You crazy?' Stu said to Mark. 'He's just messin' with you.'

Mark felt crazy. He felt out of control.

Then, maybe after a few seconds, sanity returned.

He lowered the club and said, 'I was just messing with you too,' but he knew no one was buying this, not even himself.

'I think somebody needs an anger management class,' Stu said.

Mark wanted to say something to help smooth things over, but he couldn't think of what exactly to say.

Then Richie broke the tension, saying, 'Looks like we're up.'

Mark played worse on the back nine, partly because he could tell everyone was still uncomfortable around him, and partly because he was anxious to finish up and get back to the clubhouse in time to hopefully bump into Karen. After eighteen, he rushed ahead to the clubhouse, disappointed that he didn't see Karen on the terrace where she usually hung out. The guys were lingering, talking, and he didn't want to make it too obvious that he was looking for her, so he went nonchalantly into the indoor area of the clubhouse. He didn't see her and then went into the bathroom and peed and washed up. Then he texted her: **Hey saw u playing tennis b4 @ club, was hoping to run into u How was it??**

He waited for a couple of minutes, staring at his phone, but didn't get a response. Then he went through to the café and saw Karen and her friend at a table in the back in the corner.

Mark noticed that Stu and Richie were now near the bar, and probably would see him going over to Karen, but he didn't really care what the guys thought anymore. He definitely wasn't going to let their teasing affect his friendship with her.

Mark approached Karen from the side, and she didn't see him until he said, 'Hey you.'

'Hey,' she said.

He could tell she was as happy to see him as he was to see her.

'I have a little while till I have to get back,' he said, 'mind if I join you for a few minutes?'

Karen and her friend – Jill, that's right, her name was Jill – looked at each other.

Then Karen said, 'Sure, of course.'

'Awesome,' Mark said, sitting in the seat to Karen's right. 'So how was tennis?'

'Jill won again,' Karen said.

'Well, I got lucky on a couple of shots in that last game,' Jill said.

'No, it wasn't luck,' Karen said. 'I'm secure enough to admit my inferiority to you on the tennis court.'

Mark laughed, even though what Karen said wasn't particularly funny. He couldn't help it; he always felt so upbeat and happy when he was around her. Then Jill announced that she had to get home. Karen tried to get her to stay, but Mark knew that she was just being fake-sincere, that she actually *wanted* Jill to leave. It was possible, even probable, that Karen had told Jill what a great friend Mark was – maybe even that she wished she could have more someday – and now Jill was probably just doing her a favor to give her and Mark some alone time.

When Jill was gone Karen shifted over to her seat so that she was facing Mark, which was perfect. He imagined they were alone, in a little secluded café somewhere, maybe in Italy, on the Amalfi Coast.

'We're finally alone,' Mark said, smiling.

They talked for a few minutes, just random small talk, but with Karen it never mattered what they were talking about; it was just the *talking* that was so incredible. Then he noticed that she was distracted anyway, her eyes widening in a concerned way.

'See, I told you,' she said.

Mark had no idea what she was talking about until he turned and saw Deb near the entrance to the clubhouse. She was just standing there, glaring, but Mark knew that look. She was thinking, *How dare you, how dare you.* Mark could also tell that she'd been drinking again.

Turning back to Karen, Mark said, 'Sorry, I don't know what's wrong with her lately.'

'She's looking at me like she was last night,' Karen said. 'Like she wants to kill me.'

'She's just drunk. You were right, she has a problem. A *serious* problem.'

'She's coming over here.'

Mark turned, and saw Deb marching toward them. He also saw that Stu and Richie and now Doug were at the bar. Shit, this was all he needed, Deb causing a scene, saying the things she'd said last night, putting him in an embarrassing awkward position with Karen.

Deciding he had to do *something* to ward off a disaster, he got up and tried to intercept her, saying, 'Okay, come on, let's go outside,' but Deb was too enraged, and pushed by Mark, not even making eye contact with him.

Then Deb shouted at Karen, 'You fucking whore! You fucking slut!'

Everyone in the room looked over. He'd been having this wonderful time with Karen and now, in an instant, it had all gone to hell.

Karen seemed shocked too, and mortified. She seemed to be struggling to come up with some kind of response.

But Deb beat her to it, saying, 'You just stay away from my goddamn husband. He's mine, you understand that? *Mine.*'

'Calm down, Deb,' Karen said.

'Don't tell me to be calm, bitch!' Deb shouted. 'I'll be however the hell I want to be!'

Then Mark grabbed Deb by the arm and pulled her away and whispered harshly, 'What are you doing? What's wrong with you?'

Deb yanked her arm free and said, 'Friends, my ass! You're fucking her, aren't you? Why don't you just admit it already? Why do we need *secrets* anymore?'

Deb's breath reeked of alcohol. Mark grabbed her again, trying to pull her farther from the table.

'You have to leave, right now,' he said. 'You're embarrassing both of us.'

'I'm embarrassing *you*? How about how you're embarrassing me by fucking this slut?'

'You talking about me?' Karen was standing near Mark and Deb.

Deb broke free from Mark and said to Karen, 'Somebody should tattoo a letter on your forehead!'

'Bitch,' Karen said.

'Whore,' Deb said.

'Cunt,' Karen said.

Deb pushed her, nearly knocking her down, and then Karen grabbed her, forcing her back toward the table. Deb lost her balance, tripping backward over a chair, and Karen fell with her, still grabbing her, as the tablecloth got yanked and dishes fell off and some smashed. Now Karen and Deb were wrestling on the floor, screaming, cursing at each other, and then Karen's hands were pushing down against Deb's throat. Deb said something and Karen spit in her face.

Mark watched the surreal scene for several seconds, too stunned to act, then he snapped into action and managed to separate the two. He got Deb to her feet and pulled her away as she screamed, 'Lemme go, I said, lemme go!'

Mark forced her to walk toward the exit, saying, 'Did you drive here? Did you?'

'And I was gonna go to fucking Italy with you,' Deb rambled. 'Why would I go to Italy with *you*?'

'You didn't drive here drunk, did you?'

'Where is she, huh? Where's the whore?'

'Come on,' Mark said.

He walked ahead, pulling her toward the front of the clubhouse. She kept resisting, screaming for him to let go. He knew everyone was watching them and, Jesus, some people were holding up their phones, filming. He was looking away, trying not to make eye contact with anyone. The only one he really cared about anyway was Karen, and he just wanted to get Deb away from her. He felt awful that Karen had gotten caught up in this, and he was terrified that she'd be upset and blame him.

Then, as he exited onto the terrace, still pulling Deb along, he looked back toward the table he'd been sitting at and saw that the nightmare was already happening.

Karen was gone.

5

OWEN HARRISON DIDN'T get what was up with Deb. Last week everything was so cool. They'd hooked up that afternoon in his room when his mother and stepfather were away and his brother was at school, and they were texting regularly too, and she seemed as into him as she always was, but then today, out of nowhere, she was freaking, and he had no idea why.

He'd started worrying about her attitude in the morning when he'd texted her about how psyched he was to meet up at swim practice, and she'd gotten all panicky, afraid her husband would see some texts. He was hoping that was all it was – panic – that it didn't really *mean* anything. So he just chilled the rest of the morning, driving his brother to the practice, and then slipping away up to the classroom, waiting for his naughty student. When she arrived right on time, he'd thought, *Okay, this is cool*, because, seriously, if something were really wrong, would she even show?

So they did their whole teacher-student thing, which

was as awesome as always. Well, he liked it better when they were in his bedroom and he could get her to put on the schoolgirl outfit he'd bought for her on eBay, but the actual fucking was always awesome. He loved telling her what to do, giving her orders, especially when it was stuff that he thought was really nasty. He got most of his ideas watching porn online. His favorite scenes were schoolgirl and cheerleader scenes which he knew didn't make a lot of sense because in those movies the girls were always young and the teachers and coaches and whoever were always old and in real life he was into MILFS. Well not *totally* into MILFS. He hooked up with girls his own age sometimes, and it was okay. But older women were different. There was just something about the idea of being with a woman who was as old as one of his teachers, or his mother, or one of his mother's friends, that drove him crazy. Before Deb, he'd had another older girlfriend. Well, she wasn't old-old like Deb – she was his babysitter, Melanie. She was sixteen when they'd started hooking up, and he was like twelve, and it continued until she went away to college at Oneonta and got a boyfriend up there sophomore year and wanted to stop. Owen was angry and tried hard to get her back, but it turned out to be okay, even better, because right around then he'd started his thing with Deb.

For a long time Owen had no idea Deb was even into him. Yeah, she always treated him nice and smiled a lot when she saw him but a lot of moms did shit like that and those moms didn't want to, like, get naked with him. But then, two summers ago, when he got the job at the country club, she started to talk to him more, asking him a lot of questions about school and whatever, and sometimes she gave him looks. Like sometimes they were talking and she'd look in his eyes a little too long, and one time he thought he saw her checking him out, looking him up and down, and it gave him a boner. He still wasn't sure she actually *liked* him – maybe she was just flirting or maybe the whole thing was in his imagination – but then one afternoon, her husband Mark and her kids weren't around, and he saw her sitting alone at the bar at the club, drinking – big surprise, right? – so he went over and talked to her. He just thought it would be a 'Hey, how you doing?' polite-like conversation, but then she was like, 'You want to go for a walk in the woods?' Then he knew she was into him because, seriously, why would a forty-something-year-old woman be asking a sixteen-year-old to take a walk in the woods if she didn't want to get laid?

So they were in the woods, talking about whatever, when Owen noticed that Deb wasn't walking fast, like she was trying to get somewhere. No, she was taking her time, and once or twice their arms brushed, but she didn't seem to care, which was another good sign. He wasn't going to try anything though. He was thinking things in his head, yeah, but he was afraid to come out and say them. Maybe it was because with Melanie he never had to ask. From the beginning, Melanie had always told him what she wanted.

Then he heard himself say, 'I wanna fuck you against that tree.'

He didn't mean to actually say what he'd been thinking; he wished he could suck the words back into his mouth or go back in time ten seconds and say something or nothing at all because now it was going to be a disaster. Deb probably wasn't into him at all and would get all upset and offended and tell Owen's mother what had happened, and then his mother would tell his stepfather, Raymond, and Raymond would beat the shit out of him.

So Owen was shocked when, instead of yelling at him or running away, Deb said, 'Then what're you waiting for?'

For a few seconds he thought he'd imagined it, but then

he was pushing her back against the tree and one hand was in her hair, grabbing a fistful of it, and his other hand was under her panties. He loved how she let him do whatever he wanted to do to her, how instead of just seeing a movie inside his head he was actually in the movie, or even better, it was like he was the director of the movie and she was the actress, and she had to do whatever he told her to do.

It only took that one time and, that was it, he was hooked. He wanted Deb all the time, he couldn't get enough of her and, even cooler, she felt the same way about him. He loved that she was so old – Melanie was a girl, but Deb was a woman.

Things had been going great until today, then all of a sudden shit got weird. After she was his naughty schoolgirl he saw that look in her eyes. It reminded him of two years ago, when Melanie came back from school and said, 'I'm in a relationship.' Her tone had been so cold, so distant, and Owen didn't get how a girl could change so fast, how she could be so into him one day, wanting his body so badly and saying she loved him and couldn't live without him, and then suddenly she was a completely different person, saying, 'It's over,' like none of it had really meant anything to her, like it was all just a big lie.

Owen didn't want to go through that pain again; he *couldn't* go through it again.

He was hoping he had it all wrong, that it was just something else going on, like some fight with Mark that had nothing to do with him. But then he texted her, just to make sure everything was still cool and shit, and she didn't text back.

Now memories of Melanie, how shitty and helpless she'd made him feel when she wanted to break up, were rushing back. Why was Deb acting this way? What did he do *wrong*?

He looked for her in the hallway and near the bathroom and then checked outside. Once in a while she smoked cigarettes, so she could have gone out to smoke, but more likely she'd gone to have a drink. She'd been drinking a lot lately, getting tanked at the club, and sometimes when they met in the backseat of his car in the back of the John Jay High parking lot, her breath smelled like alcohol. He'd ask her if she was drinking and she was like, 'No,' but that was bullshit. She was probably an alcoholic, just like his stupid asshole stepdad.

He headed toward her car in the lot – in the back of his mind, thinking, maybe if she was there she'd give him a quick BJ. He needed to know that everything was cool, that she wasn't angry with him, and that she hadn't actually changed the way Melanie had.

But she wasn't in her car. He was going to head back into the school when he decided to go behind the building, to the area where kids sometimes hung out, and sure enough Deb was there. He tried to act natural, get things back to normal, but then she got all paranoid about them being seen together and told him to get back inside.

So he went back into the school to wait for Kyle to finish practice, figuring he'd deal with the Deb situation the next time he saw her, when they were alone. But then he started panicking all over again, thinking, *What if there isn't a next time?* What if she didn't want to see him again and told him what Melanie had told him: *I need a clean break.* Now Owen was sweating; how had everything gone to hell so fast? Something must've happened with Mark. After all, Deb had had freak-outs about Mark before. A bunch of times over the past two years she'd told Owen that what they were doing was wrong, that they had to stop – shit like that. It had never seemed like any big deal, though, because she never wanted to stop fucking hooking up.

But this time felt different. She'd never seemed so distant; something had definitely changed. He didn't get why she'd want to stay with Mark, though. She was so unhappy with that guy, and she said they'd been living like roommates for years, and that they didn't even really like each other anymore. There was no way she could possibly pick Mark over him. Besides, everybody knew that Mark was screwing Karen Daily. Well, maybe everybody except Deb.

After swim practice he was hoping he'd see Deb down by the lockers, but she wasn't there and had probably already left. A few minutes later, driving home, Owen looked in the rearview and noticed that Kyle's eyes were red and glassy. At first he thought he had gotten chlorine in his eyes, then realized he was crying.

'What's wrong?' Owen asked.

Kyle wiped his eyes with the back of his hand and turned away.

'Hey, look at me.' Owen was concerned. 'I said look at me.'

Kyle turned back, tears gushing.

'What happened?' Owen asked. 'Come on, tell me.'

'The coach…'

'The coach? What happened with the coach?'

'He said… He said I'm too fat.'

'He *said* that?'

'He said that's why I got tired in the race last week. He said I have to stop going to McDonald's.'

'How does he know you go to McDonald's?'

'He said he saw us there last week.'

'Yeah? Well, if he saw us there, then what was *he* doing there?'

Kyle almost smiled.

'Seriously,' Owen said, 'that shit's totally inappropriate.

First of all, you're a good weight, a healthy weight. You've got muscle, more muscle than me. Second of all, if the coach has a problem with something, he should talk to me about it. He shouldn't be telling a little kid what to eat, especially when he's wolfing down a double cheeseburger himself.'

Now Kyle laughed.

'I'm gonna talk to the coach, don't worry about it,' Owen said. 'But, listen to me, from now on, I want you to be strong, hear me? I don't care who the person is. I don't care if he's the coach or your teacher or the President of the United States – don't let anybody treat you like shit. If somebody hurts you, you stand up for yourself. That's what this country's all about – fighting back. You're an American, Kyle. You understand what I'm saying?'

'Yeah,' Kyle said.

'Good,' Owen said.

Owen hoped he'd gotten through to his little brother. Somebody had to teach him values, how to act like a man in the world, and if Owen didn't do it, who would?

At home, Kyle went up to his room to play, and Owen went to the kitchen and started making a ham and Swiss sandwich for lunch when he heard, 'Save that ham for your mother.'

Owen glanced toward the entrance to the kitchen at Raymond, who was standing there shirtless, his big hairy beer gut hanging over his boxers.

'There's only a couple slices left,' Owen said.

'Yeah, and that's why you're gonna save it for your mother,' Raymond said.

Owen knew that Raymond had probably eaten most of the ham himself and now just wanted to eat the rest of it. For fuck's sake, Owen's mom didn't even eat ham. But Owen also knew that starting arguments with Raymond was usually a bad idea as any little thing could set him off. So, without saying anything, Owen removed the two slices of ham from the sandwich and put them back in the package. He was hoping that would be it but, of course, it wasn't.

'And you better clean your room before your mother gets home,' Raymond said.

Owen had no idea what the hell he was talking about. He'd just cleaned his room yesterday, and it wasn't messy at all.

'Whatever,' Owen muttered.

'What's that?' Raymond asked.

'I said okay,' Owen said.

He finished making a sandwich with just cheese, aware of Raymond standing there watching him, but not looking at him at all. Then, finally, he heard Raymond leaving the kitchen.

'Prick,' Owen said.

Raymond had no purpose in life except to make Owen and his whole family miserable. He didn't work, mooching off his mother, and Owen didn't even understand why his mother was with him except that she was afraid to be alone. Owen's dad was killed in a car crash when his mom was pregnant with Kyle – and then Raymond came along and they got married. She claimed she loved him, but was that an excuse to stay with a guy who treated her like shit and hurt her kids? It was still hard for Owen to believe that this prick was actually his stepfather. Owen didn't think of him as his stepfather, that was for damn sure. He was just some asshole they all had to put up with. Owen used to beg his mother to leave him, just kick him out of the house and call the cops and get one of those restraining orders if she was afraid of him, but she never listened. Then Owen started hating her too because what kind of mother would pick some guy over her kids, over her *family*? Sometimes Owen wished they were both dead, that they took a drive one day, and the car hit a tree and they both went through the windshield and died instantly, the way his father had died, because he knew he could raise Kyle on his own and that they'd both be a lot happier not living with a stepfather who beat the shit out of them whenever he felt like it and a mother who didn't give a shit.

Owen went up to his room with his cheese sandwich, shut his door, and locked it. He was chomping on the sandwich, still pissed off about Raymond's bullshit, when his phone chimed. Excited, thinking it was Deb, he checked the phone, disappointed when he saw it was from Elana Daily: **Hey!!!**

Owen knew Elana was into him. He'd kind of known it for years but he really knew it last month on that Friday night when he'd had nothing better to do – Deb was busy doing some family shit – so he went to a party at Jake Stefano's house and Elana was there and was all over him when they were on the couch and, then, when he was coming out of the upstairs bathroom, she was waiting there, like he knew she would be, and practically dragged him into Jake's parents' bedroom where she locked the door and pinned him down to the bed. She was on top, and he got her shirt off and he couldn't really get it up. Finally she went down on him and that worked – he came fast. He knew she wanted him to go down on her after, but he wasn't into it, so after a while they just put their clothes back on and went down to the party.

Now he texted back: **Hey, sexy!!!** Then he added: **Whats goin on???**

She told him about some party tonight at Dylan Ross' house and how great it would be if he would come. He texted back, **sounds awesome**, figuring at least he'd get another BJ. She wrote back, **awesome can't wait to c u!!!** and he wrote **can't wait to c u 2!!!** Then she was texting him about the time for the party and gave him the address too because he had no idea where the dude lived.

Then another text came in, but it wasn't from Elana; it was from Deb: **Can we talk at the club this aft?**

Owen felt the same rush he'd felt when he was in the classroom before. This was a great sign – it meant he really had been panicking for no reason and she was still as into him, that nothing had changed. She probably wanted to go into the woods for a quickie, or maybe make a plan to hook up somewhere later.

He responded: **Yeah!!! Sounds awesome!!!**

Then he texted her again to set up a meeting time and while he was waiting for her to answer back, he noticed, but didn't really care, that a few more texts had come in from Elana. It wasn't just because he wasn't that into her; it was because he wasn't really into *any* girls around his age. It didn't matter, though, because Deb would always be his number one, and other girls would always just be practice.

When he finished texting with Deb, making a plan to meet at the club at one-thirty, he checked the texts from Elana, she wanted to know what time he was going to get to the party. He texted: **Um can I text u later jus realized my mom might need to borrow my car**.

He was hoping she'd write back that this was cool, but she was like, **Me and Riley gettin lift from Sabrina we can get u!!** and he thought, *Shit*, and then sent: **K let u know later.**

It was all cool. This way he could see how it went with Deb. If she wanted to hook up tonight he'd come up with some other excuse to blow off Elana, but if Deb flaked Elana would be a good plan B.

A little later, as Owen was getting ready for work, he

was thinking how it was funny that his number one was Mark Berman's wife and his number two was Mark's girlfriend's daughter.

But somehow he knew Mark wouldn't think it was so funny.

Before Owen went downstairs he listened to make sure Raymond wasn't around. When it seemed safe he went down but it was almost like Raymond was hiding there, waiting for him – and maybe he was – because at the bottom of the stairs he practically leaped out of the kitchen and said, 'Hey, you clean your room?'

Owen didn't bother answering, just went by him on his way toward the front door. But Raymond grabbed his left arm hard, gripping almost his entire bicep.

'You deaf or something?' Raymond said.

Owen cocked his right fist, wanting to deck Raymond in his stupid, worthless face.

'Try it, you know what's good for you,' Raymond said. 'Go 'head, try it.'

Owen had hit Raymond before and, though it felt great for a second or two, it always made things worse because, yeah, maybe he'd get a couple of good shots in, but he was no match for Raymond who was probably fifty pounds heavier and six inches taller, and if he got Raymond angrier it just gave him more of an excuse to be an abusive piece of shit.

So Owen didn't hit Raymond but he should've known it wasn't going to save him a beating. Raymond slapped him in the face hard, one of his fingers or his thumb hitting Owen's right eye. As Owen screeched, Raymond grabbed him under the shoulders and lifted him up against the wall so they were at eye level.

'Shoulda hit me when you had the chance.' Raymond's

breath smelled like ham. 'You're gonna clean your room now, right?'

'Put me the fuck down,' Owen said.

'Keep talking back to me, I'll keep you up here all day,' Raymond said. 'I'll nail you to the fucking wall.'

'It's clean, it's fuckin' clean, man.'

Owen's knees were almost at the level of Raymond's balls. He wanted to do it; knee the prick in the balls, or lean forward and spit into the fat fuck's face or, better yet, bite off a chunk of it. Yeah, he actually *saw* himself biting off a chunk of Raymond's pudgy cheek and spitting it right back at him.

Back to reality, Raymond was saying, 'It *better* be clean and you better not talk back to me again when I tell you somethin' to do, or you and Jesus'll have somethin' in common.'

What Owen got was another whiff of ham, and then Raymond released his grip. Owen fell onto his knees, then saw Kyle, standing near the staircase. Owen hoped Kyle hadn't seen him acting so weak and defenseless.

Kyle ran upstairs.

Owen didn't remember leaving the house. An instant later – well, it *seemed* like an instant – he was suddenly in his car, backing out of the driveway. Then he saw Raymond on the lawn, half of his hairy, disgusting beer gut showing under his wife-beater. Raymond was saying something; Owen couldn't hear him, but he didn't give a shit. He three-point turned and was about to pass the house when he had a sudden impulse to yank on the steering wheel and run Raymond over. Just one little yank and the ugly asshole who'd been making all their lives miserable would be gone, mowed down like a fucking weed. Owen could say it was an accident, the steering wheel jammed. Maybe they'd believe him, maybe they wouldn't. Who gave a shit?

Just do it, he thought. *Come on, just fuckin' do it.*

But he was speeding up the block now. His neck still hurt from where Raymond had squeezed it and his heart was thumping. He wanted to get out of the house so badly, live on his own, but where would he go? He couldn't rent an apartment without money, and he was only making about four hundred a week as a groundskeeper at the country club, and it was a temp job. His mother always got on his case about how he should've gone to college. He could've done better in high school – he was smarter than everyone there – but he didn't see the point of trying. He didn't care about his grades because he didn't want to go to college and have to leave Deb.

He needed to see Deb – right now. When things got shitty at home, she always made him feel better, like there was a reason for living.

Twenty minutes later he pulled into the lot of the country club, spotting Deb's blue Pathfinder. He parked and when he got out he had to adjust his hard-on. It was 1:18, so he had like twelve minutes to kill before seeing her.

Heading through the clubhouse, he nodded 'hi' to Julio, a Mexican dude he worked with, then he continued past the pro shop to the employee locker room. He changed into his work clothes – work boots and a dorky Oak Ridge Country Club collared shirt.

Owen didn't know shit about grounds keeping when he'd gotten the job, but he was great at faking things, and he was a fast learner. Within a couple of days he could cut grass and landscape as well as the Mexican guys who'd been doing it their whole lives.

He was excited about Deb – she was probably really horny or she wouldn't've called for a second booty call in one day. Thinking about what fantasy he would do this time – stepmother-son? mother-son? – he headed back through the clubhouse, then out past the patio overlooking the first hole. Then he went past the far end of the club toward the storage shed.

As he approached it, maybe a hundred feet away, he could smell her. Not her perfume – *her*. He didn't know how this was possible; maybe it was some kind of sex, animal type thing.

She was waiting for him, but what was the deal? She had all her clothes on. Usually she was naked, or at least *half* naked, wearing something slinky and sexy. He smelled alcohol, which was a good sign, because a lot of the time she liked to get wasted before their hook ups.

'You just get here?' he asked, looking at the time on his cell phone.

They always arrived and left separately, a few minutes apart.

'It's over,' Deb said.

'What?' Owen asked, though Deb had spoken clearly and loud enough.

'I said it's over,' Deb said. 'We can't do this anymore.'

'What're you talking about?'

'Don't call or text or try to see me again,' Deb said. 'And stay away from my daughter.'

'Riley?' Owen was lost. 'What're you talkin' about?'

'You're pathetic,' Deb said. 'And I'm pathetic for ever getting involved with you. I'm lucky you didn't give me a disease, and if you gave my daughter a disease, I'll kill you. I swear to God I will.'

Owen didn't get this at all. It was like a nightmare.

'I have to go,' Deb said.

She tried to get by. He grabbed her by the wrist, hard.

'Let go of me,' she said, angry, not screaming, but she was about to.

'Chill,' he said. 'Just chill.'

'I'm telling you for the last time,' she said, 'get your fucking hands off me.'

Then something clicked – she wasn't actually saying this. Yeah, she was *saying* it, but she didn't *mean* it. This was just an act, one of their – what did she sometimes call it? – role plays. Yeah, it was a role play, like when he was the teacher and she was the naughty student. But now, she was Miss Innocent, and he was the Mean Stranger. Sometimes she liked it rough – wanted him to hold her down hard and pull her hair and bite her.

So he didn't let go. He tugged on her fiercely, trying to throw her down onto the floor. But she didn't fall; she slapped him, hard across the face, and he had a flash of Raymond hitting him, and he pushed her away and she fell back over an old lawnmower, onto her side. He knew he was probably going too far because this wasn't Raymond, and he wasn't really angry at *her*, but she wanted to be angry, to be rough, that was the whole point, so when she cursed at him again and told him to stay the fuck away from her, he went after her again and grabbed her and held her down onto the floor. Okay, he was right, this was what she wanted – some rough sex. He grabbed part of her skirt, tried to pull it down, and then she bit him on the side of his neck. He liked it – well, at first. Then the good pain turned to just pain and he screamed and must've let go of her because she was up, heading toward the door. He lunged after her, stumbling over the lawnmower, and tried to grab her legs, but couldn't. Then she left the shed, letting the door slam.

When he got to his feet and opened the door she was already about twenty yards away. He was about to chase after her but there were other people around – the practice putting green was off to the right and Luke, a pro at the club, was giving a lesson to some old guy. Okay, now

Owen was confused. What kind of role play was this if she was actually running away?

Whatever, he decided. She was drunk, maybe having another bad day with her husband. He knew she didn't actually mean that she didn't want to see him again, that was ridiculous.

Owen was going to get in a cart and head to the fairway near the sixth hole to do some pruning, when he heard some commotion coming from the clubhouse. It sounded like a woman screaming; was it *Deb*? So he jogged over to the clubhouse and stopped when he saw Deb screaming at Karen Daily, Elana's mom. Mark was there too, trying to calm Deb down. Okay, now it was all starting to come together for Owen. Deb's bad mood definitely had nothing to do with him – it was all because of Mark and Karen. Deb had probably walked in on them fucking or some shit which wasn't a bad thing at all, because if Deb and Mark were officially having trouble that meant Deb might be ready to kick him out of the house, and if he was out of the house, that meant Owen could move in.

Now Karen and Deb were fighting – wrestling on the floor. Ha, shit was so funny to watch, these two women, acting like crazy kids, and Owen took out his phone and filmed some of it. Karen was holding big clumps of Deb's hair and then Deb spat in her face. Then Mark was pulling Deb out of the café area, onto the terrace, Deb trying to get away, maybe to go after Karen. Then Deb looked right at Owen, and he smiled, wanting her to know that he knew what was going on, that it was all cool but, for some reason, probably because she was too angry at Karen, she didn't smile back. She just looked at Owen, with no expression at all, until Mark pulled her around the building toward the front of the club and she was gone.

6

DEB COULD HAVE killed Karen. If they weren't in public, if it had just been the two of them, she wouldn't have been able to stop herself. She would have attacked her, torn that skinny little home wrecker to pieces.

'You're crazy,' Mark said. 'You're out of your mind.'

Deb, still into the fantasy, believed Karen had said this and thought, *Yeah, I'm crazy, and I'm out of my mind, and I'm gonna kill you,* and it took a couple of seconds, or maybe much longer, till her drunken brain realized that they were in Mark's car, driving somewhere, probably home. Yeah, that's right, Deb had wanted to take her *own* car because the last place in the world she wanted to be was in a car with Mark, but he'd insisted she couldn't drive, that she was too drunk. Yeah right, she'd only had a few, but when she tried to get to her car, Mark grabbed her, she cursed and kicked him, wanting to kick him in the balls, his *cheating* balls, and then a security guy from the club came over, and she kept trying to get away, to drive the hell home, but Mark wouldn't let her go, and the security guy was talking about how he might have to call the cops, and then she finally gave in and got in the car with Mark.

Now Mark was saying, 'You know what you just did to us? You know what kind of damage you just did? We might get kicked out of the club, and you know what people will say? Those are my friends, they'll think you're crazy, *we're* crazy.'

Deb, exhausted from fighting and screaming, stared out the window, watching the scenery race by, still imagining having her hands around Karen's neck.

'You listening to me?' Mark asked. 'Do you even *care*?'

Mark's voice was so grating, Deb couldn't take it. She felt like such an idiot for staying with him for so long, listening to his lies.

'I want you to call the club and apologize,' Mark said. 'I want you to call the manager, Dave Thompson, and tell him how sorry you are. And I want you to apologize to Karen too.'

'*What*?' That had snapped Deb out of it.

'You heard me,' Mark said. 'I want you to call her right now, tell her you were drunk, you have a drinking problem, and –'

'You really think...' Deb was so upset she couldn't keep her thoughts straight. 'You honestly think...'

'You humiliated her,' Mark said.

'*I* humiliated *her*?' Deb said. 'What about *me*? What about what you did to *me*?'

'What did I do, except work my ass off for seventeen years?'

'Seventeen years,' Deb said. 'I've been putting up with your *shit* for seventeen years.'

'You mean spending my money. When was the last time you worked?'

'I sacrificed everything.'

'Sacrificed! Please. The kids are older now, you don't have to stay home. You can go back to work, but you don't want to. You want to sit around and get drunk all day.'

'My life,' Deb said. 'I threw my life away for you.'

'That's what you call raising a family?' Mark said. 'Throwing away your life?'

'Your distance, your self-involvement, your pathetic stupid everything about you.' Deb knew she wasn't making much sense, but she didn't care.

'You don't know how lucky you are,' Mark said. 'Most women would kill for a guy like me.'

'I want a divorce,' Deb said.

She hadn't planned to say this, but she liked the way it sounded, and the way it made her feel, as if a secret she'd been keeping for years had finally been told.

'Okay, let's stop with that crap again,' Mark said, staring at the road, making that expression Deb hated, the one where he scrunched up his nose and flared his nostrils.

'I'm serious.' Deb's voice was suddenly strong, certain. 'I've had it with you and this ridiculous fake life. I'm not staying married to a cheater.'

Deb had a flash of herself earlier, bent over the teacher's desk, looking back over her shoulder at Owen while he told her how naughty she was.

'I'm calling Scott Greenberg tomorrow,' she said.

Scott was a friend – well, one of Riley's friends' dad – who was a divorce lawyer.

'You know what I'm sick of?' Mark's face was red. 'I'm sick of you threatening me all the time, pulling the divorce card. And you know what else I'm sick of?' Mark looked away from the road, directly at her. 'I'm sick of your moods, that's what I'm sick of. One second you're talking about a trip to Italy, the next second you want a divorce.

You're like Jekyll and Hyde, I don't know what I'm gonna get from you next.'

'Look at the road,' Deb said.

'Mr Hyde,' Mark said. 'I'm married to Mr Fucking Hyde!'

Mark shut up the rest of the ride home, and Deb didn't say anything either. She wasn't fantasizing about killing Karen anymore; yep, she was beyond all that. If Mark wanted to spend his life with some pathetic, middle-aged, home wrecker, did it really matter? At least he'd be someone else's problem and Deb would be free; after seventeen mostly miserable years she could do whatever the hell she wanted. She could take that class at the Art Students League, or maybe go to grad school, get a Masters. She could get a job, maybe teach or work at a museum. She'd take Mark's money and the house for the kids, but she didn't need a man to take care of her – that was Mark's fantasy, not hers. And when she was ready, she'd meet someone, a real man, someone as unlike Mark as possible. He'd be sexy, adventurous, sophisticated, maybe European. Yeah, she could see herself with a tall, dark, sharply dressed European man who enjoyed the things she enjoyed – travel, theater, vineyards, literature, the ballet. It would be great to have a husband whose typical Friday night wasn't sitting on his ass, watching the golf channel, someone she could go to parties with and feel proud that he was cultured, had opinions, and when the subject turned to books he'd have something to talk about other than a John Grisham novel he'd once read.

Yeah, this had turned into the greatest day of Deb's life.

At the house, in the garage, Deb got out of the car while the engine was still running. Casey was barking, excited to see her.

'Not now,' she said to him and grabbed her iPad and

then went into the den/playroom on the second floor and push-locked the door. The page from Orbitz for Amalfi Coast vacations was still up and she said, 'Yeah, right,' as she left the page and Googled 'Scott Greenberg attorney.' As she called, she realized it was a Saturday and he wouldn't be in the office, but she didn't care. She left a message, reminding him who she was, and that she wanted to initiate divorce proceedings on her husband immediately and looked forward to talking on Monday. When she hung up she felt good for being proactive, for taking another big step toward freedom.

When she left the room, she noticed that Riley's door was open a crack, and she peeked in and saw Riley lying on her stomach in bed, propped up by her elbows, reading some soft cover teen fantasy novel.

Deb opened the door fully and said, 'Got a second?'

Riley didn't answer, so Deb went further into the room and sat on the foot of the bed and said, 'Seriously, I want to talk to you about something.'

'What is it?' Riley's eyes shifted toward Deb but she kept the book propped up.

'I want you to stay away from Owen Harrison,' Deb said.

'What?' Riley seemed confused. 'Why?'

'Because I told you to, that's why,' Deb said. 'He's too old for you and… and I just want you to stay away from him, okay?'

Now Riley put down the book and smiled. 'Wait,' she said. 'You seriously think something's going on with me and Owen Harrison?'

'I just want you to stay away from him,' Deb said.

'Yuck.' Riley looked disgusted. 'Owen's a total freak.'

Deb couldn't help feeling a little offended. 'I didn't say he was a *freak*,' she said. 'I just don't think he's appropriate for you.'

'Um, he's a freak, Ma,' Riley said. 'He's totally gross. Elana's into him, not me.'

'Elana?' Deb asked, wondering if Riley was telling the truth.

'Yeah,' Riley said, 'and I think she's crazy. I don't know why she likes him at all, but she's like obsessed, like so into him it's insane. That's why I asked you about him, because Elana's been getting suspicious, afraid he's cheating on her. You really thought *I* like him?'

Deb believed Riley, but she was suddenly confused by the whole situation. 'What do you mean by "so into him"?' she asked.

'You know, *into* him,' Riley said. 'Like seriously into him.'

Deb felt awkward and wasn't sure how to get into the conversation because, she realized, she had never really had an in depth conversation with Riley about sex. They'd *talked* about it, of course. Deb had answered most of her questions around the time she hit puberty and when she was taking sex ed, but they didn't have the kind of open relationship where they talked about sex and dating that some mothers seemed to have with their daughters.

'So you're trying to say that Elana has a crush on Owen?' Deb asked.

'No, way more than a crush,' Riley said. 'They've already, you know, done stuff.'

Deb suddenly felt unsteady, a little dizzy, as if she'd just gotten news about a relative's death. She said, 'Stuff. You mean they've… kissed.'

'Way more than kissing,' Riley said. 'They've been, like, you know… hooking up.'

Now Deb's stomach cramped, as if somebody were reaching in there and squeezing a fistful of her guts, and it was hard to get enough breath in her lungs to say, 'Hooking up,' and that was really all she could say with her brain churning, thinking about so many things at once.

'Yeah,' Riley said. 'Why? I mean like why do you even *care*?'

Deb imagined Owen and Elana in the back of his car, where *she* had been with him so many times before. She burped up the odor of vodka and stomach acid burned her throat.

'How do you know this?' Deb asked.

'Are you okay, Ma?' Riley seemed concerned.

'Did she tell you this?' Deb asked, fighting off another image of Owen as a teacher and Elana as his naughty student. 'I mean, did she actually tell you this or are you just... hypothesizing?'

'Are you sure you're okay, Ma?'

'Did she tell you or not?' Deb was losing patience.

'She didn't have to tell me,' Riley said. 'I was there. I mean not *there*, there, but I've seen them together. I mean, like, before they were together.'

'So is this something new?' Deb asked.

'Yeah,' Riley said. 'I mean kind of. But why are you asking? Why do you care?'

Deb wanted to keep grilling Riley, to find out exactly what was going on with Owen and Elana, but it hit that she'd better back off, that she didn't want it getting back to Elana, and then Elana telling Owen.

'Oh, I don't really care at all,' Deb said. 'I was curious because you mentioned him in the car, that's all, and I didn't want you dating an older guy. But I guess it was just a misunderstanding.'

Deb went back downstairs, right to the liquor cabinet, and poured a full glass of Stoli. Owen had once promised Deb that he wasn't dating anyone else and the idea that he'd been with Elana – and god knows how many other girls – repulsed Deb, but as she downed a second glass, she thought, *Does it really matter anymore*? After all, she'd dumped Owen anyway and was going to move on with her life, and at least apparently Owen hadn't been having sex with Riley so Deb should actually be *happy*.

But she wasn't happy. She felt used, lied to, played, but it was hard to blame Owen. He was young, naive, so it was understandable that he'd made a bad decision. It was actually *Elana's* fault. Like Karen had stolen Mark, Elana had stolen Owen – Deb was losing all her men to that fucking family. She was well on her way to Drunkville but, fuck it, she had a right to be angry; she wouldn't be human if she wasn't angry. She'd been humiliated twice today and she wasn't sure what to do about it.

'You're kidding me, right?'

Mark entered and saw Deb finishing the second drink. In the past Deb would have felt ashamed, defensive, but now she couldn't give a shit.

Ignoring him, she put the bottle away, then walked right past him, not making eye contact and said, 'Get ready for the fight of your life,' and went upstairs.

Ha, was that perfect or what? Mark was probably terrified, afraid he was going to lose everything, and little did he know that his fears were justified. If she didn't hate him so much for cheating on her and making her miserable, she would have felt sorry for him, because no one – not even a lying, cheating husband – deserved the hell he was about to go through.

Deb was scared too, though, and didn't want to be alone tonight. Without giving it any more thought, she texted Owen: **sory about before, can explain I rally want to c u later**

She knew she'd made typos, but she didn't want to waste time correcting them, wanting to hit send right away.

Seconds later she got: **Awesome!!!! Where u wanna meet?**

Deb felt a rush, knowing she'd made the right decision. Fuck Mark. Fuck logic.

They made plans to meet up at eight-thirty 'at their usual spot,' in the back of the parking lot of John Jay High School.

Later, in a little black dress and knee-length black boots, Deb checked herself out in the full-length mirror on the back of the bathroom door and loved how she looked. She usually didn't dress sexy, and she hadn't felt this good about herself in years; she felt like she was twenty-three years old, after college, living with friends in that small apartment on the Upper West Side. Life had been so simple then – work, shopping, and meeting guys were her only real concerns. She wanted that easy, simple life again.

She called for a car service and went downstairs when she heard Casey barking, meaning that a car had pulled up outside. Mark was sprawled in the living room, his finger in his nose, watching golf. Mark stopped picking his nose when he noticed her and, though she only glanced in his direction for an instant as he flicked away the booger, she knew he was checking her out, noticing how sexy she looked, probably wondering where she was going, looking so hot. Good, let him have his regret – he deserved it – and it felt great to be able to come and go as she pleased. For years she'd felt like a repressed teenager with Mark as her overbearing father. Well, so long, Daddy.

Riding in the back of the car down Savage Lane, past Karen's house, Deb said, 'The nose picker's all yours, sweetie. Enjoy!'

The driver, an older Indian guy, looked at her in the rearview and said, 'I'm sorry?'

'Not you,' Deb said. 'I was talking to the husband-stealing whore who lives in that house over there.'

Then she texted Mark: **Drop J at sleepover at Andrews**

That was perfect – texting about Justin but leaving her plans tonight a mystery. She wanted him to feel the loss, know that the intimacy in their marriage was gone forever.

The car service dropped her in the parking lot of the country club where she picked up her Pathfinder. Driving, she turned on her iPod and let Billy Joel, *My Life*, rip as she opened both front windows part way and felt the wind rushing through her hair. She wasn't forty-four, she was seventeen, driving along a highway in Bergen County, New Jersey, where she grew up. She had completely lost her buzz from the Stoli, but it didn't matter.

It was all good.

Owen was never late for sex and tonight was no exception. At eight-thirty headlights appeared, and then his car eased into the spot next to where she'd parked, and he cut the engine. Then he got out and got back in to the backseat. She exited her car, barely aware that it was starting to rain, and opened his car door. As usual, he had left a flashlight, turned on, on the front seat, which illuminated the entire car in a dull orange hue, but bright enough to see each other clearly. He was sitting casually, one foot up on the seat, smiling widely.

'I knew you wouldn't be able to stay away from me for long, baby,' he said.

Deb, halfway into the car, froze, not sure if she was mesmerized or just confused. It was raining harder; she felt the cold drops on her head, neck, and back.

'What're you waiting for?' he asked.

Deb didn't budge until she realized she was starting to get soaked and then she came in all the way and shut the door.

'The wet look,' Owen said. 'I like that.'

He reached under her dress and touched her thigh, and she instinctively tensed. Rain sizzled on the car's roof.

'Come here,' he said, grabbing her waist and trying to pull her toward him.

Resisting, Deb said, 'Don't.'

But he didn't listen; instead, he grabbed her harder, saying, 'Come on, what's –' and Deb had to push him away from her. He wasn't grinning anymore.

'Why'd you do that?' he asked.

Outside lightning flashed and Deb thought, *Who is this kid*? *Kid*, because that was how he looked – like a child, a baby. In this dim light he could be fifteen years old, younger than when they'd met, and there was nothing sexy about him, and he didn't even seem particularly attractive. He was wiry, awkward looking. His ears stuck out too far, and he had oddly shaped arched eyebrows. For the first time, she realized, she was seeing him the way Riley, and probably everybody else saw him – there was definitely something *off* about him. He hadn't gone to college and was living with his parents and was working at a temporary, dead-end job. Worse, he had no real interests or ambition and there was nothing particularly interesting about his personality. He wasn't funny or smart or a very good conversationalist. From her new perspective, as a separated woman, she realized there wasn't anything even intriguing about him. Though they'd had good sex, now it was hard to fathom why exactly she had been so attracted to him. Thoughts of his bony, hairless child's body seemed repulsive – she couldn't even stand the way he smelled, with his nauseating Axe cologne. This wasn't close to the suave, sophisticated Italian man she'd been fantasizing about meeting. Now it seemed absurd, completely insane that she'd been involved with him at all, and she just wanted, no, *needed* to get away.

'This was a mistake,' she said.

She reached for the door handle, but he grabbed her waist. There was another, brighter flash of lightning, as if someone had snapped a photo of the two of them, and then they were back in near darkness.

'Get your hands off me,' Deb said.

'What's wrong?' He wouldn't let go. 'Why're you freaking again?'

'I have to get home now.'

'Come on, talk to me, baby.'

His hand on her waist was like a claw. She felt like she couldn't breathe, like she wasn't in a car, she was in a coffin.

'Let go of me,' she said during a blast of thunder and she wasn't sure he'd heard her.

'This is bullshit,' he said. 'Why won't you just chill? What did I do? What did I do?'

Who was this guy? She didn't even recognize his voice.

'We're over,' she said. '*This* is over.'

His leg was on her now – how had that happened? – and with the hand that wasn't clawing her thigh he was reaching under her shirt.

'I get it.' He was smiling again. 'So this is how you want it tonight, huh?'

'Let go,' she said as lightning illuminated his crazed face.

'Like that time last year in the woods,' he said.

She knew what he meant – last summer, the time they met at Katonah Memorial Park. They'd met there a few times last summer, but she knew exactly what time he was talking about. She'd told him she wanted to pretend they were strangers, that she was walking in the woods alone and that he was following her, stalking her. The fantasy had been hers, not his, but now it seemed like no one's. It seemed as if the images in her head weren't memories of herself, they were scenes from a movie she'd once seen, or a story she'd once heard, and weren't connected to her at all.

'This isn't a fantasy,' she said. 'I want you to stop.'

He kissed her with his slimy lips. Disgusted, she spit back at him.

'I like that,' he said. 'Just like you spit at Karen today. Do that some more.'

His hand was lower now, fingers extended, digging under her panties. She tried to get to the car door but now, with the full weight of his body holding her down, he was able to remove the hand from her waist and grab her extended arm by the wrist.

Thunder blasted, but not as loud as before.

'Trying to get away, just like the woods,' he said. 'That turns you on, huh, bitch? Come on, spit on me some more.'

She spit right in his eyes, but it only seemed to excite him even more. He was yanking on her panties, pulling them down.

'You want it rough?' he said. 'You want it *nasty*?'

She was trying to wriggle free, but he was pinning her down too tightly. Her panties were down to her thighs, and he was unzipping his jeans. She knew that within seconds he'd be inside her, and she couldn't let that happen because this wasn't a fantasy; now he actually *was* a stranger in the woods.

So she did the only thing she could do to stop him. She lunged her head forward and bit down in the same motion onto the only part of his body she could reach – the side of his shoulder. She was pressing her teeth through his shirt, but there wasn't much fat there – it felt as if she were biting into bone – and he was suddenly screeching in agony. He was trying to break away, but she wouldn't let go, knowing that she had to make him feel the pain, that it was her only chance.

'Oh, god,' he wailed. 'Oh... shit... stop it!'

He let go of her wrist, and she immediately stiff-armed his neck, pressing right against his Adam's apple, and that made him pull his entire body back a bit, and she had to stop biting him. He was still on her lap, though, weighing her down, and she still couldn't get out of the car. The rain had subsided, the storm passing as quickly as it had come.

'Ow,' he groaned. 'Why'd you do that?'

He was crying – not just tears from the pain, actually crying. Now he *really* seemed like a child, and Deb had clarity about exactly what she'd done for the past two years. She was a filthy, horrible, disgusting, perverted person, no better than any child molester.

'You have to let me go now,' she said. 'It's over. Do you understand me, Owen? *Over.*'

Tears gushing, he said, 'You aren't supposed to actually hurt me. Isn't that your rule?'

Had she actually made up rules for a rape fantasy game with a teenager?

'We aren't doing this anymore, that's what I'm trying to tell you,' she said. 'I'm not pretending to get away from you, I really want to get away from you, not because I don't like you, or think you're a bad person, but because what we're doing, what we've *been* doing, is wrong. It served its purpose, but it's time to move on, for both of us. You have to be with someone your own age. Someone like Elana Daily.'

'Elana Daily?' He was still crying, but he sounded angry. 'Why would I want to be with Elana Daily?'

For a moment, Deb wondered, *Had Riley lied to her after all*? But with Owen still on top of her, this wasn't her major concern.

She said, 'You know what I mean. Somebody else... somebody more... appropriate.'

'No.' Owen took a few moments to compose himself, then said, 'No. I don't want anyone else but you. You're the most important person in my life.'

There was desperation in his voice that she'd never heard before.

'I understand why you're so upset right now,' she said. 'I'm upset too. This is hard for me too. But you knew this wouldn't go on forever, right? I mean we once discussed all that.' Had they ever discussed it? She thought they had, but she wasn't sure of anything. She continued, 'Anyway, now we have to say goodbye to each other. I know you're a smart, perceptive person. You can understand this, can't you?'

'Is it because of your stupid husband?' Owen asked. 'Did he find out?'

'No, no one found out,' Deb said, 'and it has to stay that way. It won't be good for either one of us if anyone finds out. But I know I can trust you about that.'

Actually, Deb didn't know if she could trust him. Actually, she was terrified.

Then he was kissing her, his tongue part way into her mouth.

She turned her head and said, 'Stop it, Owen,' the way she would discipline a child.

Owen, getting that she was serious about this, shook his head a couple of times, then said, 'No... No, this isn't happening. I... I'm not losing you... I *can't* lose you.'

'Don't think of it that way,' Deb said. 'We're ending, but I'm not ending. I could always be in your life. We can be friends.'

She had no intention of maintaining a friendship – that was the last thing she needed. She figured she'd email with him a couple of times, maybe exchange a few texts, then gradually distance herself. Hopefully by then he'd meet somebody else, forget about her.

'I'm not your fucking friend,' Owen said.

'Okay,' Deb said, trying to calm him. 'Friend was a bad word. We're more than friends, we just can't be...' She was going to say 'lovers,' but went with, '... like we've been. We just need to take a break from all this, but everything will be okay. I promise you that.'

He was crying again. She didn't feel like she was getting through to him at all.

'You have no idea,' he said. 'You don't know. You just don't.'

The rain had completely stopped. She just wanted to be in her car, driving, hitting the gas.

'Yes, I do know,' Deb said, touching his hand in a sweet way.

'No, you fucking don't.' Owen swatted her hand away. 'Raymond makes my life hell.'

'I understand,' Deb said, 'but it'll get better. You're young, your future's bright.'

'Bullshit,' Owen said. 'Raymond's a fuckin' asshole.'

Owen had told Deb about his abusive stepfather. Deb used to feel sorry for him, wanted to help, but now she couldn't get in touch with those feelings. She just didn't want to be here, in a parking lot in the dark, counseling a teenager.

'You can move out,' Deb said. 'You can get help. You have options, Owen.'

'You don't get it,' he said. 'He doesn't just hit me. He does more, *a lot* more.' He sobbed, seemed out of control, on the edge of a breakdown. Then he said, 'It started when I was a kid, like, ten years old. I was just a kid and didn't know what was going on and sometimes Raymond, he'd come into my room when my mom was sleeping and... and he'd...'

Owen was so upset he couldn't continue. As he cried,

holding his hands over his face, he shifted off her a bit, and Deb thought if she reached for the door handle and moved fast enough, then she could get out, and if Owen came after her, she could slam the door, maybe giving her enough time to get to her car, start it, drive away. She wasn't sure she could make it, but if she had a chance she had to take it. Later, she could call him, text him, calm him down, which would be better than trying to calm him down here.

Then Owen said, '... he'd get in bed with me. I'd feel his big, hairy, disgusting body next to me, and he told me if I told my mother, if I told anybody, he'd kill me. So I did what he said, I never told anybody, except you, right now.'

He was looking at her, eyes widened, not saying anything. She knew he was waiting for some kind of response, but, thinking about the door, she wasn't sure what to say.

When she felt too much time was going by, she had to say *something*, so she said, 'I'm so sorry that happened, Owen. Maybe you should talk to someone about it.'

He was still staring at her. He looked angrier, unless she was just imagining it.

Then he said, 'I am talking to someone about it. I'm talking to you.'

'No, I mean maybe you should get professional help,' Deb said. 'You know, from a psychologist.'

'Why can't *you* help me?'

'I have to go now, Owen.'

'No. You can't.'

Deb knew she wasn't imagining it – his eyes had narrowed, and she could see his jaw shift as his teeth grinded. Worse, he'd shifted his weight back onto her, and he'd grabbed her shoulder, pinning her back again.

'Say you need me,' he said.

'*What?*'

'You heard me. Say you *need* me. Say it.'

'You need help, Owen.'

'Say it, you old fucking bitch.'

He was looking at her, but he wasn't there anymore. It was like she was looking at the eyes of a dead person. Her instincts screamed: *run!* She glanced at the door handle, wishing she'd reached for it ten seconds ago, and then she couldn't breathe.

'Say it,' he said. '*Say it.*'

It took a few seconds before she realized *why* trying to gasp was useless, but she still didn't understand what was actually happening because, even as full blown panic set in and she was staring at Owen's crazed face, trying to kick and flail her arms, do *anything* to get free, she kept telling herself that this was just a fantasy, a game, like the games they always played, and the game would end soon and everything would be fine, because everything was always fine, but then she got weaker and dizzier and could hardly move, and then, near the end, she knew it was real, all of it, and her life and the whole world had never seemed so stupid.

7

WE NEED TO TALK
      The text Karen sent Mark when she got home
from the country club.

Following the crazy, drunken scene Deb had caused
she'd wanted to call Mark immediately, but she was too
upset and didn't want to say something that she'd end up
regretting. Despite how furious and humiliated she was,
she knew it was always best to let things settle and think
before responding in these sorts of situations.

She went into the kitchen where Elana was standing,
leaning against the breakfast bar, FaceTiming, saying to
whomever, 'Wait, can you hold on?' and then going past
Karen, toward the stairs.

'Hello to you too,' Karen said to her back.

'Hello,' she said and went upstairs, saying, 'Sorry, it was
just my mom.'

While Karen didn't appreciate Elana's sassiness, she
figured she'd deal with it later; one drama at a time.

Mark hadn't texted her back – to be expected. She knew him well and knew he liked to avoid conflict, which was probably how he'd managed to stay married to Deb for so long. As Karen flashed back to her and Deb on the floor of the restaurant, clawing at each other's faces, she had a surreal moment, thinking, *Was that really* me? She was probably still in shock, she realized. She had no idea why Deb was so convinced that something was going on between her and Mark, but she needed Mark to set her straight because she couldn't have a scene like today happen ever again. Karen worked at an elementary school, for god's sake; she had a reputation to protect. There were several members of the country club who had kids at her school and, thank god, they hadn't been at the club today, and Karen was glad Jill hadn't been there either. Jill was a friend, but Karen didn't want *anyone* she knew to see such an ugly side to her.

Still no response from Mark. She imagined he was panicked, overwhelmed, trying to figure out how to deal with his out-of-control wife and appease Karen at the same time. Mark was the type of guy who liked the status quo, who wanted things to be *okay*, but Karen wasn't about to feel sorry for him.

Karen went into the living room and did some light stretching and then got into a few yoga positions – Plank, Pyramid, Mountain. This usually relaxed her, but she had too many worries, and it barely had an effect. She had her phone near her on the floor and when there was a chime indicating an incoming text, her heart raced, as she thought it was Mark but then she saw 'Steven' on the display. Then she saw the message – **Can we talk for a sec when you have a chance?** – and she thought, great, that was all she needed now – drama with a guy she'd just broken up with. She had no idea what Steven wanted, but after she ended the relationship with him just last night she didn't think he should be texting her the next day.

In Downward Facing Dog, Karen contemplated the Steven situation for a while, then her anxiety drifted back to Deb – what exactly had gotten her so suspicious and paranoid lately? Karen couldn't think of any particular conversation they'd had, but last night at the Lerners' dinner party, Deb had definitely been acting weird.

And then it hit – god, it was so obvious, she couldn't believe she hadn't caught on sooner. Deb had been acting odd at the Lerners because that was where the misunderstanding had happened. During dinner, Karen had excused herself and gone to the bathroom. When she came out, Mark was there, waiting – the way he seemed to accidentally run into her lately. He seemed serious, concerned about something, and said, 'Come on, I need to talk to you for a second.' Karen, a little uncomfortable, just wanted to return to the dinner table, but she wanted to make sure that he was okay. So she went with him outside to the garden and stopped and asked, 'What is it?' and he'd said, 'Come on.' Again she resisted her instincts and went with him toward the pool and asked, 'What's going on?' and he said, 'So what do you think?' and she asked, confused, 'Think about what?' and he said, 'The Lerners. Are they out-of-control pretentious, or what?' Wait, so this was why he'd led her out here, to *gossip*? She'd said something like, 'We should go inside,' or maybe, 'Let's talk about this later.' And that was when it happened. She didn't even know what exactly was going on until a few seconds later, because she had been caught so off-guard. Then she was surprised because it was so 'un-Mark.' He'd been a good friend to her for years, but he'd never held her hand, and it wasn't just the hand holding. It was the way he was gazing at her, romantically, looking at her lips. She said, 'Um, what are –' and, as if snapping out of it, he said quickly, 'Sorry, sorry. I guess we should go back inside.'

That was the end of it, and Karen hadn't given it much thought afterward because it really hadn't seemed like a big deal. He'd held her hand for maybe five seconds tops and, on the way in, back to the party, he'd seemed almost embarrassed about it. She figured he'd had a couple of drinks, got a little too flirty with an old friend – what was the big deal? But that was exactly when Deb's attitude had changed, when they got *back* to the table. So Deb must have seen them. Maybe she'd gotten up to go to the bathroom herself, or was looking for Mark, but she must have looked out through the patio door at the moment Mark had held her hand, and that was why she'd jumped to a completely wrong, ridiculous conclusion.

Now Karen was angrier with Mark because, even if he had nothing to do with Deb getting a wrong idea, he must have known, or at least sensed, what his wife was upset about, and had blatantly lied, telling her that everything was fine and it had nothing to do with her, when it had everything to do with her.

Karen's phone chimed, a text from Mark: **So so sorry, sweetie!**

Sweetie? Was he fucking serious?

Pulse pounding, she hit back with: **Please stop calling me sweetie!!**

Then added: **And erase these texts!!!**

Several seconds later she got: **Erased!!**

Then: **So so sorry, but don't worry, it'll all be okay**

Then: **Promise!**

Calmness was officially out of the question now. Her anger was dominating, controlling her. She texted: **It is not okay! You have to talk to her immediately, tell her absolutely nothing is going on with us!!**

Maybe a minute later she got: **Done babe! Already talked to her! Will all be okay, trust me!**

Karen didn't trust him and didn't even believe he'd spoken to Deb. Mark was wimpy and spineless, especially when it came to his relationship with his wife.

She fired back: **You better talk to her, or I'm going to talk to her myself. I won't get sucked into your drama, Mark! I won't!! And don't call me babe!!!**

She had a feeling this would get through to him. The last thing he probably wanted was her and Deb getting into an ongoing fight about this, which would make his life at home even more difficult. Sure enough she got back a meek: **ok**

The rest of the afternoon, Karen did her best to put the situation out of her mind. She did chores – laundry, some straightening up. She didn't hear anything further from Mark, but she got another text from Steven: **r u around today?** Now she was certain that Steven wasn't acting appropriately – texting her *twice* after a breakup? She wasn't sure how to respond, *if* she should respond, and definitely didn't feel like dealing with it today. Then she checked her email and got a nice note from Richard the dentist, asking her if she wanted to talk on the phone or get together sometime. She didn't respond, but planned to later, when she felt more settled.

This whole being single, dating thing had been fun for a while, but not so much lately. Maybe if she lived in the city, she would've felt differently, but in Westchester there seemed to be a giant spotlight on her all the time – she was a single, divorced woman, *the* single, divorced woman. Dinner last night at the Lerners' had been an exception; she'd been excluded from many social events that couples were usually invited to, and even her close female friends – mainly moms of her kids' friends – whom she'd gotten close to while she was married, had left her off of guest lists recently. The country club was the worst as there were only a few single, divorced female members, and it was hard not to feel self conscious, especially when she was around happily married people. She could get over her insecurities, but she was getting tired of being alone and shopping for men on the internet. Besides, dating was a huge time suck, and she'd rather spend that time with her family and with someone she loved.

After laundry, she whipped up a quick dinner for the kids – macaroni and cheese and a salad. When she called them downstairs, Matthew immediately came to the table. He was excited about the sleepover party tonight with a few others boys at Andrew Waxman's house, and he was gobbling his dinner up, as if figuring the sooner he finished, the sooner he'd get to see all of his friends. Elana didn't come down right away, and Karen had to call for her a few times before she finally sashayed into the kitchen in a tight red strapless dress and high heels. Karen thought the dress was way too sexy, even borderline slutty.

'Wow, that's some dress,' Karen said, letting the implication linger.

'Thanks,' Elana said, texting somebody.

'Please put the phone away, it's rude,' Karen said.

'Sorry,' Elana said. Then, glancing at the plate of food on the table, added, 'I'm not hungry.'

'It's not healthy to skip meals,' Karen said.

Karen didn't think Elana was anorexic but had been concerned about her weight for some time. Especially the last few months, Elana's body – in particular her arms and shoulders – looked bonier.

'I had lunch,' Elana said.

'What did you have?' Karen asked.

'Yogurt and a piece of fruit.'

'That's not enough.'

'That's what *you* have for lunch.'

This was true, but Karen said, 'You didn't have enough breakfast either.'

'I'll eat at the party.'

'I want you to eat now.'

Elana sighed and said, 'Fine, but there's no way I'm eating all those carbs.'

She joined Matthew – who was busy gobbling down his food – at the table.

Karen watched her take a few bites of salad, mostly lettuce, then asked, 'Are you comfortable wearing that?'

Confused, Elana asked, 'What?'

Karen's look explained it.

'Oh,' Elana said. 'It's cotton.'

'No, I mean are you comfortable with that outfit?'

'I look sexy.'

'But don't you think you look *too* sexy?'

'How can you look too sexy?'

'Please change into something else.'

Shaking her head, Elana continued eating her salad.

'Done,' Matthew announced and stood up. 'Can I play XBox?'

'No, we have to leave for Andrew's party soon.'

Matthew left the room, sulking.

'What was I doing?' Karen asked herself. 'Right, loading the dishwasher.'

Karen did some more chores in the kitchen and around the house and when she returned Elana had finished her salad and some of her mac and cheese. She checked the garbage to see if Elana had tossed some of the food, but all seemed clear.

'Okay, a few more bites and you can go change,' Karen said.

She glanced at her phone and remembered that she

owed Richard an email, so she opened the Match app and, keeping it simple, wrote that she'd love to chat on the phone sometime or get together and sent him her number. She remembered how Mark had bashed Richard earlier. Was he trying to protect her, or was he just jealous? The idea of Mark getting jealous would have seemed crazy just twenty-four hours ago, but after what had happened at the Lerners' last night and at the country club today, it made Karen question his intentions all along. All those times he'd helped her with divorce and financial issues, was he actually *hitting* on her?

The doorbell rang. Karen opened the door and saw Riley Berman there in a flimsy black dress, so short most of her butt cheeks were exposed. Well, it didn't seem like there was much great parenting going on in *that* household.

'Hey,' Riley said. 'I just texted Elana from my friend's car.'

Karen glanced toward an idling Honda and Sabrina Feldman at the wheel, busy texting.

'I'm here,' Elana said in the monotone she spoke in when she was angry.

Elana was behind Karen and had just come downstairs in jeans, heels, and a nice tank.

'Much better,' Karen said.

But Elana ignored this, saying to Riley, 'C'mon, let's go,' as she headed toward the car.

'I want you home by eleven the latest,' Karen said to their backs, 'and you better keep your phone on.'

Karen's phone chimed – she didn't recognize the number on the display.

She tapped, said, 'Hello?'

'Karen?' A man's voice.

She didn't know who it was, said tentatively, 'Yes?'

'Richard Gross from Match.'

111

'Oh, hello,' she said, trying to sound upbeat.

'Hope I didn't get you at a bad time,' he said.

'No, I'm just getting my kids out, but it's not a bad time at all.'

Sitting on the living room floor in a half lotus, she chatted with him for a while. He was charming, had a good sense of humor, and seemed genuinely interested in her and her career. He suggested meeting for dinner on Tuesday at an Italian restaurant in New Rochelle and Karen said that sounded like a wonderful idea.

A few minutes later, in the car on the way to the sleepover at Andrew's, positive feelings about Richard had overwhelmed negative feelings about Mark and Deb. Today's drama, and the whole situation, seemed so meaningless. So Mark had a crush on her, and Deb had exaggerated the situation in her head and things had gotten a little out of control. What was the big deal?

The sleepover was in Golden's Bridge, the next town over from South Salem, at a nice, contemporary house. Andrew's father, Tom, did something on Wall Street, and his wife Sarah used to work in the city, also in finance, but had been a stay-at-home mom the past several years and was active on the PTA at Meadow Pond, the school where Karen taught. Karen and Sarah had never been great friends, but they'd always been friendly whenever they ran into each other, usually at play dates, sleepovers, and other events for their boys. This evening, though, something seemed off. Sarah usually greeted Karen with a warm kiss on the cheek and had a short conversation with her, but today when she opened the door she barely smiled and said to Matthew, 'The boys are upstairs.'

Matthew dashed up to his friends and Sarah said to Karen, 'You can pick up any time tomorrow before noon,' but she wasn't making eye contact, maybe distracted by something or someone to her left in the house's living room. It was also unusual that Sarah hadn't invited her in, as she usually asked her if she wanted coffee or something else to drink. Eh, Karen figured, maybe she was just overwhelmed, having to host a party for about ten prepubescent boys.

'I'll get him by eleven,' Karen said.

'Great,' Sarah said, now looking beyond Karen, toward the street.

Karen turned and saw Mark approaching with Justin.

'Hey you,' Mark said, smiling widely at Karen.

Karen was surprised to see him, and she was also thinking, *Is he for real?* After everything that had happened today, and all the texts, was he really saying, 'Hey you' to her? She wasn't sure what to say, when he reached out and grabbed her hand and said, 'Wait one sec, I wanna talk to you.'

Flustered, Karen didn't react right away. Maybe a few seconds went by. Then it registered – Mark was holding her hand again.

Karen yanked her hand free, but it was too late. She looked at Sarah, who was still at the door, and it was obvious she had seen what had just happened. Great, this was all Karen needed, another misunderstanding, this time right in front of Sarah who had a reputation as a major gossiper.

While Mark dropped off Justin with Sarah, Karen lingered. She didn't want to talk to Mark – not here anyway. She just wanted to get into her car and drive away, but she thought that could come off as too dramatic, and she didn't want to make a bigger scene than she already had.

After Mark exchanged goodbyes with Sarah – she'd been very smiley and outgoing with him – Mark came over to

Karen and, seeming excited, almost hyper, said, 'Wow, it's so great running into you here.'

'What the hell?' Karen sneered.

'What?' Mark was instantly defensive. 'What did I do?'

'What is it with you lately? Seriously.'

'I have no idea what you're talking about.'

'You can't do things like this.'

'I was just excited to see you.'

'But you can't be excited to see me. I'm not someone you should be excited about. And you can't just –' Karen realized she was raising her voice, and the last thing she needed was Sarah overhearing and/or watching a dramatic conversation through a window. In a more controlled tone she said, 'You grabbed my hand. Why did you grab my hand *again*?'

'I grabbed your hand?' He sounded lost.

Straining to maintain an even, non-agitated expression, Karen said, 'I told you I'm not getting sucked into the middle of anything, and I meant it. Did you talk to her yet?'

'Yeah, don't worry, sweetie, it's all taken care of.'

'Please don't call me sweetie, and what did you tell her?' Keeping a calm expression seemed to involve every muscle in her face.

'I told her what you wanted me to tell her, that nothing's going on.'

Karen didn't think he was lying.

'Fine,' she said. 'That's good.' She looked toward the house and thought she saw the blinds on the living room window rustle. She added, 'Well, this isn't the place to have this conversation, so I'll talk to you later.'

But she wasn't planning to talk to him later. She was angry and frustrated and just wanted him to leave her alone.

As she walked away toward where her car was parked, Mark came up behind her and said, 'Wait, hold up.'

She didn't stop, but he'd caught up to her and walked alongside her.

'I have to tell you something,' he said.

'What is it?'

'Can we go in your car?'

She didn't want him in her car, and she had no idea why he wanted to get in with her. Well, she didn't want to think about the reason why anyway.

'I'm in a rush, I have to meet someone,' she lied.

'A date?' he asked.

Did he sound jealous?

'Kind of,' she said, thinking, *Why not* make *him a little jealous*? Maybe it would help him realize that they were just friends, and that's all they would ever be.

'How do you kind of have a date?'

Karen stopped in front of her car. 'Seriously, what's this about?' There was no one around so she felt freer to talk.

Now Mark had a weird, overly sincere expression. 'It's kind of about what we were talking about before,' he said. 'As you know, my marriage has been, well, pretty stormy for a long time, and Deb's drinking has been out of control.'

'Okay.' Karen was impatient.

'I'm just saying,' Mark said. 'I mean maybe today, what happened, maybe it was a good thing. You know, I mean, for us.'

'Us?'

'Yeah, for our, you know… connection.'

'Connection?' Karen couldn't believe she was actually hearing this. 'What *connection*?'

'Whatever you want to call it,' Mark said. 'The thing we have going on.'

'The *thing*? What *thing*?'

'You know, the thing. I mean, I'm not sure where things are going with Deb so, you never know, me and you, maybe we'll get a chance to spend more time together. You know, in the future.'

'Are you out of your fu –' Karen checked to make sure there wasn't anyone around then continued, 'You're crazy, you've totally lost it. There's nothing going on with us, nothing at all, and there never was anything going on with us. We're friends, that's it. *Friends,* F R I E N D S. I don't know what this is about, I honestly don't. I'm clueless.'

'Okay, never mind, never mind,' Mark said, trying to calm her down. 'I know this isn't the best time to talk about this. Talk to ya later, okay?'

He moved in quickly and kissed her on the cheek. She reacted late, jerking her head back away, but the kiss had already ended.

When she got in the car she saw Mark outside in front of her. He was holding his hand up to his ear like a phone and, though she couldn't hear him, she could read his lips: *I'll call you.*

Ugh, Karen couldn't take this anymore. As she drove away, she wiped her face where Mark had kissed her. There wasn't any saliva there, but it felt like there was. It felt like her face was covered in his spit.

Then, a couple of minutes later, her phone chimed. Shit, it wasn't Mark already, was it? On top of everything else she had to deal with in her life – taking care of her kids, her work, trying to meet the right man, worrying about finances and the future, now she had *this*? But no, the dashboard display showed that it was Steven calling.

'Fuck,' Karen said.

This day was out of control. This was, what, the third time Steven had contacted her today, and now he was *calling*? As his name continued to flash she couldn't help feeling a little frightened. This behavior definitely didn't seem normal. Jesus, this was all she needed now, to be *stalked*. Could this day possibly get any worse?

She was going to let voicemail pick up, but she didn't want to be passive about it; she wanted to take control.

So she answered with the speaker, 'Hello,' going for a severe, okay *bitchy* tone.

'Hey, it's Steven,' he said.

'Yeah, I know,' she said. 'What do you want?'

'Did you get my texts?'

'Yes, sorry, I'm in a hurry right now.'

'Oh, okay, I just wanted to talk about –'

'Look.' Her patience was officially gone. 'I thought you were okay with everything yesterday. The relationship wasn't working for me, we have to move on, and that's that, okay?'

'No, I understand, it's not that,' he said. 'That's totally cool. It's about something else.'

'What?' Now she was clueless. Was this just bait, a ploy to try to suck her back into the relationship?

'Are you on speaker?' he asked.

'Yes,' she said.

'Are your kids in the car?'

'No.' She was definitely getting a weird, stalker vibe now. Maybe he couldn't handle rejection after all; maybe he was a psycho. She flashed back to the trepidation she'd had on their first date when he'd mentioned an ex he'd had 'a hard time letting go of.' Were there other red flags she'd missed? She said in her authoritative, no-bullshit tone, as if she were disciplining one of her kids, 'What is this about, Steven?'

'Well, this morning, I… uh… saw something.'

'You saw something.'

'Yeah, well, *noticed* something, yeah. So… I… um…

went to see somebody this afternoon, and... god, this is so hard.'

'What is? What's hard, Steven?'

'Please don't hate me for this.'

'Hate you for what?'

Shit, what was he getting at? Her pulse was pounding.

'I'm really, really sorry.'

'Just tell me.'

'Okay.'

'Okay?'

'You...'

'I? I what?'

A deep breath then, 'You have to get tested for crabs, Karen.'

8

At first Owen didn't know Deb was dead. He didn't really know what he was doing or what the hell was happening. He was just angry – at Raymond, at his mother, at Deb, at everybody – and he wanted the whole world to shut up and leave him alone.

Then it was silent and that was when he knew. He removed his hands from her neck, was looking at her eyes, so totally still, like the eyes of a stuffed animal. He liked her eyes like this, how he could see nothing in them except his own reflections – a little pale Owen face in each pupil. He knew it should probably bother him that she was dead, but it didn't. He was actually glad she was gone, that she couldn't talk back anymore. Then he remembered how she'd said she wanted to be friends, how she told him he needed help. Friends? Yeah, right. She was not his fucking *friend*, and how the hell did she know what he needed? He felt the anger, the rage, wanted to kill her all over again, and then he was doing it, squeezing her throat so hard he could feel her neck bone between his clenched hands. Telling him he needed help after he told her that Raymond had been fucking him? Actually he'd been lying, Raymond was a prick but there had never been any real abuse – no ass-fucking anyway – but this didn't matter because Deb hadn't known that. As far as she knew he'd been getting ass-fucked for years, and she still didn't care. She was such a bitch; he wanted to kill her again and again forever.

He stopped, not because he was through being angry, but because he was scared – not of how she looked or what he'd done, but of what might happen next. He was in a high school parking lot with a body in the back of his car – well, his mom's car, but that made it even worse. There was no way he was going to jail because of her, because of *this* – that just wasn't happening. He needed a plan, some way out, but he wasn't panicking. Coming up with plans, *acting*, was what he did best.

At least no one was around. The rain had stopped and the only sounds were cars going by on North Salem Road, way at the other end of the lot. If it was during the day and they were somewhere else, like in that classroom, this could have been a lot worse so he had to keep thinking about the bright side, or at least the not so dark side. But he had to be smart about this – think through everything every which way before he made any moves. He knew what cops were like, what kinds of questions they asked, and he'd seen enough CSI to know his hair fibers, or spit, or whatever, were probably all over her body. Even if he got her out of his car and put her somewhere else, like in her own car, and even if he cleaned his car ten times and took ten showers he'd be fucked. He had sex with her before, at the school, with no condom because she had one of those IUD things, so tons of his sperm were probably swimming around inside her, and if they found one sperm, one fucking sperm, he'd be fucked.

He hadn't moved this whole time. He was still on her body, a few inches away from her face and her stuffed-animal eyes, which probably wasn't the smartest thing in the world, he realized, because what if he coughed or sneezed and got even more DNA on her? Her body was already getting stiff, or at least it seemed like it was. It was weird how he wasn't scared at all; he actually *liked* this. He loved that Deb was here, but gone at the same time, and that he was in total control of everything now.

'I own you now,' he whispered to her. 'You're mine.'

He knew what he was saying didn't make much sense, and he wasn't even sure why he was saying it, but he didn't care because it was making him feel good.

'I know you like it like this,' he said. 'This is what you wanted all along, isn't it?'

He would've loved talking to her like this for hours, it was such a rush, but he knew the sooner he got out of there the better. Eventually Mark or somebody would come looking for her. She also had a phone, *two* phones, and her iPhone had GPS, so eventually somebody could track her down. He maneuvered off her, then found the phones in her purse and turned them off, but that wasn't the most important thing. The most important thing was figuring out what to do with *her*.

He had to get her out of there. Okay, this was good, he was thinking, making progress. It was only a matter of time till the answer came to him, till everything clicked.

He got out of the car. No one was around – he was sure of it, and the cars on the road were so far away that no one could possibly see, and it was so dark that even if someone did happen to look from so far away they wouldn't be able to tell what was going on. So he grabbed her by her arms, up by her shoulders, and dragged her out. He liked holding her this way, feeling her cold skin. He tried to carry her, but she was too heavy – he probably should have expected this – so instead he dragged her toward the back of the car and then, as he reached into his pocket for the car keys, he suddenly panicked, thinking, *Fuck, security cameras.* He didn't know if there were cameras in the parking lot – he hadn't even thought of checking – he was angry with himself for not thinking of such an obvious thing. Cameras were everywhere these days and if one was on him now, it was over, he might as well just figure out a way to kill himself.

Looking around frantically, he didn't see any cameras, though. There weren't any attached to the fence near the football field and even if there was on the actual school building, it was so far away it wouldn't matter. The biggest danger was the trees near where the car was parked. He didn't think there would be a camera in a tree, but it was too dark to see, so there was no way of knowing for sure. He continued looking around, searching for cameras, not seeing any, and then started to relax, realizing there probably weren't any and even if there was one in a tree, it was so dark where he was, barely enough light from faraway lampposts to even see where he was going, that it wouldn't pick up much.

Confident he was okay, that he wasn't being filmed, he popped open the trunk and saw he had another problem. His mother had put those old PCs in the trunk the other day to take to a computer store so they could remove the hard drives, but she hadn't gotten around to going. The PCs didn't take up a ton of space, but he wasn't sure the body would fit with them; it would've been a tight squeeze anyway. He thought about moving the PCs to the back seat but was afraid the body would fall down if he left it and maybe some blood would come out or skin would scrape off and the forensics guys would find it. So instead he did the smart thing and tried to stuff the body into the trunk.

She was definitely too big to fit in straight across, so he put her in diagonally, feet first toward the back right corner. Her legs – with high heel boots still on – fit in nicely, but it was hard to twist the rest of her body around the PCs. He wedged it in the best he could, then added her purse. He tried to close the trunk a couple of times but, nope, it kept popping open. Then he figured out the problem – her head wasn't fitting over the PCs. So he pulled her out and turned her around, forcing her head into the tight space in the back of the trunk. He was sweating and just wanted to get her the hell in already when there was suddenly bright light shining right on him.

He had no idea what was going on – was somebody shining a flashlight on him? Was it a cop or a security guard? Holding Deb by the waist, right above her ass, he was terrified and numb, unable to move or think, as if somebody had shot him with a stun gun. Then maybe his brain jumpstarted and it clicked that it wasn't a flashlight, it was the headlights of the car, and the lights weren't on him anymore because the car had turned away and pulled into a spot maybe fifty yards away. Shit, this was fucked up, but first things first – he had to get the body into the car.

Using his body to shield what he was doing from where the other car had parked, he forced her legs in, but the trunk still wouldn't close. He was sweating worse now, like he was in the sun on a hot summer day, and he was afraid somebody was going to get out of the car and come over and see what was going on. He reached in and grabbed Deb's hair, turning the head sharply to the left. He thought he heard something crack, but he'd managed to squeeze her head deeper into the trunk, creating more room for the rest of her body, and that was all that mattered. He closed the trunk, maybe letting it slam a little too hard, and got into the driver's seat of the car – worn out and relieved.

But he knew he wasn't out of trouble yet – he still had a lot of work to do. The other car was still in the light, but the headlights were off now. With a clearer head, Owen now realized that it was probably a couple of teenagers, out getting laid. While he was still worried that somebody could've seen him, he thought, *Yeah, but what did they see?* Maybe they saw him standing up in front of the trunk but most of the body had been inside, they couldn't have seen what he was doing. Besides, when people are out to hook up do they really *see* anything? They were probably so busy thinking about getting into each other's pants they didn't give a shit about anything else.

Feeling better, Owen did the smart thing and didn't leave right away. He wanted to think it through first, make sure he wasn't forgetting anything. Deb's car would stay in the lot, of course, but he didn't see any way around that – he couldn't get rid of her car. He didn't want to take a chance with the teenagers, though, so when he was convinced everything was going according to plan, he backed out of the spot and drove away, going a different way than when he'd arrived, going around the whole football field, so he didn't have to pass the teenagers and give them a chance to get a closer look at his car.

A few minutes later, he was out of the lot, driving away, his confidence back in full force. He knew everything was going to work out, and he loved having Deb's body in the trunk – just knowing she was back there, that he could take her anywhere, anywhere he wanted, and she had no choice at all, gave him an amazing rush. He actually liked it better when she was dead than she was alive; when she was alive she could be a pain in the ass. He wished there was a way he could keep her back there for a long time – a few days at least – but he knew this was impossible because it was his mom's car and because the smell would get awful. Could he freeze her? He liked that idea a lot, but it sucked that it was just a fantasy. That was the shitty thing about fantasies – they were only there when you thought about them, you couldn't stay in them forever.

He didn't see why he had to get rid of her right away, though, why there was a serious hurry. Nobody was going to miss her for a while – dumb, clueless Mark wouldn't notice until maybe around midnight, and no one was going to start searching for her until probably tomorrow morning or afternoon. The body would be okay in the trunk for a while – it wasn't rotting or smelling yet – so why not party?

He drove for about ten minutes, to Dylan Ross's house.

Owen was a year older than Dylan and kind of knew him from just around. They'd never gone to the same schools, but when Owen was maybe five years old, they went to the same day camp, and they'd seen each other around at other places. Dylan seemed like a popular guy; he had a lot of friends anyway. Owen knew they must have talked to each other at some point in their lives, but he couldn't remember ever saying a single word to the guy.

The house was on a street with lots of big houses – it was a good neighborhood, better than Owen's – and Owen parked on the grass alongside the street and then walked on to the house, already annoyed by the loud party music. Owen hated music. He knew this was weird, because he was *supposed* to like music, but he couldn't change how he felt. To him, music just sounded like loud, fucked up noise. He didn't get it at all.

The beat was throbbing from right outside the house,

and then, after he rang the bell and some too-thin blonde girl he'd never seen before answered, it got even more annoying.

'Hey,' the girl said, smiling widely.

Not in a smiling mood, Owen said, 'Hey,' and went into the house, looking for Elana. There were maybe twenty people in the living room, and some more over by the stairs, but he only recognized a couple of them – this guy Jake, who Owen only knew because he had a brother Kyle's age, and a girl with curly dark hair he'd seen maybe in high school. Owen knew people were looking at him, the way people always looked at a new person who comes into a room, but he wished they would just look the fuck away.

'Hey,' a guy said.

Owen felt a hand on his shoulder and turned around suddenly, as if somebody had punched him. Then he saw it was just Dylan.

'What's up, man?' Owen asked, the music so loud he could barely hear his own voice.

'Not much, bro,' Dylan said. 'So, like, what're you doing here?'

Now Owen remembered that he'd always hated Dylan.

'Oh, um, my friend told me about the party,' Owen said, scanning the room for Elana. He didn't see her, but there was Riley Berman coming out of the kitchen. She kind of smiled at Owen so he smiled back while thinking, *Man, her mom was so much hotter than her, it's not even a contest.* Owen had always thought this, but now that Deb was gone the difference in their looks was somehow even more startling. It made Owen miss Deb, but it made him feel better when he reminded himself that even though she was dead, she wasn't really *gone*; she was right outside in the trunk of his car.

126

'Who's your friend?' Dylan asked.

Owen hadn't really made eye contact with Dylan, but he did now. Oh, man look at this jerk-off – short hair with pieces sticking up in front, probably some new hip style, in an Aeropostle shirt and baggy American Eagle shorts. He probably thought he looked so awesome, but he looked just like every other stuck-up asshole he'd gone to school with.

'Elana Daily,' Owen said.

'Elana's my girl,' Dylan said.

Owen didn't have any expression but inside he was laughing like hell. He knew he could have whatever girl he wanted – old or young – that it was all up to *him*. It was so easy to get girls to like him – all he had to do was smile, be polite, say nice things. Girls were such suckers for that shit.

After Owen finished staring at Dylan he went over to Riley and said, 'Hey, is Elana here?'

'In the kitchen,' she said.

'Thanks,' he said.

Owen wanted to say, *I just had so much fun strangling your mom*, but instead he smiled, knowing he looked hot when he smiled like that, at least Deb used to tell him he did.

When Elana saw him enter the kitchen she came over to him and hugged him tightly and said, 'Oh my god, it's so great to see you.'

'Yeah, you too,' he said, feeling her ass, missing Deb's bigger, softer ass.

Then she pulled back and, squinting, looking toward his neck, asked, 'What's that?'

He knew exactly what she was talking about. He'd felt some irritation on his neck while driving here in the car, but was so distracted he hadn't give it much thought; now, though, it hit that Deb had scratched him there. She must have done it while his hands were around her throat.

Touching his neck, feeling the sting, he said, 'Oh, my cat scratched me before,' because it was the first excuse that came to him.

'I didn't know you have a cat,' she said.

He didn't have a cat, but said, 'I guess there's a lot you don't know about me,' as he had a flash of strangling Deb.

On to something else already because she was so obviously turned on by him, Elana said, 'I'm so glad you came. Seriously, I was so bored before you showed up.'

'Of course I was going to come,' he said. 'I wouldn't blow a chance to hang with you tonight.'

'Really?' she asked.

God, how could anyone be *that* insecure? That was something he never got from older women – Deb always knew what she wanted and never doubted herself, which was so, so hot.

Missing Deb, Owen said, 'You know how into you I am.'

Elana blushed, then with a flirty look said, 'Wanna go hang someplace else?'

'Sure,' Owen said, as he was dying to get away from this music – some song by some singer he was supposed to know – and all of these assholes.

Elana went and said something to Riley, probably, 'I'm leaving with Owen.' Riley nodded, like she expected this, but she didn't seem happy about it. Then when Owen passed her she didn't even look at him, pretending to get distracted. Owen had no idea what her problem was, what he'd ever done to piss her off, but whatever, she was a girl and sometimes it was impossible to figure out what girls were thinking, so why even try?

Then, when Elana opened the front door and Owen was following her out, Dylan rushed over, all panicked and shit, and went, 'Hey, Elana, where you goin'?'

'Oh, have to head out,' she said, 'but I had an awesome time.'

'Wait,' he said, 'can we talk for a sec?'

'She said she wants to go home, dude,' Owen said. 'What's your problem?'

'You're my problem, loser. You weren't even invited to this party.'

As he spoke, Dylan had sprayed spit in Owen's face. It also annoyed Owen that Dylan's breath smelled like alcohol because it reminded him of Deb.

But it was the word *loser* that really set off Owen.

Owen grabbed Dylan by his Aeropostale shirt, and pushed him up against the door, and then Owen had a flash of Raymond holding him up against the door before and how Owen had wanted to knee him in the balls. Without thinking, Owen kneed Dylan in the balls as hard as he could. Dylan groaned in agony and then, when Owen let go of his shirt, Dylan crumpled to the floor.

Owen pulled Elana along over to his Sentra.

Later, in the car, Elana was talking a lot, complaining about Dylan. Owen wasn't really paying attention to what she was saying, picking up words here and there – 'Asshole,' 'So much, ' 'All the time.' Then he zoned back in hearing her say, 'I mean I know he's into me, but I've told him like a million times I'm so not into him, but he won't stop trying. It's like he's got some kind of problem or something.'

'It's cool,' Owen said, and he knew she was saying something else, but he'd stopped listening again, too distracted by the rush he'd gotten from kneeing Dylan, and now he was thinking about Deb in the car again.

'I miss you so much, baby,' he said.

'Really?' Elana asked.

Owen had meant to say this to Deb, but he snapped back

to reality – having to leave a fantasy really sucked – and said, 'Yeah. You're so hot.'

'I want to touch you and kiss you all over too,' Elana said.

'Wanna park someplace?' Owen asked.

'We can hang at my house.'

'Is your mother home?'

'Yeah, but it's cool.'

Owen remembered the scene this afternoon at the country club – Deb and Karen having that crazy fight. It made sense that Karen and Mark had something going on. Everyone at the club knew that Karen had been slutting around since her divorce, or maybe even since before her divorce. Owen overheard people talking about Karen and the guys she was with all the time so it made sense that she'd be cool with her daughter bringing a guy back to her place. Like mother like daughter, right?

'Yeah,' Owen said. 'Okay.'

On the way there, Elana was doing shit to him – kissing his neck, putting her hand over his crotch while he was driving, telling him how 'unbelievably cute' she thought he was.

They parked in the driveway, then went into the house through the garage.

Owen had never been to Elana's, but had gone past it lots of times on the way to Deb's. Well, maybe not lots of times, but during the two years they'd been hooking up, he'd go over to her house whenever she was home alone. Like if Mark took her kids into the city, Deb would text him and he'd drop anything and zip over there as fast as he could.

'I'm gonna miss that so much,' Owen said.

'Miss what so much?' Elana asked.

Shit, he had to stop saying what he was thinking; it

would get him into trouble if he didn't watch out.

'What you were doing to my neck before,' he said. 'That felt so awesome.'

Yeah, okay, this didn't really make sense, but it didn't matter because Elana wasn't paying much attention anyway. Meanwhile, this made him think about Deb's neck, how he'd had her hands around it, and how into it she'd been. Right up to the point she let go and was gone, he could see it in her eyes, how she wanted more, how she was *begging* for more.

They went up some steps to the first floor of the house. Damn, it was a lot nicer than Owen's house. Wasn't Elana's mom a schoolteacher? Yeah, something like that. But he didn't think teachers made enough to pay for a place like this; the place had to be worth more, what, maybe a half a million bucks. But she was divorced so she was probably getting money from her ex too. She had a good set-up going all right.

In Elana's room, Elana put on some music. Owen didn't know what it was, had never heard it before, but he said, 'Oh, cool, I love this song,' because he knew that was what he was supposed to say.

'I love it too,' Elana said.

She turned out the main light, put on a little lamp on her night table, and then grabbed his hand and pulled him onto the bed. He should've been totally psyched. He had a sexy girl – she looked sexier and prettier in the dimmer orangeish light – all primed and ready to go, but he just couldn't get into it.

They got totally naked – maybe that would help? He was kissing her, his hands all over her, but it wasn't doing anything for him because he couldn't stop thinking about Deb.

'What's wrong?'

'Sorry,' he said. 'Just can't get into it.'

'Oh.' She sounded upset. 'Okay.'

'It's not you,' he said. 'I mean I think you're hot.'

'Want a BJ?' she asked.

'Nah, it's cool, I gotta go.'

He got out of bed and started getting dressed.

'Come on,' she said. 'I mean, how do you know you won't feel better in a few minutes? Maybe it's just, I don't know, passing?'

She was still talking, going on, trying to get him back into bed with her, and he wasn't really listening to anything she was saying. Then he heard, 'Wanna hang again sometime?'

'Um no, not really,' he said.

As he headed downstairs, he was proud of himself. How many guys would have bullshitted her, said 'I'll text you later' or some shit like that? But not him – no, he was an honest guy, *good* guy, and there were so few good, honest guys left in the world these days.

Downstairs, he heard, 'Hello.' It wasn't a friendly hello. It was an angry, threatening hello.

He turned, and saw Karen Daily near the entrance to the kitchen, hands on her hips. It was funny, he'd never really thought Karen was sexy. She was pretty, yeah, had a nice body, but he'd never really *noticed* her before. But now he saw her in a whole different way, and he wasn't sure why. He remembered watching her fight with Deb before at the club; did it have to do with that? It was definitely hot, seeing a schoolteacher on the floor, wrestling like an animal, but maybe it was just her looks. Did she do something different to her hair? She wasn't wearing anything fancy, just a tank top and, what were they called? Gym pants? No, yoga pants, yeah, yoga pants, but she still looked sexy as hell. No wonder so many guys were so into her.

'Hey,' he said, smiling, the way he used to smile for Deb.

Karen was squinting. It was kind of dark, the only light coming from the kitchen.

'Do I know you?' she asked.

Owen was offended. How could she not recognize him right away even in the dim light? She'd seen him all the time at the country club, and even before he'd started working there, at school pick-ups and from just around.

'Yeah, you know me,' he said.

'Wait, you're the one from the country club,' she said. 'You work there, don't you?'

Owen wasn't crazy about 'you're the one,' he wasn't sure what that meant, but he said, 'Yep, that's me. I'm not sure I ever said hi to you before, though. I'm Owen.'

'How do you know Elana?' she asked maybe suspiciously.

'Oh, just from, you know, around,' Owen said.

'No, I don't know,' she said.

Owen liked the bitchy attitude; it was so hot.

'You know,' he said, 'parties, hanging out, school.'

'How old are you?'

'Eighteen.'

'Do you know how old Elana is?'

'Um, sixteen?'

'You're too old for her.'

Thinking, *But you're not too old for me, baby*, Owen said, 'Don't worry, nothing happened.'

'I didn't ask if anything happened,' she said. 'She's not allowed to have boyfriends over to the house, especially boyfriends who aren't appropriate for her.'

'You really have to learn to chill,' Owen said.

'Excuse me?' Karen asked.

'I can see it in your eyes,' he said, knowing he was winning her over already. 'You're so stressed out, I can hear it in your voice too.'

He saw her look to her right, at a mirror. So she was insecure – okay, he'd have to remember that, play up to it.

'Are you always this way?' Owen asked. 'Or is it because of me?'

'I think you should go now,' she said.

'Seriously,' he said, 'do you know how to relax? I mean, I can tell by your arms that you do yoga, maybe Pilates. You're in great shape, I can see that.'

He knew he was getting through to her. This was the way he always got the woman he wanted – *tell them what they want to hear.*

'And about Elana,' he said, 'I just want you to know, I'd never do anything to disrespect you. I thought it was cool with you for me to come by. If I knew it wasn't I wouldn't've come.'

'It's okay.' She was calmer now. 'I understand, and you're right I've just been a little… agitated tonight, and I didn't mean to take it out on you. Thank you for driving her home.'

'No, thank *you.*'

He knew he had her – she was vulnerable, opening up. He reached out and held her hand and he knew, by how she was looking at him, that she felt it too – a connection. Her eyes were saying: *I want you.* No, *I need you.*

Then she yanked her hand away and snapped, 'Why did you just do that? What's wrong with people?' but it didn't matter because he knew her first reaction had been her true reaction.

'Sorry,' he said. 'Goodnight.'

Driving away with Deb in the trunk was as exciting as before but not nearly as sad. After all, it would be so much easier to say his final goodbye to Deb knowing he already had a new GF.

9

IN HIS BASEMENT, gasping, into his third set of bench-presses, Mark had an epiphany: yeah, today had been a total nightmare, but everything would work out in the end. He'd been stressed all afternoon, especially about Karen. Things had been kind of weird at the drop-off for Andrew's pajama party, but now – maybe because exerting energy exercising was clearing his head – he had a much more positive take on things.

Karen wasn't actually angry with him – that was the bottom line. Yeah, she'd *seemed* angry, but he remembered her once telling him that it was a pattern for her in relationships to have emotional responses when she got upset, and it didn't mean she had any loss of love.

A relationship. Pushing through the tenth rep, Mark liked the sound of that.

After downing a bottle of PowerAde he checked his cell and was disappointed there was nothing from Karen yet, but he knew the make-up text would be coming soon.

Then they'd probably talk on the phone later, and she'd tell him how excited she was about the idea of he and Deb getting divorced and him being free. Well, she might not come out and *say* she was excited – she wouldn't do that in the current situation, and risk putting the kids in the middle of it, but the excitement would be in her tone, it would be obvious. She would probably say she was going to stop dating now, implying that she'd wait for Mark, and once the divorce got underway maybe Mark would move out to his own apartment – take a short-term lease – and then he and Karen could actually be together. They'd have to keep it under wraps, of course, they didn't want people talking, but Karen could start discreetly coming over to his new place, maybe a few evenings a week.

When Mark's cell rang he was so excited he almost dropped the bar of weights on his head and crushed himself to death. He managed to rack the bar, and then rushed to his phone that he'd put on the ping-pong table, disappointed that it was Stu, not Karen.

'Hey,' Mark said.

'You okay?' Stu asked.

'Yeah, fine. Why?'

'You sound, I don't know… down, man.'

'I was just lifting weights,' Mark said, as if that explained it. 'What's up?'

'Just checking in on you,' Stu said. 'I saw what happened at the club today and wanted to make sure you were okay.'

'The club?' Mark was lost, still disappointed he wasn't speaking to Karen right now. 'Oh, that, sorry. Yeah, I'm okay, thanks. It's just a lot of stuff's going down with me and Deb, and I'm trying to deal with it, you know?'

'Trust me, I know what it's like when things get weird at home, bro,' Stu said. 'If there's anything you need, give me a call.'

'Thanks, I appreciate that,' Mark said. 'See you on the train Monday.'

Mark resumed bench pressing, thinking about what Stu had said, about knowing what it's like when things get weird at home. Were Stu and Janet having trouble as well? That would be a big surprise, if it were true – they seemed so happy – but you never knew what was going on in other people's lives.

Mark's cell rang again, and he rushed to it, thinking this time it had to be her, but it was from a restricted number.

'Hello?' he asked excitedly, hoping Karen was calling from another phone, maybe from a friend's cell.

'Mark?' It was a woman, not Karen.

'Yes,' he said, feeling the letdown.

'He just wet himself,' the woman said.

'Who's this?' Mark asked.

'Sarah Waxman, Andrew's mother. Justin just wet himself.'

'Seriously?' Mark was surprised; Justin hadn't wet himself in years. 'How's he doing?'

'Not well,' Sarah said. 'He's extremely upset actually.'

'Okay, I'll be there as soon as I can,' Mark said.

Mark felt bad for Justin, the poor kid. On his way out, he called Karen and after four rings got her voice mail, though there was an extra tone after each ring meaning that she was on another call and wasn't getting off to speak to him. He thought this was strange, but it didn't necessarily mean something was *wrong*. She had her kids this weekend, right? Maybe she had an emergency with a kid or had some other crisis she was dealing with. She'd probably call him later or at least text him.

When Mark arrived at Andrew's house his mom, Sarah, looking nervous, said, 'Come in, he's very upset.'

Then Mark went further inside and saw Justin sitting

on the bottom step of the staircase, his head bent over between his legs, shaking, maybe crying. His knapsack was next to him.

Crouching, holding Justin's hand, Mark said, 'It's gonna be okay, kiddo. Don't worry, I promise it'll be okay.'

Justin, continuing to shake, didn't respond.

Sarah whispered to Mark, *Can we talk for a sec*?

'We're going home in two minutes,' Mark said to Justin. 'Two minutes, okay?'

Then Mark went with Sarah toward the kitchen, far enough away so that Justin couldn't hear, and then stopped.

'I had him take a shower and change into the clothes he brought with him for tomorrow,' Sarah said.

'That's great, thanks,' Mark said.

'It was very difficult for him,' Sarah said, 'and I'm afraid the other boys weren't very nice to him. Andrew, especially, wasn't very nice, and I just want you to know he's going to be punished for it – severely.'

'What can you do?' Mark said. 'Shit happens. Or, in this case, piss happens.'

He smiled, trying to make a joke out of it, but he knew he'd misfired.

'I'm kidding,' he said. 'I mean, I don't want to make a big deal about it, you know? I mean, something like this is hard enough already, you know, psychologically.'

Mark wasn't sure he was making sense. He just wanted to get Justin home, in bed, and then hopefully have a nice relaxing chat with Karen.

During the car ride home, Justin was crying a lot, and Mark said all the right things, like, 'It's gonna be okay, I promise,' and, 'It happens to everybody,' and, 'You're a big, strong kid, you'll get through this.' Meanwhile, Mark was bummed because Karen still hadn't gotten back to him.

He was dying to talk to her again, just to hear her voice.

At home, Justin was still having a hard time. Mark tried to get him to talk about it, asking him if he was upset because of things the other kids had said, and he said that was part of it. He also mentioned that it had happened a few times before and that Deb knew about it. This wasn't the only time Mark had felt in the dark about a situation at home. When Riley was having trouble in school last year and was in danger of failing a couple of classes Mark didn't find out about it until he happened to pick up the phone when the school guidance counselor called. Deb was also behind on taking the kids for physicals and dental appointments. Mark had no idea what Deb was doing with her free time, but she had certainly let the household go to hell.

Mark tried to get Justin to bed, but Justin was still saying, 'I didn't want to go to the party. You and Mom made me go, why did you make me? Why? Why?' and Mark snapped, 'I didn't make you – your mother did!' This made Justin cry even harder. Mark apologized, but Justin was still upset. After a while, Mark got into bed with him and held him until he calmed down and fell asleep.

The kids needed Mark, that was for damn sure, and not just because he brought home a paycheck every two weeks. They needed him because he was a father, a caretaker, and he needed a woman who appreciated him, didn't take him for granted. When was the last time Deb had asked him anything about work? Yeah, it was true, Mark hated talking about work at home, but it would still be nice if she asked once in a while, said, 'Hey, anything new at work?' just to show she wanted to care even if she actually didn't. And he needed some taking care of himself sometimes. Like when was the last time Deb came into the shower and gave him a blowjob? Years ago, when they were dating, and before Riley was born, she used to blow him in the shower all the time.

Later, Mark left Justin's room, his neck sweaty from where Justin's head had been leaning on him. There was still no message from Karen. Just so she knew that he was thinking about her and cared he texted: **Can I call you to say goodnight???**

He expected her to text or write back with *Yes*!! or *Of course*!! or maybe she would just call him. But fifteen minutes, then a half hour, and an hour went by and she hadn't responded. It was almost eleven o'clock. Maybe she'd turned her phone off or fallen asleep. She'd had that late night last night, ran this morning, and she always complained that she was wiped out on weekends after long days during the week working with autistic kids. He waited for a while, watching the rest of the golf tournament he'd TiVo'd. He wanted, no *needed*, to hear her voice, but he wanted to do the smart thing. If he called now, she might get the wrong idea, think he was pressuring her.

In bed, Mark watched more golf. At some point Riley came back from wherever she'd been, and he heard her go into her room. He was surprised Deb wasn't back yet. She hadn't told him where she was going, but she probably went out with a friend. Maybe Kathy; was she still friends with Kathy? She'd probably stay out late, to try to make him jealous. Yeah, right.

Mark must have fallen asleep because when he checked his phone he saw it was past three a.m. He was upset that Karen hadn't texted – it made him unsettled. Then he realized that Deb wasn't in bed next to him. She'd probably come home and gone to sleep in the guestroom, or crashed drunk in the living room.

'Fuck it,' he said to himself, as he lay back in bed, clutching his cell phone.

10

'CRABS!' KAREN SCREAMED so loud her ears stung. 'You have *crabs*?! Fucking *crabs*!'

She jerked onto the steering wheel, veering into the oncoming lane, and then veering back when she realized she was speeding toward oncoming headlights.

'Well, actually pubic lice,' Steven said. 'I mean that sounds better... I guess.'

'Oh my god, oh my god,' Karen said, touching herself over her jeans; suddenly she was itching like crazy.

'I'm sorry,' Steven said. 'You have no idea how sorry I am.'

'*Sorry*?' Karen said, thinking, *Oh, my god, I have crabs. Crabs, insects, are living on me.* 'Are you fucking kidding me?'

'It's unlikely you have it,' Steven said. 'I mean, my doctor said it's not a definite thing that you'd get it too and that you definitely shouldn't panic.'

'You're joking.' Karen was lightheaded, felt outside

herself. She heard herself say, 'This is a sick joke. Please tell me this is a sick joke. When women break up with you, you tell them you have crabs as some kind of payback, right?'

'I wish,' Steven said. 'I'm sorry. You have no idea how sorry I am.'

Her rage overflowing, she screamed, 'Fuck you, you stupid fucking prick! How could you do this to me? I have children. I'm a schoolteacher, not a hooker.'

She felt like she was losing control, not making sense.

'I didn't know I had it,' Steven said. 'I mean that. Honest. I had no idea. When I was peeing last night I saw one of them. I mean it, like, crawled onto my hand.'

Totally disgusted, Karen said, 'I have to go to a doctor.' Then, thinking out loud, she said, 'It's Saturday, how am I going to find a doctor?'

'You can go to an STD clinic, they're open twenty-four hours a day,' Steven said.

'How do you know their *hours*?!' Karen screamed at the dashboard, hating that it was displaying: STEVEN; it might as well have been displaying: CRABS. 'How are you a fucking STD expert? Have you gotten STD's before?' She swerved again, narrowly missing a collision with a speeding, honking car. 'What's that?!' She hadn't heard the last thing Steven had said because of the honking.

'I said I know you're upset, but there's no reason to get hysterical,' he said.

'Don't you dare tell me how to act,' she said, imagining big, black, disgusting crabs with their pointy claws and snapping mouths infesting her vagina. 'I can't believe this is happening. This is a fucking nightmare.'

'Look, this is difficult for me too,' Steven said. 'You think I want to have this? You think I'm *enjoying* telling you this?

I don't know how I got this, it just happened, and I'm just trying to do the right thing, notifying all my recent sex partners.'

'*All*?' Karen had to get a breath; she was starting to hyperventilate. Then she said, 'All? Exactly how many women were you fucking?'

'I just meant the women I've been with the past couple of months.'

Karen couldn't believe this. 'Who *are* you?' she asked.

'Relax,' he said. 'I don't deserve this.'

'*You* don't deserve this?'

'We never had a conversation about exclusivity.'

'Oh my god,' Karen said. 'Oh my god.'

She didn't remember how the call had ended – she'd probably hung up on him – or much else of the car ride home. She didn't even remember entering her house – she just seemed to wind up sitting on the toilet seat, her jeans and panties down, legs spread, holding a compact mirror over her vagina. She didn't see anything unusual there, but would she see, actually *see*, them? What if they were microscopic? What if there were thousands, no *millions*, of little bugs down there, sucking her blood, eating her alive? She didn't have much hair down there, just a landing strip. She'd thought about going bald. Fuck, why hadn't she gone bald?

Though she couldn't see any bugs, she could *feel* them. The itching was getting worse and worse; it was almost unbearable. She tried reminding herself that at least some of this was in her head because she hadn't been itching at all before Steven had called, but she was so frantic that logic was useless right now.

She went upstairs, stripping along the way, letting her clothes fall wherever, and went right into the shower and put the shower head between her legs. She sometimes did this to masturbate – she swore to friends it worked better than any vibrator she'd ever used – but now it didn't give her any pleasure and, worse, she knew it wasn't killing any bugs. She needed medicine, a crab picker, *something*. god, she hadn't even used condoms with Steven; what if she'd caught something else? What had he told her? Oh yeah, *Don't worry, I'm clean*.

'Clean,' she said out loud, turning the shower head to its strongest, most pulsating setting. 'Yeah, you're really fucking clean!' Her voice was so loud and piercing, echoing off the walls of the shower, that it actually hurt her ears. 'Die, you motherfuckers, die!' she screamed at her pussy and then she calculated that she and Steven had had sex at least ten times, and spent overnights at each other's places. They'd spent nights cuddling and spooning and the whole time the asshole had had crabs? And she didn't believe that I-didn't-know-I-had-it bullshit. How could you not know you have crabs? *Crabs*. Jesus, it sounded so disgusting, so filthy; it was something that hookers got, not average people. Wait, maybe Steven went to hookers. Didn't he mention he went to some strip club in Vegas one time? If he went to a strip club, why couldn't he have gone to a hooker? After all, he was a fucking liar. And if he'd gone to a hooker, *hookers*, he might have other diseases – syphilis, gonorrhea, fucking AIDS.

In full-blown panic, Karen rushed out of the shower, not even bothering to towel off, and sat on her bed, and Googled for STD clinics in the area. There was one in Bridgeport, one in New Rochelle. She was going to call to see if one was open or had weekend hours but then she stopped herself, thinking, *Do I really want to sit in the waiting room of an STD clinic with a bunch of teenagers*? She was a schoolteacher, after all – if someone saw her there and the news spread, it would be a disaster for her career. She knew she was probably just being paranoid but, fuck it, she had reason to be paranoid – she had insects in her vagina!

She'd be better off going to her gynecologist during the week, keeping it discreet. In the meantime she had to do something, so she searched for remedies online. It seemed like the treatment was pretty much the same for head lice, which both her kids had had more than once, which made her feel a little better. She'd used peppermint oil on the kids, but fuck all that holistic bullshit, she needed medicine, chemicals, so she made a beeline for Walgreens and came back with a container of Rid. Back in the shower, as she treated herself, she started sobbing. It wasn't just because of the crabs, it was because of the plight of her life, from her fairytale wedding day at the Boat House in Central Park to being keeled over in the shower, scrubbing her pussy with lice-killer. How had her life come to this? She knew, intellectually, that it was a compilation of decisions she'd made and external events that had nothing to do with her, but it still seemed absurd how everything had gone so horribly wrong.

She treated her hair and put in a laundry of all her dirty and recently used linens and towels. It was a good thing the kids didn't use her bathroom, but she hoped they didn't catch anything. How awful and humiliating would it be to pass along crabs to your child? Horrified, she imagined having to let Matthew's teachers know that Matthew may have spread crabs into his classroom.

Later, in yoga pants and a T shirt, sitting on the bed on clean sheets, Karen felt a little more relaxed – if the bugs weren't dead at least they were *dying* – but she didn't feel any better about herself. She logged onto Match on her iPad and deleted her account. She also deleted her accounts on OkCupid, PlentyOfFish, and HowAboutWe. She needed a break from dating and, if the way she felt at this moment stuck with her, she might remain celibate for the rest of her life. There were women who did that – focused on their kids and gave up on sex and romance; she could become one of those women. She could pleasure herself with the shower head and read erotic novels about sexy werewolves with washboard stomachs to make up for the deficit.

She checked her phone, a text from Mark: **Can I call you to say goodnight???**

'Are you fucking kidding me?' she said, tossing the phone away onto the love seat.

She had no patience for Mark anymore – zero, none. Did he really think she was going to get on the phone and *chat* with him, as if nothing had happened last night and today? Yeah, he probably did think that. It was clear to her now that something was seriously wrong with Mark, he needed help, but she didn't want to try to analyze him or the situation anymore. She'd wasted too much time on this ridiculousness already and, besides, compared to crabs, she couldn't care less about Mark's drama and acting out. What had happened to Mark? How did he get like this? It was sad because she really did like having him as a friend, and it sucked that he'd ruined everything. When he wasn't overstepping boundaries, he was funny, supportive, and understanding. In a way, what Mark had done to her was as bad as what Steven had done to her. Mark hadn't given her an STD, but he'd violated the trust in their relationship. Karen didn't know how she'd be able to trust any man ever again.

Feeling itchy again, she took another shower, using more Rid – she hoped she wasn't overdoing it, making it worse. Then she went down to get the laundry and the clean bed sheets when she heard someone in the house. Was Elana home? She went through the kitchen and saw a man – well, a boy – coming down the stairs.

'Hello.'

Karen was angry – not at the boy, whoever he was, but at Elana. First she'd tried to leave for the party in some slutty outfit and now she'd brought a guy home with her? How many times had she had that talk with her about how boys weren't allowed in her room? Worse, this boy looked older, definitely not someone she went to school with. They'd probably come in while she was in the shower, but Karen had spoken to her many times about dating rules. Karen understood that Elana was getting older and she wanted her to make her own decisions about when to have sex, but she had to have respect for her mother.

Karen gave the boy a hard time, then recognized him. He was that kid who worked at the country club – Owen, that's right, his name was Owen. Karen had seen him there many times and she thought she'd seen him other places before too – maybe at school pick-ups? – when he was younger, but out of context she hadn't recognized him right away.

She felt bad for lashing out at him – he probably didn't even know he'd done anything wrong; it was Elana whom Karen needed to speak with. The boy's – Owen's – attitude surprised Karen, though. She didn't think she'd ever spoken to him before, so she hadn't really had much impression of him except that he was 'the local kid who worked at the country club.' He was cocky, yeah, telling her, 'You have to learn to chill,' but his self-assurance was charming. He caught her off-guard; she wasn't expecting him to have such a strong personality. It was hard to take him seriously, though, because there was always a twinkle in his eyes, an undercurrent of something, maybe sarcasm. He was very cute – not gorgeous, but charming, definitely charming – and Karen understood why Elana liked him because he was definitely the type of mysterious boy whom Karen would have liked at her age.

And then he was holding her hand. It was so unexpected, she was caught so off-guard, that she didn't know what to do so she didn't do anything. It took awhile – well, several seconds – for it to register that it was happening *again*. After Mark had held her hand not once, but twice, now *another guy* was doing it. Not even a guy. A *kid*.

Finally she jerked her hand away and said, 'Why did you just do that?'

Staying cocky, Owen didn't offer any real explanation. Karen should have been upset, furious even. Especially after everything she'd been through today, this should have put her over the edge, but it was hard to muster up much anger about it. Owen holding her hand just didn't seem nearly as violating as what Mark had done to her. After all, Owen was just a boy. Mark was a forty-four-year-old married man who should know better.

Later, when Karen was carrying the folded laundry upstairs she heard music on low in Elana's room and through the space under the door saw that a light was on. While she wanted to have a talk with her to refresh her on the dating rules, she decided it could wait till morning.

In bed, Karen's vagina still felt itchy, but only when she thought about it. She considered another treatment of Rid, but she really didn't want to overdo it. As she wriggled around, trying to find a comfortable sleeping position, she told herself that a positive about the past couple of days was that at least she had reached such a low point in her life that things couldn't possibly get any worse. Okay, today would be a day to forget, but tomorrow would be better than today, and the day after would be better than tomorrow.

She had to have faith anyway.

11

OWEN WAS PUMPED. He had one beautiful dead MILF in the trunk of his car and another beautiful live one revved up and ready to go. Was he the luckiest guy in the world or what?

If he hadn't totally scored his next mom, Karen Daily, saying goodbye to Deb would have been so much harder. But now it would be sad, yeah, but it wouldn't be tragic. And he was amazed how easily it had all happened, how he didn't even have to try. Seriously, after that lame-ass attempted sex with Elana what were the odds that when he was leaving the house her mom would practically throw herself at him? And sealing the deal with her would be so much easier than it had been with Deb. Deb had been married with two kids, but Karen was a divorced mom; she was already a player. He could come over to the house one day at a time when he knew Elana wasn't home and be like, 'Is Elana here?' and Karen would go, 'No.' Smiling, showing him that she knew exactly what he was thinking.

She wouldn't have to invite him in, they wouldn't need words. He'd probably bang her right there in the foyer, up against the front door. Then they'd christen the rest of the house and before long they'd have a regular thing going on. They wouldn't even have to hide it. So she had a young boy-toy boyfriend, why would anybody give a shit?

He thought about dumping Deb in the Hudson – that would be quick, easy – but he decided it was a bad idea. He wasn't sure how to weigh a body down enough to make it sink, and he didn't want to take any chances of it popping up tomorrow and somebody finding it. No, burying it in the woods was a much better idea and it had worked that other time, so if it ain't broke don't fix it, right?

As he drove, hearing Deb shift in the trunk every time he made a sharp turn, he was proud of himself for coming up with such a great plan so quickly. Seriously, how many people would be able to pull that off? On TV, they always talked about how cool-under-pressure some basketball players were when they could make a foul shot with the game on the line, or how a golfer in the Masters had 'ice in his veins' because he could make a big putt on the eighteenth hole when it was do-or-die. Or what about the President, having to make big decisions about bombing countries or whatever, dealing with all that pressure and shit? He was like the President, like an NBA superstar. He had ice in his veins, was the coolest guy on the planet, Mr Chill, and no one could take him down, absolutely no one.

'Fuck you!' he shouted. 'Fuck all of you!'

Owen had never done drugs, but he thought this was how it must feel as he pulled into the grounds of the Oak Ridge Country Club. There were only a couple of cars in the lot – the night security dudes – Pedro and Johnny – but that was cool, he could deal with them. They hung out in the clubhouse most of the night and almost never went onto the grounds of the club, where Owen was planning to go. So he drove past the main entrance to the club, way down to the end of the road. No security cameras to worry about here – that was for damn sure. Sometimes grounds crew guys came here at night, but there were no cars parked in the area and Owen doubted anyone was around. There was no major work going on at the club, and no reason anybody would be working OT, especially on a Saturday night. So he drove through the maintenance gate and backed into a spot near the sixth and seventh holes of the golf course, right near the beginning of a dirt path that led into the woods. He'd been on the path at night a couple of times last summer with Deb. They'd met up over here then gone into the woods and screwed under the stars. What had Deb said? Oh, that it was romantic.

Weirdly, he could hear her now, saying, 'It's so romantic here.'

'Yeah, I wouldn't bury you anywhere else, baby,' he said out loud as he got out.

Lots of cricket noises, fireflies, an almost full moon – the rain had totally passed – but not much else. He went to the storage shed and, using the flashlight app on his phone, found what he needed – a wheelbarrow and the biggest, strongest looking shovel he could find. Then he returned to the car and looked around, not worried at all – he was so cool under pressure it was crazy. He didn't see anyone or hear anything except crickets, so he popped open the trunk. He yanked Deb up and out by her feet and then grabbed her hair and propped her up next to him. Holding her like that, face to face, they could've been dancing. He maneuvered her on top of the wheelbarrow, centering her the best he could, and, taking her purse with him, carrying it over his shoulder, he went into the woods.

The flashlight app wasn't bad – it made a long stream

of whitish light and Owen had no problem seeing where he was going. The issue was that Deb's head was hanging off to the side, dragging in the dirt and mud and, once in a while, bouncing on rocks. He didn't care if her face got fucked up, it was just the CSI shit he was worried about. He knew that if the cops looked around here they would definitely find some blood or hair. But then he thought, *Yeah, but they won't look here.* He was proud of himself for not getting caught up in bullshit worrying, for sticking to the plan. It showed him again how strong he really was.

Once Deb had said to him, 'I didn't think I'd ever feel this way again.'

'You were right about that, baby,' Owen said, out loud, pushing the wheelbarrow. Then he laughed – he didn't care, because no one was around to hear, so why not laugh, why not *enjoy* this? He didn't know if he believed in all that life after death bullshit, but he knew that if Deb was up there somewhere looking down she'd probably be getting a kick out of this too. Who knows? She was so kinky, she might think that being dead and wheeled out to their spot in the woods was the hottest thing ever.

Then something weird happened. Along with the crickets there was another noise – it sounded like a woman giggling. Naturally Owen freaked. He stopped, aiming the light from his phone in every direction, expecting to see a woman. He had no idea what he'd do when he saw her, but he wouldn't be able to just let her get away.

Then he heard the giggling again. It sounded the same as before – not very loud, at the level of a whisper, but there wasn't anyone here – at least there didn't seem to be. At the same time, he knew he was hearing it, that he wasn't just imagining it. There it was again. It sounded familiar; he'd definitely heard it before. Was it Deb? He shone the light at her face and she was dead, with those

153

wide-open teddy bear eyes, no doubt about it. Then where was the giggling coming from?

He just wanted her gone, buried, as fast as possible. At the spot in the woods where they'd hooked up that time, he started digging a hole with the shovel. Like last time, it was hard work. There was enough moonlight through the trees to see what he was doing, but it would take a long time before the hole was big enough to fit a body. In the movies they always made it look so easy – a guy goes into the woods with a shovel and boom, a few minutes later there's a big grave there. Not the case in real life. The dirt was heavy, maybe heavier because of the rain before, and after digging for like ten minutes it was maybe a couple of feet deep and, worse, he seemed to be hitting something hard, like a root of a tree – you never see that happen in movies either; in the make believe world, nothing ever gets in the way.

He kept working, digging in a different spot, away from the root and finally, after like a half hour, he was exhausted and sweating like crazy, but at least it was starting to look like a grave. He knew it wasn't deep enough yet, though, so he kept digging, sweating his ass off, getting blisters on his hands for maybe another half hour, and then he dragged the body off the wheelbarrow and then kind of rolled it into the hole. It fit and there seemed to be about two feet of space on top. Deeper would have been better, but this was deep enough to cover a body and he didn't want to spend any more time out here.

He took her cell phones out of her purse and tossed them into the hole, smashing them with the shovel until they were crushed. Then he took her cash out of her purse – seventy-three bucks – and then dumped the purse and everything else in it into the hole. He wanted to take off the jewelry she'd been wearing – a wedding ring, bracelets, a necklace – and try to sell the stuff at some point, but he knew that would be too dangerous. He wanted to do this right, have zero chance of getting caught.

He dumped dirt onto her face, covering all of her head. The rest of her body was easier to cover and soon her whole body was buried. There was a lot of leftover dirt so he spent some time flinging it away in different directions, and then he covered the gravesite with some leaves and twigs and, he had to fucking admit, he'd done a damn good job, at least as good as the other time. He didn't leave so fast, though; he added a few twigs here, a few more leaves there, like he was doing the finishing touches to a painting. When he knew there was nothing else he could do, and sticking around was only torturing himself, he headed along the path, pushing the empty wheelbarrow, hating that he was starting to cry.

When he got home he was through crying; he just hoped he didn't have to deal with any bullshit from Raymond. Though it was almost one in the morning, Raymond was sometimes up late, drinking beer and stuffing his face with whatever food he could get his hands on. The TV was on in the den, which got Owen nervous, but then he peeked in and saw Raymond passed out on the couch, the TV on to some black-and-white movie. The whole downstairs reeked of beer farts.

Owen went up to his room and took off all his dirty, muddied clothes and put them in the hamper. He'd do laundry in the morning, but he wasn't worried about the dirt because his clothes were always dirty from the country club. He was more worried about CSI shit, like if Deb's hairs were on the clothes, or in the trunk of his car. There was no big rush now, though; he had plenty of time to clean up and make sure everything was perfect.

In the hot shower, Owen was thinking about Karen looking so sexy in her yoga pants. He wished he'd kissed her, just gone for it, what the hell? He knew she'd wanted him to, that she definitely would have been into it. Going with the fantasy, he pictured them making out in the hallway, getting her so turned on she was practically panting. Then they somehow wound up in the kitchen, and she was bent over the table, and he was pulling down those yoga pants, and then they were doing it from behind, and he was grabbing onto her hair, pulling on it, the way Deb used to like it pulled.

It was weird – now he felt like Deb was in the shower with him. He didn't see her there – he wasn't totally schizo – but he could *hear* her. She was giggling, like in the woods. Why wouldn't she leave him alone? Was she jealous of Karen? Yeah, probably. After all, she wasn't exactly happy with Karen when she was alive, screaming at her at the country club, so it figured she wouldn't be thrilled with her when she was dead either. Owen didn't like this sudden change in the giggling though. It reminded him of how she had changed in real life – loving him in the morning when they were playing student-teacher at the school and then turning and becoming so cold and distant in the car. It was like that game his mother used to play with him when he was a kid – moving her hand over her face, her expression turning from a smile to a sad face. He loved it when his mother had a happy face, but hated it when her expression changed, and it was the same way with Deb. He wanted her angry giggling to stop, he wanted to shut her up the way he had when he'd strangled her, but he couldn't strangle her again.

He still heard the giggling when he got out of the shower and later in bed when he was trying to sleep it was still there. It wasn't loud, he could barely hear it actually, but it was just loud enough to annoy the hell out of him, like a dripping faucet. It was worse than a dripping faucet though, because you can fix a dripping faucet, or put in ear plugs, but even with two pillows over his ears, he couldn't make this stop.

In the morning, he still heard it. It wasn't as loud as last night, but it still bothered him when he focused on it; maybe that was the key – to not focus on it. If he just ignored it, didn't give it any attention, hopefully she'd give up and leave him alone.

Luckily he had a lot to do this morning so he had plenty of distractions. He figured Deb's husband Mark had probably called the cops by now and soon they'd look for Deb, find her car in the parking lot, and then start searching everywhere for her. He put in a load of laundry along with his clothes from last night. Raymond wasn't on the couch anymore – the fat fuck had probably crawled into bed with Owen's mother in the middle of the night – but the whole downstairs still smelled like beer farts. After a quick bowl of Frosted Flakes, Owen went out back and vacuumed the inside of his mother's car, especially the backseat, and then he vacuumed the trunk. He could still hear the giggling – the noise of the vacuum didn't help block it out much – but it was okay; he could deal. When he didn't think there could possibly be any hairs or fibers left, he was about to go back into the house, through the garage, when Kyle came out with his jacket on, looking angry.

'Where you goin'?' Owen asked.

'Out,' Kyle said.

'Where?'

'I don't know.'

Owen remembered when he was Kyle's age, eleven

years old, and realizing how shitty life at home was. Back then he'd wanted to get out of the house all the time, get as far away from Raymond and all the bullshit as he could. Then one day he decided he had to get out permanently, and he packed his backpack with everything he thought he needed for the rest of his life – a few pairs of jeans, some T-shirts, his toothbrush, and a bunch of comic books – and he took a shuttle bus to the Metro North train station in Katonah and bought a one way ticket into the city and planned to never see his mom, his little brother, or his asshole stepdad again. It was November, maybe December, and sunny when he left, but when he got out at Grand Central it was cloudy and much colder and he didn't have a jacket. He walked to Times Square because he didn't know the city that well and it was the only place he knew how to get to. Using some of the money he'd brought – his life savings, about forty bucks – he bought a hot dog and knish. When he finished it he couldn't think of anything else to do so he just walked around, back and forth along the crowded streets, until it got dark and colder. He was tired and realized he had nowhere to sleep. He went down to the subway, figuring he'd sleep on a train, but the station smelled like piss, and he saw a couple of rats on the tracks. He decided that it sucked big time, and he went back to Grand Central and took a train back to Katonah. He called his mom to come pick him up. She was worried and crying, and he told her he was sorry, but he really wasn't; he just said he was sorry because he knew that was what he was supposed to say. He knew Raymond was going to give him hell for running away, and he did. Later, Raymond came into his room and beat the shit out of him and even though his mom was right across the hall and heard him screaming for help, she didn't do anything about it. Owen was used to it, though, and he'd learned an important lesson that day. He'd learned that, yeah, life at home sucked, but life in the rest of the world sucked too, so he might as well stick it out at home for as long as he could stand it.

'Hey, wait a sec,' Owen said to Kyle.

Kyle, half on his bike, about to leave the garage, looked back.

'You okay, bro?' Owen asked.

Kyle looked down, toward his Nikes. 'Mom and Raymond are fighting again,' he said.

Owen knew this was why Kyle was taking off; he didn't know why he'd bothered asking.

'So just ignore 'em,' Owen said.

'It's really bad,' Kyle said.

Owen could tell Kyle was scared, just wanted to get away. He knew how that felt.

'Did Raymond say something to you?'

'No,' Kyle said.

'Did he *do* something to you?' Owen's fists clenched, his fingernails digging into his palms.

'No.' Kyle was looking at his Nikes again.

Owen knew Kyle was lying about something, but he didn't know what.

'Okay, but you remember what I told you,' Owen said. 'If he ever does anything to you, if he ever lays a hand on you, you come to me, okay?'

Kyle got fully onto his bike and rode away.

Owen knew that Kyle needed him, and he was always there for his little bro, looking out for him. He took him to swimming practice, play dates, and brought him to the country club on weekends. He liked Kyle, thought he was the coolest kid in the world, and wanted to keep him away from Raymond. It was one of the main reasons why Owen had stayed living at home the past couple of years. Owen was afraid if he left, Raymond would start picking on Kyle, and Owen would rather take the hit himself than see Kyle get hurt. The way Owen saw it, it was his job to take care of his little brother; it was his main reason for living.

Back in the house, Owen heard his mother and Raymond fighting – yeah, they were really going at it, but it was no worse than usual. He was yelling like a lunatic – maybe cause he *was* a lunatic – calling her a cunt and a whore and, like always, she was just taking it, not saying anything back. It always amazed Owen how his mother could be that way, how she could take so much shit. Meanwhile, Owen was trying to figure out if there was anything else he needed to get rid of. He'd put the laundry in the dryer soon, so he didn't have to worry about that anymore. He'd do some more cleaning up later, then he'd be able to chill.

Ignoring the giggling, he was pouring a glass of Pepsi in the kitchen when his mother came in. She was forty-six but looked more like sixty. A few years ago she found out she had breast cancer and had to go through chemo, radiation, all that shit, but it wasn't the cancer that was sucking the life out of her – it was living with Raymond, putting up with bullshit every fucking day. Even before she was diagnosed, she'd looked older, thinner, more stressed out than other moms. Her face especially looked old – she had permanent wrinkles on her forehead and she looked like she was making a sad face even when she wasn't.

But now she was sad – crying, her face wet with tears.

'I hate him,' she said. 'I hate him so much.'

She went to the door leading to the deck in the backyard, like she was going to go out, but she just stood there, staring out.

Owen gulped down some more Pepsi, then said, 'So leave him already.'

Her mother didn't turn around or answer, but Owen heard her crying. He also heard Deb giggling, but the crying was louder.

'I'm serious,' Owen said. 'It's time already. What's he going to have to do before you walk out, kill me?'

'Stop it,' she said.

'Or kill Kyle?'

'I said stop it.'

'You know it's gonna happen,' Owen said. 'It's a miracle it hasn't happened already. And what about you? How much more abuse can you take?'

Now she turned, whispering but it seemed like she was yelling, 'Keep your voice down.'

'What, you're afraid he's gonna hear me?' Owen said. 'Ooh, I'm so scared, Big Bad Raymond's gonna beat me up. See, I don't have to run away from him anymore. I used to be weak, but I'm bigger now, I'm stronger. I can stand up to him now, and you can too. You can say, "Enough," and do what you should've done years ago. Kick him the fuck out.'

'I can't do that.'

'Of course you can,' he said. 'You just do it, don't even think about it.' He whispered, 'When he's out of the house just change the locks, the fat fuck won't be able to get in. If he comes back you get a restraining order. He won't be able to hurt you or us ever again.'

'I'm sorry, Owen.' Sobbing, his mother came over and wrapped her arms around his waist, hugging him tightly. It was weird, freaky – he couldn't remember the last time his mother had hugged him and it was shocking how skeleton-like her body was.

'I'm so, so sorry,' she said, still sobbing.

His mother never apologized to him before for anything, and he didn't know what to say, so he didn't say anything. It was silent except for his mom's crying and Deb's giggling.

Finally, feeling nothing, Owen said, 'I'm sorry too, Ma. I mean I want to forgive you for everything you did to me, for not being there for me all the times I needed you, but I can't. I wish I could, but I can't.'

More silence, then his mother said, 'That's not why I'm sorry.'

Owen was confused. 'It isn't?'

'No,' she said. 'I mean I'm sorry about that too, but now I'm sorry that...' She waited then said, 'I'm sorry that you... that you have to move out.'

Now Owen was completely confused. He wasn't sure he'd heard her correctly.

'What did you say?' he asked.

'It's for the best, it really is,' she said. 'It's causing too much trouble for all of us with you living here. It'll be better for me, it'll be better for Kyle too.'

Owen felt a rush of pain, of hurt, and he didn't know where it was coming from or what it meant. All he knew was that he'd felt this way before, and he was feeling this way again, and that it sucked.

'Why are you doing this to me?' he said, feeling like he'd asked this question dozens of times before, because he probably had.

'Please don't make this any harder, just try to understand,' she said. 'I did the best I could, I tried to protect you, but things are different now. You're working now, making money, and you can find something else over the winter. You should have your own space, be independent.'

'Bullshit.' Owen's face was hot. 'This isn't about me, it's never about me. It's about you, you and that stupid asshole. You're afraid of him so you take it out on us.'

'Quiet,' his mother said.

'Fuck you.' Owen sprayed spit in his mother face. Deb's

giggling was suddenly louder, and he shouted at her, 'Shut up!' and then back to his mother, 'You don't care about me or Kyle. You're the worst mother in the world cause you don't give a shit about your kids.'

'I only want to do what's best for everybody,' she said.

Owen was maybe five years old, throwing a bowl of macaroni and cheese at his mother, the bowl shattering on the kitchen floor, and then he was back in the present, saying, 'So this is *your* idea for me to move out? This is what *you* want?'

'Yes.'

He grabbed her bony arm. 'You're full of shit. He told you to do this, so you're doing it. You're like his fucking pawn. You have no life of your own.'

'That isn't true.'

'You have no idea how much I hate you,' Owen said, and then he smelled Raymond's reeking sweat as Raymond grabbed him by his arm from behind and yanked him away. Owen let go of his mother's arm, knowing that he'd need to defend himself, but it was too late, Raymond had already hit him in the nose. There was a crunch but the pain didn't hit yet. Then Raymond hit him again, in the cheek, and Owen lost his balance. He reached back with his hands, trying to brace his fall, but he was going down too fast, and his head slammed against the stove. Dazed on the floor, he couldn't tell if the back of his head hurt or not because his nose and face hurt so much it was hard to feel anything else.

Raymond was over him saying, '... out of this house tonight, you hear me? I see your face around here again, I'll break the rest of it.'

Owen was squirming on the kitchen floor, touching his face, feeling all the blood, then seeing it on his hands. He was groaning in pain, but telling himself that he couldn't cry, he couldn't give Raymond the satisfaction. He wanted his mother to hit Raymond, or at least scream at him, but when he looked up his mother wasn't even there. She'd probably gone upstairs, and left him alone with Raymond, the way she always did. He'd once heard Raymond tell his mother, 'The boy needs a man's discipline.' Now Raymond was standing over him, hands on hips.

'Come on, get up,' he said. 'You've got some packing to do.'

The pain in his nose was still out of control, but he struggled to his feet. Raymond hadn't budged, his big gut sticking out, and Owen cocked his fist and tried to hit him in his stupid face, but Raymond moved out of the way at the last second and the punch totally missed and, worse, Owen lost his balance again and fell back on the floor.

Then he was up again, but this time he didn't get up on his own. Raymond had grabbed him and was pulling him, by the hair, through the kitchen, out toward the front door. Owen was practically running to keep up and not get a big chunk of hair of his hair pulled out. Then Raymond opened the door and shoved Owen out of the house. Owen stumbled off the stoop and fell hard onto the stone path leading up to the house.

He struggled, finally got up. The door was closed, but Owen had his keys. He could try to go back in, but Raymond had probably put the chain on; then he thought, why bother? He'd had it with Raymond and his mother and he just wanted to get away from them. But this time he wouldn't just go into the city for a few hours. This time he'd stay away forever.

He got in the Sentra and sped away. Blood was dripping over his mouth, down his chin, and some went onto the steering wheel. For a while he was too busy cursing Raymond and just wanting to get the hell away that he didn't bother to wipe up the blood. Finally, at a red light, he checked the glove compartment, looking for some napkins or some shit to wipe himself with. Nothing, so he reached under the front seat and grabbed an old rag he used sometimes to check the oil. As he drove, he pressed the rag against his face, not caring that he was barely soaking up the blood and smearing himself with oil. Deb's giggling was bothering him now, and he occasionally screamed 'Shut up!' or 'Shut the fuck up!' but it didn't stop.

He realized he didn't know where he was going – on Route 684, weaving through traffic, but with no destination. He didn't have to get to work for another hour and wasn't far from the car wash place on North Bedford Road.

There was no line, so he pulled right up and got out. By the way one of the workers was looking at him, he knew his nose was still bleeding or at least had a lot of blood around it.

'Fender bender,' he said.

He didn't think the guy would believe this when there was no damage to the car, but he didn't really care either.

After he wiped down the steering wheel with the rag the best he could, he watched as a couple of guys vacuumed the inside of the car, trying not to think about what had happened at home or Deb's giggling. He had to stay positive, think about the future, not the past, and the future was going to be awesome. The car would be clean soon, and there wouldn't be a speck of Deb left.

He needed to see Karen, right now, so he took out his phone and played the video from the country club yesterday. Jeez, look how sexy she was, wrestling with Deb. It was hot watching these two older women, *his* two older women, fighting on the floor like animals. It reminded him of all the wild times with Deb, and Karen was so into him already it would probably only take a couple of days before they were a couple and then – like Deb – she'd get addicted to him. She'd realize how she'd been wasting her time with those old dudes she'd been hooking up with and how awesome it was to have a hot, young boyfriend. And then, because she was a single mom and had nothing holding her back, she'd invite him to move in with her. He'd say yes and bring Kyle with him, get him away from Raymond. They would be such a happy family – Owen, Karen, Elana, Kyle, and Elana's little brother, Matthew. Matthew and Kyle were about the same age, and Kyle would love having a step-bro, but what would Elana say when she found out that Owen was going to be her *stepdad*? Owen laughed, thinking it could turn into an even cooler situation when Elana got older. Yeah, he wasn't into her now, but years from now that could all change. When Owen was an old man, like fifty, Elana would be forty-eight, and she might be hotter then, more MILFy anyway. Karen might be too old then, so he could trade her in for Elana. Or if Karen still had it going on, Owen could have both of them. That would be so awesome, having threesomes every night.

The inside of the car was done and the mechanical brushes were scrubbing the outside.

Later, driving to work in his clean car, Owen was still thinking about his happy future with Karen and the kids. Maybe they'd have another kid together. Karen was old, but not *too* old; she could probably still squeeze out one more. They'd call the kid Owen – Owen Jr. Owen had never really thought about being a dad before, but he knew he'd be a great father. He couldn't wait to teach Owen Jr. how the world worked, and do whatever else dads did with their sons. Then, someday, he'd have grandkids. Grandpa Owen. Yeah, he liked the way that sounded.

Then the giggling started again. Maybe the machines at

the car wash had blocked it or he'd been too busy thinking about other stuff. But, wait, there was something different about it now, or something he hadn't picked up on before anyway. It was familiar, yeah, he'd heard it before, but it wasn't Deb, he was sure of it. He knew who it was, though; it made so much sense.

Shit, he should've known.

12

MARK THOUGHT, *Okay, seriously, what's up with Karen?* He'd understood why she didn't feel like talking or texting last night, but he didn't get why she was still ignoring him this morning. Okay, it was only 8:32 on a Sunday and there was a possibility she was sleeping, but this didn't really make sense since he'd decided that she hadn't called him last night because she'd gone to sleep early and, besides, she was an early riser. She'd told him lots of times how she woke up every day at dawn, 'like a rooster,' to do yoga and shit. She'd probably been up for about two hours already, and she must've seen his text from last night. Mark wanted to believe that she was working out, running, doing work for her job, involved with the kids, but he knew that only one explanation made actual sense – she was blowing him off.

Mark was in the kitchen, contemplating what to do, when Justin came down.

'There's my big boy,' Mark said. 'How're you this morning, kiddo?'

''Kay,' Justin said flatly, sitting at the table.

'Well, you look a lot better,' Mark said. 'You look rested, you look happy. How about some pancakes for breaksticks?'

''Kay,' Justin said.

Mark made Justin a couple of just-add-water buttermilk pancakes and served them to Justin with syrup. Justin took a bite, seemed a little disappointed, and said, 'Mom makes them better.'

''That's not a nice thing to say,' Mark said. 'You just hurt my feelings.'

'Sorry,' Justin said.

Mark left the kitchen, checking his cell, annoyed that Karen still hadn't contacted him. Then it occurred to him that it was weird that Deb wasn't up yet either, as she also wasn't usually a late sleeper. When Mark woke up he'd noticed that she wasn't next to him and then when he left the bedroom Casey started jumping on him because he hadn't been let out yet. Mark assumed Deb had come home late, maybe one or two in the morning, and fallen asleep on a couch in the living room, or slept in the guestroom. She wasn't in the living room so – just out of curiosity, not because he actually *cared* – he went up to the guest room, but the couch hadn't been opened and there was no sign that she had slept there. Weird, yeah, but wasn't it to be expected? The way she'd sashayed out of the house last night, obviously trying to make him jealous, it made sense that she'd sleep at Kathy's or wherever to make him think that she was with a guy. It was a sad way of trying to make him jealous and upset, but as a mother of two kids it was also ridiculously irresponsible of her to play these games. Mark was going to have to remember to tell his lawyer about this too.

Ten o'clock and still no texts or calls from Karen – now *this* was getting Mark seriously concerned. He could deal with Deb checking out because his marriage had been dying a slow death for years, but he couldn't handle even the possibility of losing Karen. He had to smooth things over, make her understand that everything was cool. He knew that if they just talked and he heard her voice he could get her to laugh and see the lighter side of the situation. She'd once told him, 'You make me laugh. Joe hardly ever made me laugh. That's what I love about you.' *Love* – her word, not his. That was proof that their connection was real, *special*. She was having a hard time admitting it to herself, though, and was just taking some time to process things before opening up completely. That was okay; it was all good. He wanted to give her all the space she needed and didn't want to come on too strong.

But after another twenty minutes went by and there was still no word from her, he was starting to get paranoid again. Maybe he should go see her in person, just to say hi and make sure everything was cool? He loved the idea – in a few minutes he'd be with his future wife. Yes, yes, this was amazing.

He went upstairs and changed into jeans and a white button-down. He knew he looked good in white; it always contrasted nicely with his dark, Mediterranean skin. He slicked his hair back and sprayed on some of the new cologne he'd bought – Driven by Derek Jeter – and thought he looked hot, just like Javier Bardem.

He said to the mirror, 'Go get her, Javier.'

Riley, who was in the living room, doing something on her iPad, looked up and said, 'Why are you so dressed up at eleven o'clock in the morning?'

'Dressed up?' He made a confused expression, but felt

like he was overdoing it. 'Who's dressed up?'

'Um, you are, Dad.'

'I'm just going for a walk, be back in a few,' he said.

As he headed toward the door, Riley said something, but Mark was distracted, checking out his sexy, brooding profile in a mirror, and didn't hear.

'What?' Mark asked.

'Where's Mommy?' Riley asked. 'Your wife.'

'Oh, I don't know.'

'Did she come home last night?'

Opening the door, Mark said, 'Not sure,' then left before hearing whatever else Riley was saying.

Walking to Karen's, Mark was rehearsing in his head – and occasionally out loud – what he'd say to her. He'd play it cool, not act at all concerned that he hadn't heard from her last night or this morning, making her think it was no big deal, that he wasn't worried or doubtful about their relationship at all. Confidence was key. She'd probably apologize, say, 'Sorry for the way I acted outside Sarah Waxman's yesterday. I was just in a really bad mood, 'cause of you know, and it had nothing to do with you.' He loved the 'cause of you know' part; as a woman, Karen would have to understand how hard it was to go through a separation, she'd have to have sympathy. Then they'd sit at her kitchen table, no in the living room, on the couch, yeah, the couch. Her kids wouldn't be home, they'd be out with friends or wherever – it would just be the two of them all alone, and romantic music, Sinatra, would be playing; it was his fantasy, why couldn't he pick the music? They'd talk about the future, how they wanted to be together forever, and the timing for when Mark could move in. And then – or actually probably before then – they'd kiss. Mark's heart raced. It was actually going to happen today, within minutes; what he'd been dreaming about for years would be a reality. Soon he'd actually be kissing Karen Daily.

He rang the doorbell, licking and sucking on his lips, hating that they were so dry, and his whole mouth was sticky; why didn't he have a glass of water before he left? He felt sweat building on his neck and chest and then, with panic, noticed that he had big sweat marks on his shirt from his armpits. Shit, why hadn't he worn a T-shirt underneath or a thicker button-down?

The door opened. It was Elana, who seemed disappointed when she saw it was him. Her eyes were red, glassy, had she been crying? Yeah, probably.

'Hey, is your mom home?' Mark asked, actually hoping she wasn't, that she was out doing errands, so he'd have a chance to dash home and drink a glass of water and put on some Chapstick and a different shirt.

'Ma!' Elana called out. Then she said, 'Come in,' and walked away up the stairs, doing something on her iPhone.

Mark was blowing on his underarm areas as he went into the house and then saw Karen coming downstairs. He was expecting her to smile, say, 'Wow, what a pleasant surprise,' so he was confused when she stopped two or three steps from the bottom and, towering over him, said, 'What are *you* doing here?'

For a few seconds, he was distracted, noticing how perfect her body looked in leggings and a sports bra, then he snapped out of it, saying, 'Oh, just dropped by to say "hi."'

'This isn't a good time,' she said.

For an instant, Mark panicked, thinking she might have a guy over, but he relaxed, realizing that this didn't make much sense with Elana home.

'Oh, okay,' Mark said. 'Is everything cool?'

'No actually, everyth… This just isn't a good time.'

'No problem,' Mark said. 'Do you want to go for lunch or coffee late –'

'No, okay?' Karen said. 'No, I do not.'

Mark looked at her face closely, noticing she looked tired and/or upset – her eyes bloodshot with puffiness around them.

'You don't seem like yourself,' he said.

'I just can't deal with any more drama in my life right now,' she said.

'Oh, I get it,' he said. 'I told you, we don't have to worry about that anymore. It looks like what I told you yesterday is happening for real. My marriage is over, *finito*.'

Karen's eye widened and her jaw clenched. She looked back over her shoulder, probably checking to see if her kids were there, then she marched down the rest of the stairs, went by Mark, motioning with her hand for him to follow her. They went through the kitchen, into the dining area at the other end of the house, Mark trailing, knowing by the way she was shaking her head that she was seriously upset. This visit wasn't exactly going as planned.

At the end of the dining room, near the sliding doors leading out to the deck, Karen stopped and looked at Mark and whispered harshly, 'Are you crazy? My kids are home.'

'Sorry,' Mark whispered. 'I wasn't thinking, but you're right. We probably shouldn't tell them yet.'

'Tell them *what*?' Still angry as hell. 'What are you talking about?'

'Us,' Mark said, like it was obvious, because it was.

'There's no us,' Karen said. 'What's wrong with you? Why can't you…' She was shaking her head. 'Look, I can't deal with this right now. I have to function for my kids and this whole thing is driving me crazy. You have to go. Please, just go.'

Mark couldn't remember ever seeing Karen so agitated.

'I'll go, I'll go,' he said. 'But I think I get why you're so angry.'

'Can you keep your voice down?'

'I'm trying to say, I understand, I get it,' Mark whispered. 'It's because you think you're responsible, but you're not. Me ending my marriage has nothing to do with you, okay? This has to do with me and Deb. It's *our* decision.' Mark was smiling, saying to himself, *It is because of her. You're so full of shit. Who are you kidding?*

'Why are you smiling?' Karen asked. 'You think this is funny?'

'No,' Mark said. 'I'm just... happy.'

'I don't want to hear about your fucking happiness.' She was waving her hands in front of her face. 'You need help, not from me, from a therapist.'

Mark knew she didn't mean any of this. She was just scared. She didn't want to be the bad one, the home wrecker.

'I know what you're going through right now,' Mark said.

'Just go home,' she said. 'If you like me at all, if you respect me at all, you'll just do this. Please. *Please.*'

He knew she didn't mean this either. So he said, 'Fine, talk to you later when you chill out,' and left the house, thinking there was no way she'd be able to stay away from him for long.

At home, Mark tried to not think about Karen, which turned out to be easy because there was a crisis at work. Two major systems were down in Hong Kong and programmers were emailing him, like he was a fucking help desk, and he resented that he had to deal with this shit on a Sunday. There were supposed to be people in Hong Kong to handle these problems, and even if they were understaffed there, why were they calling him? He was middle management, he wasn't supposed to be doing hands-on work, but he had to suck it up and be the Company Man. Bonuses had been shitty enough lately, and he didn't want to give his boss any reason to fuck him over at Christmas time.

During the calls, while he was on hold, he went on Facebook and wound up on Karen's page. He looked through her recent pics, including one of her with Steven. Look at the guy, with his ponytail; why had Karen gone for a guy like that? To feel better, Mark went to the photos of himself with Karen. There were some on her page – one from maybe ten years ago when she was married to Joe, of him and Karen with Deb and Joe at a barbecue in their backyard. He was next to her in the photo, both smiling widely, arms around each other's waists. The other photos were from a couple of kids' birthday parties and one at a New Year's Eve party Mark and Deb had had maybe five years ago.

He had the enlarged pic of him and Karen with their arms around each other up on the screen when Riley appeared behind him and asked, 'Where's Mommy?'

He immediately X'd the page and said, 'Out still, I guess.'

'Did she come home last night or not?' Riley asked.

'I don't think so,' Mark said.

'Before you said you weren't sure.'

'What difference does it make what I said?'

Sometimes Riley reminded Mark of Deb, the way they both tried to nudge information out of him.

'Her car's not here,' Riley said.

'She left it at the country club yesterday,' Mark said. 'I'm on hold on a work call.'

'Why?'

'Because sometimes I get work calls on Sundays.'

'No, I mean why did she leave her car at the club?'

Mark was going to explain that she'd been too drunk to drive but didn't want to get into it and said, 'It doesn't matter why.'

'I don't get it,' Riley said. 'How did she go anywhere without her car?'

Mark thought he remembered hearing a car pull up before she'd left yesterday.

'I think a friend picked her up,' he said.

'A friend? What friend?'

'I don't know… Kathy?'

'Kathy *Davidson*? I don't think Mommy even talks to her anymore. They had some falling out or something two years ago.'

Now, vaguely, Mark remembered hearing about that. He had no idea what Deb had been doing with her time lately, who her current friends were; all he knew was that she could've gone back to work years ago, but hadn't, and it had caused a strain on them financially.

'And besides,' Riley went on, 'Mommy, *Mom* never stays over with friends. She always sleeps at home… Did you and Mommy have a fight? I mean, I know you always have fights, but did you have a big fight? Is that why she's not home?'

Mark didn't want to have a conversation about the divorce with Riley. Well, not yet.

'Aren't you getting a little old for that?' Mark asked.

'Old for what?' Riley seemed confused.

'Mommy,' Mark said. 'Shouldn't you call her "Mom" or even "Ma"?'

'Don't you even care that she's not home?' Riley asked.

'Of course, I care,' Mark said. 'I'm sure she'll be home soon. In the meantime, don't you have homework or term papers to do? When are your finals?'

'In two weeks.'

'Well, do some work. I have work to do too.'

'Why were you on Karen's Facebook?'

'I wasn't.'

'I saw you,' Riley said, 'when I came in.'

'I was just surfing,' he said, not sure why he was lying about this.

'Surfing?' Riley said sassily. 'Nobody says *surfing* anymore.'

'Can you just go and do some work please?'

Riley breathed deeply and headed upstairs.

Mark returned to Karen's Facebook pictures, checking out some beach shots she'd posted of herself in various bikinis at various beaches. Then, after he finished troubleshooting with the morons in Hong Kong and got the systems up-and-running, he went upstairs. Justin was contentedly playing on his XBox, so the bedwetting crisis seemed to be over, and Riley was in the bedroom with her door closed, listening to whatever pop music she was into these days. Mark was aware of how calm, how *normal*, the house was without Deb around. He'd definitely been in denial lately, maybe for years, not realizing how Deb had been disrupting everybody's lives. There was no doubt her drinking had been out of control and when she was around there was generally an overall tense, anxious vibe in the house. This had been making Mark extremely unhappy – he was so aware of this now – and was probably why Justin was wetting himself, and Riley was sometimes confrontational and difficult to get along with. The divorce was going to be the best thing for everybody – even Deb. She'd be happier, not bickering with her husband all the time in a disintegrating marriage, and maybe she'd meet some guy – a rich guy, who was into traveling and art and all the other shit she was into. Meanwhile, Karen was going to be an awesome stepmom and a great role model for the kids. No doubt about it – it would be a win-win situation for everybody.

A little later, Mark took a drive to the strip mall down the road to pick up some pizza for him and the kids for lunch. When he left, he slowed passing Karen's house, noticing her car in the driveway, but couldn't catch a glimpse of her in the house. On his way back he slowed again but still couldn't see her and her car was still there.

Back home in the kitchen, Justin was gobbling up his second slice, eager to get back to XBox, and Mark was having some Greek yogurt with pieces of banana in it. He'd taken a bite of pizza then reminded himself that he needed to lose ten pounds to get into shape for Karen, so he opted for the less caloric lunch.

Then Riley came in and said, 'I'm really worried about Mommy.'

Mark glanced at the clock: 2:26. Okay, he admitted this was getting a little odd now. It definitely wasn't like Deb to just not come home. Then again, she didn't usually ask for a divorce before she left either. Then again, why wouldn't she at least call or text the kids?

'You didn't get any texts from her?' Mark asked.

'No,' Riley said.

'Did Mom text you?' Mark asked Justin.

With his cheeks stuffed with pizza, Justin mumbled, 'No,' as he rushed past Mark and Riley on his way upstairs.

'I'm really worried,' Riley said. 'I think you should call the police.'

'Oh, stop it,' Mark said.

'Maybe she was in a car accident or something.'

'She wasn't in a car accident.'

'How do you know?'

'Because the police would've contacted us if she was in an accident.'

'Then where is she?'

'I don't know. Maybe she and a friend went into the city.'

'The city?'

'Yeah, maybe they stayed overnight, got a hotel room in Times Square or something.'

Mark remembered how he and Deb used to do that, like fifteen years ago, when they first moved to the 'burbs and wanted to have romantic nights in the city. Jeez, now the idea of a night in the city with Deb seemed like torture.

'Why would Mom go into the city and stay overnight without telling anybody?'

'I'm not sure,' Mark said, 'but it's not a responsible thing to do… *if* that's what she did.'

If it did turn out Deb had gone off to the city, on a drinking binge, Mark was going to tell this to his divorce attorney; at this rate he was going to have a long list of ammo for his divorce. Forget about any chance of her getting full custody, she'd be lucky if she got *any* custody.

'What if she's not in the city?' Riley said. 'What if it's something else? I want to call the police.'

'Whoa, let's not panic and get ahead of ourselves here,' Mark said. 'Somebody has to be missing twenty-four hours before they start looking, right? If we call the police they'll probably just tell us to wait and keep trying to contact her. Did you text her?'

'I texted and called like five times.'

'Call again,' Mark said. 'Maybe her phone ran out and she just charged it now. I'll make a few calls. I'm sure we'll hear from her soon.'

Actually Mark wasn't planning to call anybody. He knew Deb would show up soon and admit that she was out drinking in Manhattan. Yeah, she'd try to apologize, but as far as Mark was concerned there was nothing Deb could say now that could save their marriage. Acting out with some drama at the country club was one thing, but disappearing and not calling and getting everyone, including the kids, upset was taking it way too far.

Sure enough about an hour later, Mark heard a car pull into the drive. Mark marched to the front door, ready to give his soon-to-be-ex some hell.

13

WHEN DETECTIVE LARRY WALSH of the Bedford Police Department got the call to go into work, Stu Zimmerman, who was naked in bed with him, said, 'Come on, man, not again.'

'Sorry.' Larry turned on his side to kiss him, holding him tightly. Then he let go, clapped his hands twice, got out of bed and said, 'But you know how it is.'

Larry went across the bedroom to the bathroom and peed with the door open.

'How long you gonna be gone?' Stu asked.

'Don't know,' Larry said. 'Hopefully just an hour or two.'

'I won't be here when you get back. Sorry, I gotta be home for my kids.'

'I understand.' Larry flushed. 'I'm gonna shower, wanna come in with me?'

Larry looked in the bedroom, saw Stu was at the edge of the bed getting dressed, had already pulled on his boxer briefs.

'No, I think I'm just gonna take off,' Stu said, sounding pissed off.

'Come on, don't be a dick about this,' Larry said, back in the bedroom. 'You know my job's unpredictable.'

'So what's the big emergency today?'

'I don't know, but my sergeant said he needs me.'

'More than I need you?'

Larry headed back toward the bathroom.

Stu rushed over, grabbing his hand to stop him and said, 'Okay, sorry, sorry, I didn't mean it like that. That shit was wrong.'

Larry and Stu were facing each other.

'If this is getting too hard for you, I understand,' Larry said.

'You'll never be too hard for me,' Stu said, smiling.

'Ha ha,' Larry said, smiling with him.

They kissed, Stu's hands on Larry's ass. It felt good – too good.

'Down boy,' Larry said.

'I can't help it, you turn me on too much,' Stu said.

Looking into Stu's eyes, feeling lost in them the way he always did, Larry said, 'You're lucky you're so fuckin' hot or I'd dump you.'

'Bullshit,' Stu said. 'You'll never dump me. Even when I'm eighty with bitch tits and my pants pulled up over my bellybutton.'

'Yeah, you're probably right.' More kissing then Larry pulled back and said, 'I really have to go.'

'I don't know when I can see you again,' Stu said. 'Luke has swimming all next weekend, and the weekend after that we're taking the kids to Janet's parents' in the Hamptons.'

'Well, I guess we'll figure something out,' Larry said, feeling bad about the situation himself now.

'Hey, I'm doing whatever I can to get free to see you,' Stu said, pulling on his jeans, 'but it might be harder to get away over the summer when the kids are in camp 'cause Janet'll be in my face all the time.'

'I understand,' Larry said. 'You're doing what you can do.'

'And I know you're doing what you can do. I didn't mean to give you a guilt trip before, that was wrong. I just love seeing you so much, man. I think about you all the time, and I want to see you more, and it sucks that I can't even pick up the phone and call you when I miss you. It's like I'm in prison.'

Larry didn't say anything, absorbing this. Then, wrapped in a towel around his waist, he waited until Stu was fully dressed with shoes on. Then he walked him to the door, making sure he was out of view when it opened. He lived in a community of semi-attached houses and had neighbors close-by on both sides.

'I'm gonna miss you, you sexy motherfucker,' Stu said, a little teary-eyed.

'Yeah, me too,' Larry said.

They snuck a kiss goodbye behind the door and then Stu left.

Larry rushed into the shower, trying not to feel the letdown, but it was hard not to. It always felt like a loss when Stu left, and his life felt bleak and empty without him. Emotionally, Larry wanted Stu to tell Janet the truth, that he was in love with a man, and leave his marriage, but rationally he knew that a total clusterfuck would ensue. She would be devastated, his kids would hate him, and he would become resentful of Larry, and it would probably ruin their whole relationship. Even if Stu could figure out a way to ease out of his marriage, he wouldn't be able to be in an out-in-the-open relationship with a dude. When it was revealed that the affair had broken up a family in the community, Larry would be pressured to leave his job with the department.

Since they'd started seeing each other, over a year ago, Larry and Stu had run through every possible scenario for how their relationship could work long term to the point where they were both sick of the conversation. There was no point in even discussing it anymore as they kept coming back to the same conclusion – that the only solution was to stick to what they called their 'eight year plan.' Stu's youngest kid, his daughter Maddy, was ten years old. When Maddy went to college Stu planned to leave his marriage. At that time Larry would be fifty-three years old and would take an early retirement package. Then Larry and Stu could leave Westchester, move to the city, get married. As partner of his law firm, Stu could work out an early retirement deal of his own, or reduce his hours at least, and Larry and Stu could travel, live in South Beach part of the year, and do all the other things they wanted to do together.

It was a great fantasy, but a fantasy that wouldn't become a reality for eight years, and who knew what could happen in eight years? Stu could decide he didn't want to hurt his wife, or didn't want to put his kids through any turmoil, or he didn't want to come out after all and he wanted to stay in his marriage. Or maybe they wouldn't last eight years – the sneaking around and secretiveness would get to be too much and Stu, or even Larry, would bail.

But Larry doubted he'd ever bail. How could he ever want to dump the love of his life?

As he got dressed for work and later, driving to the police station, he was aware of how the situation was already draining him. He was ruminating about it all the time, replaying conversations he'd had with Stu in his head and thinking up scenarios for how they could be together happily long term. He knew he was doing this by choice. He didn't have to stay with a guy who was in a committed relationship with a woman. He could break up with Stu, meet somebody else. Most of his previous boyfriends had lived in Manhattan as he preferred not to shit where he ate. But he didn't intend to meet Stu that day at Whole Foods in Port Chester – it wasn't exactly a cruising spot – and he didn't expect to fall in love with him either; it had just happened. Now this was the situation, and Larry had to be cool with it and deal with his jealousy – Stu didn't talk about having sex with his wife, but Larry knew it was happening – or move on. Staying meant having Stu in his life, but with eight more years of torment and no guaranteed happy ending. Moving on meant losing Stu, maybe forever. Larry had been struggling with the dilemma for months and was no closer to finding a solution.

When Larry entered the station at Bedford Hills, a young police officer, Robert Kelly, came over and said, 'Thanks for coming in. Been slow so far today, but we're undermanned.' Kelly explained that Charlie Wilson, another cop at the station, had to go home with food poisoning, which was why Larry had been called in for OT. Larry, seeing a flash of Stu's body, was irritated that he hadn't been called in for a more urgent reason, but he didn't want to get into it with his subordinate.

'No problem,' Larry said. 'I had some paperwork I needed to get done anyway.'

It was true he was way behind on paperwork, and it would be good to get it out of the way, but he wished he was still in bed with Stu. They'd had fewer opportunities to see each other lately, and they had to make the most of them if this relationship had any chance of working out.

185

At his desk, Larry sipped coffee, trying to focus on the reports he needed to file, ignoring the images of the sex earlier that kept coming to him. Then he smiled when his phone chimed and he saw a text from Stu: **You were awesome this afternoon, bro.** Smiling, Larry texted back, **I'm the luckiest dude in the world**, trying to fight off some tears, aware of how tenuous this relationship was and how he was all-in emotionally – potentially a lethal combination.

'Hey, Larry.'

Shit, it was Officer Kelly. Larry looked down immediately and concealed the cell phone behind the desk. Larry didn't want the young cop to see that he was crying over a text.

'Yeah,' Larry said, trying to sound casual, hoping his voice wasn't cracking, giving his mood away.

'There's a girl on the phone,' Kelly said. 'Says she thinks her mother's missing.'

'A girl?' Larry asked.

'Yeah, you know, a teenager,' Kelly said. 'She sounds pretty upset.'

'Okay, put her through.'

'Right, boss.'

When Kelly left, Larry wiped the tears away with the back of his hand. Then a few seconds later his phone rang.

He picked up and said, 'Bedford Police, Detective Walsh speaking.'

'He-hello.' The girl did sound upset, as if she'd been crying.

Hiding his own tearful tone, Larry said, 'What's your name please?'

'Riley. Riley Berman.'

'And how can I help you, Riley?'

'I-I think my mother's missing.'

'And what makes you think that?'

'Because she didn't come home last night.'

'Okay.' Larry wasn't sure what to make of this. 'How old are you, Riley?'

'I'm sixteen.'

'Is there an adult or another relative at home I can speak with?'

'My father's here.'

'Can you put him on please?'

'No.'

'Why ca –'

'Can you just look for my mother, please? Can you do *something*? I'm really scared. She didn't come home or call or text or *anything*. This isn't like her at all.'

'Okay, you're going to have to calm down,' Larry said. 'I want to help you, but I'm going to need you to stay calm and answer some questions, okay?'

'Okay, I'm calm, I'm calm.'

'Good. Now is your father home or not?'

'He's here, but he doesn't care, okay? He's barely worried at all.'

'Maybe he's not worried because he knows she's okay.'

'No, he's not worried because he's mad at her. My parents are getting a divorce. I saw my mom's iPad. She was looking up divorce lawyers.'

'I understand,' Larry said, thinking this sounded like a lot of teenage drama. 'So how do you know your mother's not staying with a friend?'

'Because my mother wouldn't do that. She'd never just go someplace and stay overnight without telling us. I'm telling you, she wouldn't.'

'Okay, I understand,' Larry said. He wasn't very concerned – this girl's mother hadn't been gone long enough to be considered missing – but he was glad to have a distraction from thinking about Stu. 'What's your mother's name?'

'Deborah.'

'And your father's name?'

'Mark.'

'Berman, right?'

'Right.'

Mark Berman, why did that name sound familiar? Wait, didn't Stu play golf with a Mark Berman? Larry was pretty sure he did.

'And can I have your address, please?'

The girl gave him her address, on Savage Lane in South Salem. Larry knew exactly where it was and it was sort of on his way home.

'I'll tell you what,' Larry said. 'I'll stop by in about an hour to check in on you and look into the situation. In the meantime, you let me know if your mom comes home, okay?'

'Okay.' The girl was crying again. 'But something happened to her. I'm telling you something happened.'

Larry didn't get a call from the girl so after he put in another hour or so doing paperwork he swung by the house off Lake Shore Drive. He parked in the driveway at the end of the cul-de-sac on Savage Lane, then went around to the front and rang the bell. Inside a dog was barking.

A stocky, middle-aged dark-haired man opened the door. Larry watched the man's expression morph from anger to surprise. He'd obviously been expecting someone else.

'Mark Berman?'

'Yeah.' He was squinting, confused.

While Larry still didn't know whether this Mark Berman was the Mark Berman who played golf with Stu, he seemed to be about the right age – mid-forties – and seemed like the suburban golf-playing type. But what straight guy out here didn't?

Larry showed his badge, said, 'Larry Walsh, Bedford Hills Police.'

Now Mark's surprise became concern.

'Is your wife home?' Larry asked.

'No,' Mark said. 'Actually I thought it was her when I heard the car in the drive. Is everything okay?'

'I don't know,' Larry said. 'That's why I'm here.'

'I don't understand.'

'I called him, Dad.'

A teenage girl, hair back in a ponytail, had appeared from behind Mark.

'For Chrissake, Riley,' Mark said.

'I'm scared, and you weren't doing anything,' Riley said.

'This is ridiculous,' Mark said to Larry. 'There's no reason for you to be here.'

'So you've located your wife,' Larry said.

'No, but she doesn't need locating,' Mark said. 'She's probably in the city with a friend.'

'She wouldn't go to the city overnight without telling us,' Riley said.

Now a boy, holding a gaming remote, came down, asking, 'Is Mommy home yet?'

'Kids, I want you to go upstairs right now,' Mark said.

'But I'm the one who called him,' Riley said.

'It's okay,' Larry said to Riley. 'Why don't you go upstairs? I want to talk to your father alone for a few minutes, okay?'

Riley muttered, 'Okay,' and went up with the boy. Larry heard the boy asking, 'Where's Mommy?' and Riley telling him, 'We don't know yet,' and the boy saying, 'I miss her.'

When the kids seemed out of earshot, Mark said, 'I'm really sorry about this. I had no idea she was calling you.'

'It's okay, I was passing through anyway and just wanted to check the situation out.'

'The situation is she's probably with a friend, and she'll be home any minute.' Mark sounded annoyed.

'Is that what she told you? That she was meeting a friend?'

'No, she didn't really tell me anything.'

'Have you tried calling her friends?'

'I didn't want to make a big deal about this for no reason. You know, get people all worked up.'

'Have you tried to call her yourself?'

'I did before you got here, yes.'

'And?'

'It went right to voicemail.'

'Does she usually have her phone off?'

'No, not usually, but sometimes it dies.'

'Can you try to call her again right now?'

'I don't see why –' Then he let out a breath and said, 'Okay, okay.'

Larry followed Mark into the kitchen. Mark picked up a cordless, tapped in the number, then ended the call and said, 'Voicemail again.'

'So when exactly was the last time you saw her?' Larry asked.

'I don't know,' Mark said, running a hand through his thinning hair. 'I guess yesterday at like seven, seven-thirty.'

'That's significant,' Larry said. 'It's getting to the point when we'll probably have to start getting concerned.'

'Concerned about what?'

'Let's not worry about that right now. Let's just try to locate your wife.'

'Shit,' Mark said.

Now Larry thought Mark seemed genuinely worried.

Larry took out a pen and a small pad from the pocket of

his Windbreaker, flipped to a fresh page. After jotting, 7, 7:30? in the pad he asked, 'And she gave you no indication where she was going?'

'No,' Mark said.

'Is that unusual?'

'I didn't think so at the time,' Mark said. 'I figured she was just going out for a while.'

'Were you concerned when she didn't come home last night?'

'A little but, like I said, I figured she was with a friend.'

'Who's this friend?'

'I don't know. I heard a car pull up.'

'So she didn't drive her own car?'

'No, her car's in the lot of the Oak Ridge Country Club where we have a membership.'

Stu's club.

Writing in his pad, Larry asked, 'Did you get a look at the car she got in?'

'No, I just heard it.'

'And what was she wearing?'

'Is that really necessary?'

'Maybe, maybe not.'

Another deep breath then Mark said, 'I didn't notice.'

'Did she look like she was going someplace special?'

'I really have no idea.'

It seemed odd to Larry that he didn't notice how his wife was dressed; Larry could name every outfit he'd seen Stu wear for the past two months.

'And behaviorally,' Larry said, 'did you notice anything unusual yesterday?'

'What do you mean?' Mark asked.

Larry thought Mark suddenly seemed nervous, uncomfortable.

'I mean was there anything off about her, anything that

seemed out of the ordinary, or did anything happen that may have gotten her upset, made her want to leave for some reason?'

Larry was trying to hint about Mark and Deborah's possible divorce situation.

'No,' Mark said. 'Not really.'

Larry noticed Mark's right hand was clenched into a fist.

'Do you know where she was earlier in the day yesterday?' Larry asked.

'Nowhere special,' Mark said. 'Just around.'

'Did she leave the house?'

'She picked up the kids, ran errands, went to the country club. Shit like that.'

'And is everything...' Larry wanted to be sensitive here. '... okay in your marriage?'

'What's that supposed to mean?' Mark sounded defensive.

'I mean are you and your wife... divorcing?' Larry asked.

'*What*? Where did you get that idea?'

'From me.' Riley Berman had entered the kitchen.

Mark's face was pink. 'You told him that? Why? Where did you even get that idea?'

'Oh come on, it was so obvious,' she said. 'She wasn't talking to you yesterday, and I saw her iPad. She was looking up divorce lawyers. I saw Scott Greenberg's page on there.'

'Okay, that's enough, Riley,' Mark said. 'Go upstairs.'

'Well, she *was*. You can't lie.'

'I said that's enough.'

Riley left the room slowly, shaking her head.

'Look, this is getting out of control,' Mark said to Larry. 'I don't know why Riley told you that. Teenagers, they get these ideas in their heads, you know?'

'So you aren't getting divorced.'

'No, I… Look, I don't know what was going on, okay? Did we have a fight yesterday? Yes, we had a fight. Was it any more unusual than any other fight we've ever had? No, not really. And she was always threatening me with divorce. That's just what she did when she got mad. So, no, we were not *planning* to get divorced, that is absolutely untrue.'

'I understand,' Larry said.

'And you know,' Mark said, seeming more agitated, 'I'm getting pissed off at you for coming here even asking me these questions. I mean, I get why you're here and, honestly, I'm getting very concerned myself right now, but that doesn't give you the right to pry into my personal life. What was going on with me and Deb has absolutely nothing to do with any of this except she might have gone out with a friend and stayed overnight to prove a point, to try to get my attention or something. I'll call around now, check with all her friends, and I'm sure I'll track her down. When I do I'll call you and you'll be the first to know. How's that sound?'

'Sounds good to me,' Larry said, putting his pad away and taking a business card out of his wallet and placing it on the breakfast bar. 'I'm sorry for any stress I caused you, and I hope your wife turns up shortly.'

On his way out, Larry saw the kids, scampering upstairs, so they'd probably listened in on the whole conversation.

From outside, Larry heard the dog barking again. He felt bad for the family and hoped Deborah Berman came home soon, but driving back along Savage Lane he was much more concerned about this situation than he'd been a half hour ago. He had nothing solid to go on – it was just instinct – but he had a feeling that Mark Berman was hiding something, and Larry could spot a man with a secret better than just about anyone.

14

A T WORK ON SUNDAY afternoon Owen was in a great mood. Walking through the club he smiled and said 'hi' to everybody he passed which was unusual for him because he usually kept to himself and didn't give a fuck about people. But today was different; today he wanted to spread the love.

As he worked, pruning the shrubbery near the clubhouse and along the back nine, and then watering the greens and setting up sprinklers in the rough, he was still thinking about Karen. He didn't think about Deb at all until later. During a break, he went to the storage shed and, after making sure nobody was around to see, hosed down the wheelbarrow the best he could, just in case there was some kind of evidence from last night, even though he didn't think there was any or that anybody would have a reason to check.

The rest of the day, Owen went about his business. Every now and then he heard the giggling, but now that he knew it wasn't Deb, it didn't bother him as much. It was actually, like, comforting, like he had an angel following him wherever he went. The angel wasn't mocking him; it was letting him know that, *It's okay, I'm here, and nothing can hurt you when I'm here.*

When Owen's workday ended, at eight p.m., he left the country club, imagining what was going on at the Berman's. Mark had probably called the cops by now and maybe Deb was officially missing. They'd find her car in the high school lot, but so what? The cops would look around for months, maybe years for her, but it didn't matter because they'd never find her.

Owen drove with the front windows open, loving the rush of cool air against his face.

Several minutes later, as he approached his house, Owen's great mood turned to shit. What was up with all the boxes and garbage bags in front of the house? He parked on the street, ran around the car toward the lawn, and saw that it was stuff from his room in boxes and his clothes in the bag. He picked up one of the bags and flung it toward the house, shouting, 'Fuck you! Fuck you, you son of a bitch!'

Then he tried to open the front door but his key didn't fit and then he noticed that the lock had been replaced. Owen marched around the house, telling himself that he didn't care that Raymond was bigger and stronger – he was going to do whatever he had to do to get him out of his life, once and for all. If his mother wouldn't leave him, Owen would have to do it himself.

He rang the bell a bunch of times and banged on the door. The door didn't open, and Owen didn't hear any movement in the house, but Raymond's car was in the driveway and when he backed away from the house he saw the light was on in the master bedroom. He was probably up there with his mom, both of them ignoring the ringing and banging. He hated his mother so much; he didn't understand why she was doing this to him. He couldn't let this happen; he had to do *something*. The light wasn't on in Kyle's room, so maybe Kyle wasn't home; maybe he was away on a play date or sleepover or something.

Owen went to the trunk of his car, took out the heaviest object there – the carjack. Then he stormed back toward the house, ready to smash one of the living room windows. He imagined himself climbing in, going upstairs, finding Raymond and…

He stopped himself, with carjack cocked behind his back like an axe. He was telling himself, *You gotta be smart, bro. You gotta be chill*. He remembered everything else that was going on in his life, the big picture, and knew that getting into a fight now with Raymond and then maybe some neighbor calling the cops wasn't the smartest idea in the world. It definitely wouldn't make his life any better anyway.

So he put the carjack back in the trunk and then filled up the car with the rest of his stuff, making a bunch of trips back and forth to the car. He didn't know what he'd done to deserve this. He knew Raymond hated him – that was different, Raymond was just a prick – but what about his mother? How could his mother do this to him? His mother was his *mother*; wasn't a mother supposed to love her kid no matter what? Yeah, Owen knew he'd given her a hard time over the years, but he was still her kid. Wasn't that supposed to mean *something*?

As he drove away, he looked toward the house and saw his mother, watching from one of her bedroom windows. He couldn't see her face clearly, but he knew she wasn't crying or even sad. He glared at her, wanting her to see him, but she moved to the side, out of view, and, just like that, was gone, out of his life, probably forever.

He went to a motel off the Saw Mill River Parkway, not too far away, where his family – and Raymond – had stayed for a few days once after a Nor'easter had taken out the power at their house. There were vacancies and no problem for Owen getting a room for as long as he wanted, but it wasn't cheap – ninety-five dollars a night plus tax. He had a bankcard, with about two thousand bucks in savings, and his paychecks from the country club, but that wouldn't be enough to last very long at a motel, or anywhere. He'd planned to take it slow with Karen, try to woo her a little first before he made his big move, but he'd have to move faster now. If he didn't hook up with her soon and move into her house he'd be in trouble in the fall when his job ended – he was a seasonal employee – and his savings ran out. He didn't have any friends, and his relatives were all in Arizona and California. He wasn't close with them and, besides, they probably wouldn't want to put him up anyway after Raymond and his mother finished badmouthing him.

As he pulled a couple of changes of clothes out of the Hefty bags in the car and went up to his room, he was scared about the future, and he hated being scared, being weak. He wanted to hear the giggling now, to know he wasn't actually alone, but there was just silence.

'Come on,' he said. 'Now, when I need you, you disappear on me?'

Still nothing. Angry and hurt, he wanted to break something so he did – grabbing a lamp, yanking the cord out of the wall, then tossing it against the wall. The bulb shattered.

It figured that she'd take off when he needed her, that

she'd *change*, because that's what she did the last time. But he didn't need *her*, or Deb, or anyone else because he had a new woman in his life now – Karen Daily. Karen was here, she was alive, she was real, and soon she'd be his.

It was only a matter of time.

15

WHEN LARRY GOT word early Monday morning, via state troopers, that Deborah Berman's Pathfinder had been discovered in the parking lot of John Jay High School in Cross River he knew this case wouldn't have a happy ending. He also knew that it wouldn't be his case for long.

Sure enough, at around ten a.m., after he'd been in the office for about an hour, he got a call from Nick Piretti, a squat, graying homicide detective from the Westchester County Police in Bronxville whom Larry had met before. Nick said he and his department would be taking over the investigation, and he was on his way over to be briefed. In the past it would have bothered Larry when a detective from County took over one of his cases, but over the past few years – well, the past year especially – he'd lost most of the ego and ambition about his job. His career used to be everything. He used to dream of scoring a promotion to detective at County and had even thought about relocating to the city, to pursue opportunities with the NYPD. But now Larry had lost his career ambition because he'd found something that was more important to him. His new dream was of riding out eight more years in Bedford Hills, getting an early retirement package, and then living happily ever after with Stu. The fact that he'd sacrificed his career ambition, and a major part of himself, for a fantasy that might never come to fruition was fucked up, but it was what it was.

Later, at Larry's office at the Bedford Hills precinct, Larry filled Nick in about the discovery of Deborah's car and the search for her.

'Her husband said she'd left her car at the Oak Ridge Country Club,' Larry said. 'He said a friend picked her up at the house.'

'Well the friend may have driven her to the club to get her car,' Nick said.

'To drive to a high school parking lot?' Larry asked.

'I heard it's a popular hookup spot.'

'Yeah, for teenagers, not forty-four-year-old married women.'

'Well, if she doesn't turn up soon, we'll need to expand the search beyond Westchester,' Nick said. 'Connecticut, New Jersey, New York City, and Long Island for starters.'

'I'm already on it,' Larry said. 'We have a description of her out already, and we're getting a photo to go along with it from her husband.'

'Have you gotten any calls?' Nick said. 'Any possible sightings?'

'Nothing yet.'

'And what about her family and friends? Have they been contacted?'

'Deborah's husband said he made some calls yesterday evening.'

'We can't rely on that,' Nick said. 'Let's get somebody down there to get all that contact information immediately. What's your take on the husband?'

Larry knew why Nick was asking – the husband was always the first suspect.

'I talked to Mark Berman yesterday evening, but it wasn't a long conversation,' Larry said. 'He seemed upset and I think hopeful that his wife would return soon.'

'You think?' Nick asked.

'Honestly, my instinct was that something seemed off,' Larry said. 'I'm not sure what it was or why I felt that way. He seemed upset, yeah, but maybe not as upset as he should have been. He seemed a little aloof about the whole thing, but apparently there was trouble in his marriage. He and Deborah were apparently getting a divorce, or talking about getting a divorce, so maybe that's what I was picking up on. I don't really know for sure.'

'So he's divorcing his wife and then his wife disappears,' Nick said. 'Does he have an alibi?'

'I didn't interrogate him,' Larry said. 'It was just a preliminary conversation.'

'Well, he definitely should be a focus right now,' Nick said. 'I'll talk to him again when I leave here, see what his whole story is, and we'll take it from there. Now what's this about this woman, Karen Daily?'

When Larry had arrived at the precinct this morning he'd heard about Karen Daily from a few reporters who were assembled outside.

'I swear, sometimes it feels like these reporters are one step ahead of us,' Larry said. 'When word got out we're searching for Deborah, they started getting calls about Karen. Apparently there was an incident Saturday afternoon at the Oak Ridge Country Club.'

'And this has been confirmed?' Nick asked.

'Yeah, people filmed it on their phones,' Larry said. 'Right before you got here I spoke to the woman the reporters spoke to, Jenna Frisco, a waitress at the club – she filmed the end of the fight. She confirmed what the reporters are saying. Karen and Deborah were having an argument and it escalated. The film shows Karen and Deborah wrestling on the floor.'

'Ooh, a cat fight,' Nick said, smiling. 'Does the waitress know what the argument was about? One reporter was saying that there were rumors that Mark Berman and this Karen Daily were having an affair. Is that true?'

'I don't know,' Larry said, thinking he would ask Stu if he knew anything about this. 'Jenna said names were exchanged – they were calling each other bitch, cunt, etcetera.'

'Sounds like a fun afternoon in Westchester,' Nick said. 'We need to know more about the incident, though. Was Mark there at the time?'

'Yes, he was,' Larry said.

'But he didn't tell you about this yesterday,' Nick said.

'No, he did not,' Larry said, knowing what Nick was hinting at.

'That sounds unusual, doesn't it?' Nick asked. 'Why keep it a secret if you don't have to?'

'Maybe he was embarrassed or didn't think it was important,' Larry said.

'Or maybe he had another reason not to talk about it,' Nick said. 'Like maybe he was having an affair with Karen Daily and is trying to protect her.'

'It's possible,' Larry said.

'Well, let's look into all of that,' Nick said. 'I'll talk to Mark Berman and this Jenna at the club again and you track down Karen and get a statement from her. If we don't locate Deborah soon, within the next couple of hours, we'll have to expand the investigation. But after we get firm timelines for Mark and Karen, that might tell us something right there. We also need to find any witnesses who may have seen her in that parking lot where the car was discovered. How did she get out of the car? Walk? Probably not, there's not much in that area. We need a description of another car – anything we can get. Let's be wide open with all this with the press, we need as much publicity as possible to get as much help as possible from the public. The next couple of hours will be crucial.'

Nick left and Larry got Karen Daily's home number and called her and got her voicemail – not very surprising since it was Monday morning and she probably worked. He was going to track her down, maybe at work, but realized there was a quicker, much more appealing way to get some of the info he needed.

'Um, I only have a few minutes,' Stu said. 'What's going on?'

Stu sounded uncomfortable, but Larry had expected this. He normally didn't call Stu at work, at his law office, because Stu had asked him not to. Still, as always, just hearing Stu's voice was exciting to Larry, made him feel more alert and, yeah, more alive.

'Can you talk for a sec?' Larry said.

'Hold on,' Stu said. Then several seconds later added, 'Okay, I just locked the door to my office. What's going on, man?' Now he sounded much more relaxed, like his usual self.

'It's nice to hear your voice,' Larry said.

'You don't know how good it makes me feel to hear you say that,' Stu said. 'So is this really about work?'

'Unfortunately, yeah,' Larry said. 'You know Deborah Berman, right?'

Pause then, 'Deb Berman? You mean my buddy Mark's wife? Yeah, I know her. Why?'

'She's missing,' Larry said.

'*What*?' Stu sounded shocked. 'What the fuck do you mean?'

Larry explained how her car had been discovered and that she hadn't been seen since Saturday evening.

'Jesus Christ,' Stu said. 'I can't believe this. I guess that's why Mark wasn't on the train this morning. How's he doing? He must be a total mess.'

'He was okay last night when I talked to him, but I don't know about today,' Larry said. 'What about a woman named Karen Daily? Do you know her?'

'Yeah, I know her,' Stu said. 'I used to know her ex-husband Joe better than her, but I know her. She's a member of the club too. She's divorced now. What about her?'

'I heard she had an argument with Deborah on Saturday at the club,' Larry said.

'Oh yeah, she did,' Stu said. 'I was there.'

'You *were*?'

'A lot of people were there. They were really going at it. Cat fight, you know?'

'Do you know what the argument was about?'

'No, not really,' Stu said. 'I mean we guessed it had to do with something going on with Mark and Karen, but that was just a guess. Actually, that's right, I called Mark after on Saturday just to check in on him, make sure he was all right. I thought he was in the dog house, you know?'

'Mark and Karen were having an affair?'

'I don't know,' Stu said. 'To be honest, I don't know Mark all that well. I mean we play golf, ride into the city together sometimes, but we just bullshit with each other, you know on-the-surface type shit. But we don't discuss our personal lives at all. Obviously.'

'He talk about Karen a lot?' Larry asked.

'Yeah, sometimes,' Stu said. 'I mean, I know they're at least friends, neighbors, hang out a lot. But me and the guys, we kid around with Mark about it. I mean, just usual guy type talk, you know? I have to keep up a good front, right?'

Larry pictured Stu smiling with those incredible dimples.

'But actually, yeah,' Stu went on, 'when we were playing golf on Saturday the guys were teasing Mark about it, and he flipped out.'

'Flipped out how?'

'Was gonna whack this guy Doug over the head with a golf club. I mean, I don't know if he was *really* gonna do it, but he made like he was gonna do it, so let's just say Mark seemed a little sensitive about the subject... wait, why? You don't think Karen has something to with Deb being missing, do you?'

'We don't know anything yet,' Larry said. 'But, yeah, her name has come up.'

'Wow,' Stu said. 'Wow, I can't believe that.'

'You can't believe that she has something to do with it, or you can't believe she was having an affair with Mark?'

'The affair part I can believe,' Stu said. 'I mean Mark always denies it, yeah, but it's pretty obvious *something's* going on with them. I mean she lives right down the road from him, and she's a good looking woman, and he always seems to be around her at the club, hovering.'

'But you don't know if they've actually been having a relationship?'

'No, but I know she's been playing the field, doing a lot of online dating,' Stu said. 'She has a reputation.'

'What kind of reputation?'

'You know,' Stu said. 'Divorced woman, going a little crazy with dating, playing the field. She's had a lot of boyfriends, and she's a good-looking woman.'

'Yeah, you mentioned that,' Larry said, pretending he was joking, but he actually wasn't joking. Well, not totally joking anyway.

'Don't worry, you have nothing to get jealous about, bro,' Stu said. 'You know who I think the hot one is. But people definitely talk a lot about Karen. I guess because she dates a lot and women don't seem to like her very much. I mean, my wife thinks she flirts too much with married men. I don't see the big deal about it, but my wife doesn't like it, and maybe she sees something that I don't. I think it's because of Karen's looks to be honest. She's in great shape, and she's definitely a well-endowed woman, it's hard not to notice *that*. Actually, something else happened the other day at golf.'

'What?' Larry asked.

'The guys were joking around about Karen,' Stu said, 'and somebody, I forget who, made a comment, wondering if Karen's tits were real or not. You know, usual dumb guy talk. But Mark made a comment that Karen's tits were definitely real, that Karen had told him they were real. That struck me as kind of odd, you know? I mean, why would she just tell him that? I mean, I know they're friends, but you see what I mean. Maybe he said it because he knew, because he's having sex with her. Jesus, maybe they really are having an affair. I mean, when you think about it, it makes sense.'

'Do you know where Karen works?' Larry asked.

'Yeah, actually I do,' Stu said. 'She's a schoolteacher at Meadow Pond. She's a speech pathologist, works with autistic kids, I think. But she has nothing to do with what happened to Deb, I'm telling you that right now. I know people talk about her, say things, but she's a teacher, a mother, a good normal woman. She wouldn't hurt anybody.'

'Thanks,' Larry said. 'This has been enormously helpful.'

'What should I do now?' Stu asked. 'Should I call Mark again? I feel awful. The poor guy's probably a fuckin' mess. And his kids? Jesus.'

'Do whatever you feel comfortable doing as a friend,' Larry said. 'But I don't think you should tell him that you and I spoke – for more than one reason, if you get my drift.'

When he ended the call with Stu, Larry didn't waste any time. He coordinated with his people over at the John Jay High School parking lot and informed them that Detective Piretti and the Westchester Country Police were taking over the investigation, and then went down the hallway to Sam Allen's office. Sam handled communications issues for the Bedford Police and Larry asked Sam to set up a press conference as soon as possible. There already had been a couple of reporters by the precinct and Larry assumed there were more in the area, or certainly would be more as the story continued to spread.

Although Larry was involved in getting the investigation underway, something – some underlying anxiety – was gnawing at him. For a while he wasn't sure what was causing it, then it hit that, of course, it had to do with the conversation with Stu. He'd gotten some great information, but it was always hard for Larry to not get insecure when Stu made innuendos about women. He knew that Stu was still having sex with his wife and, though Stu claimed that he didn't enjoy it, how did Larry know if this was true or not? Larry wished this didn't matter to him, but it did, and it reminded him of how fucked up the situation was. Larry had been tormented by the relationship since, well, pretty much since the relationship had started. Sometimes it seemed as if he couldn't go five minutes without replaying conversations they'd had or trying to analyze Stu's behavior. Was Stu really into him or was he just experimenting, having a midlife crisis? How could they be happy and together without hurting people around them and ruining their lives? Larry had once gotten a fortune cookie that had read, 'No problem can withstand the assault of sustained thinking,' and unfortunately that pretty much summed up his biggest fears about his relationship with Stu.

But Larry did his best to put Stu out of his mind and stay focused. The longer Deborah Berman remained missing, the more serious this case was going to become. Because of the situation – an affluent woman, a mom disappearing – this had potential to blow up; it was already getting more media attention than any case Larry had worked on in a long time, maybe ever, and Nick had been right – the next few hours could be key to the whole investigation.

On his way out to talk to Karen, Larry held a mini press conference in front of the precinct. There were several reporters and TV crews, including NBC and CBS. After a general statement about the case and the status of the investigation – providing information about the time Deborah Berman was last seen on Saturday evening and giving a description of her SUV that had been found at the John Jay High School parking lot – he took questions.

'What about Karen Daily?' the young male reporter from NBC asked. 'Would you characterize her as a person of interest in the case?'

'The investigation is just underway, and we aren't focused on any one individual at this time,' Larry said.

'But you do consider Karen Daily a suspect?' the reporter persisted.

'There aren't any suspects,' Larry said. 'Our focus is on finding Deborah Berman.'

'But you've spoken to Karen Daily?'

'We're speaking to everyone who may have a connection to the case and Ms. Daily is one of them, yes.'

A female reporter asked, 'Can you tell us about the incident that took place between Karen Daily and Deborah Berman on Saturday afternoon at the Oak Ridge Country Club?'

'I can't really comment on that at this time,' he said.

'Are you aware of any specific threats that Karen made to Deborah?' another reporter asked.

'Again,' Larry said, 'I can't comment on that, and I want to stress that the investigation is fluid and ongoing, and we haven't reached any conclusions at this time. Our focus is on following up leads related to the whereabouts of Deborah Berman.'

'Was Karen Daily having a relationship with Mark Berman?' the NBC reporter asked.

'I'll say it again,' Larry said. 'We're looking at multiple scenarios. We don't know what's relevant and what isn't at this time.'

'Is it true that during their argument Karen Daily called Deborah Berman the C-word?' the CBS reporter asked.

'I can't take any more questions at this time,' Larry said. 'But we're asking that if anyone has seen Deborah Berman, or been in contact with her, that they contact the police immediately. Thank you very much.'

As Larry headed to his car, the reporters shouted more questions, mostly about Karen. Larry wasn't surprised that the media was so focused on her – a speech pathologist involved in a missing persons case was certainly a provocative story. But that was all it was at this point – a story. It was way too early to speculate.

Driving away, Larry was thinking about Stu again – how hard it was to hear his voice without seeing him – and then what Stu had said, about how Karen definitely didn't have anything to do with Deborah's disappearance. While Larry trusted Stu's opinion, in cases like these you always had to throw opinions out. During his time as a cop Larry had learned two things – you never know who's lying to you, and anyone is capable of anything.

16

OWEN WOKE UP, happy and hopeful, still fantasizing about Karen. He loved that it was so quiet and dark in the room, the thick curtains blocking the light, because the darkness made his fantasies more intense which made him feel closer to Karen, made his future life with her seem more real. He didn't want his fantasies to ever stop – it was the opposite, he wanted to fuckin' *live* them – but he turned on the TV, just to see if anything was going on with Deb. He didn't expect there to be – not yet anyway. The police were probably seriously looking for her by now, but he doubted a woman who'd been missing – what, a little over a day? – would be a big news story. He flipped around, past sports and sitcoms and talk show shit, and stopped on a news station.

He was watching, bored, about some new war breaking out in the Middle East, and then there was suddenly a picture of Deb on TV. Owen was surprised and said out loud, 'Holy fuckin' shit.'

It was so weird seeing Deb on TV he seriously thought he was dreaming. He blinked hard a couple times and now there was a whole news story about Deb – this definitely wasn't a dream. A reporter was holding a mike, talking in front of the Bedford Hills Police Station, and then there was a shot of Deb Berman's house. It was hard to focus, so many thoughts were hitting Owen at once, but he heard the reporter say that the police had found Deb's car in the John Jay High parking lot and that the police already had a 'person of interest' in the case. A person of interest already? How was that possible? Owen's heart was thumping like there was a gerbil trapped in his chest. How could the cops have found out about him already? Did he leave something at the parking lot, some CSI shit? Or did somebody see him, somebody in that other car that showed up?

But, wait, now a reporter, a blonde, was saying something about a woman Deborah Berman was arguing with at the Oak Ridge Country Club earlier in the day on Saturday. Then they showed some footage of Deb and Karen fighting, taken on somebody's phone. It was so funny, Owen had to laugh. Was Karen really the person of interest?

The news report ended, sports came on, and Owen was still laughing. It made sense that the cops thought Karen did it. Everybody at the club always saw Karen and Mark hanging out together, and were talking about them behind their backs. One time Owen heard guys talking in the men's room about how Karen and Mark were screwing. Even Deb was suspicious, telling Owen a couple of times how she didn't like how Karen was flirting all the time with her husband. Obviously the cops thought Karen was jealous so she went out and killed Deb.

Owen continued laughing for a long time, as if he'd just heard the funniest joke in the world. Man, this couldn't be working out any better for him. If the cops thought Karen did it that meant they wouldn't think anyone else did. It also meant that Karen would be upset, feeling alone and needy, which meant she'd want a man to come along and comfort her. Not just any man, though – a *young* handsome man, somebody pure and innocent who was – wait for it – *caring*, and really *got her* in a way no older man could, and Owen knew that he was that man. He was actually the only man in the world who could help her now, give her what she needed. Was this the luckiest break or what? He'd thought it would take weeks, or months, to get Karen to love him the way Deb had, but now it would only take a few days or, fuck, a few hours. Karen was going to be desperate, she'd need support, and he'd be there, ready to give her everything she needed.

Oh, yeah baby, this was gonna be perfect.

Karen was happiest in a routine. On days when her life went according to a predictable schedule – waking up, going for a run, doing yoga, getting the kids off to school, going to work, coming home, making the kids dinner, helping them with their homework, then getting them to bed and unwinding reading or watching TV, she felt the most at peace. Since her divorce, life had become more unpredictable, with many new responsibilities and concerns, and it had become more challenging to establish a routine, but she strove to find regularity in her life and cherished the times when she did.

So when she woke up, she decided that to counter all of the recent chaos in her life, she would try to make today, the beginning of a new work week, as simple and normal as possible. Her itching had subsided and she was apparently crab-free so, hallelujah, she already had one thing to be grateful for. After a nice Mark-less run around the beautiful misty lake, she did some light yoga, and then she made sure that Elana and Matthew were up. In the kitchen she made the kids' lunches and fixed her usual morning cup of green tea. The first sip felt warm and relaxing in her throat and she felt energetic and optimistic and ready to take on the day.

Then she heard voices. Not in her head – yes, she'd been stressed lately but, no, she wasn't totally whacko – there were voices, real voices, definitely coming from the direction of her living room. She figured it was the TV – was Matthew watching Pokémon when he was supposed to be getting ready for school? She went toward the living room, and said, 'Matthew, what're you...' and then realized the voices were actually coming from outside.

Outside? That was weird. This was the suburbs; there were never a lot of people outside, unless some sort of party was going on. But how could there be a party at around eight o'clock on a Monday morning? Then she peeked past the window shade and saw all the reporters and news trucks and she was even more confused. *What the hell*? She knew it couldn't have anything to do with *her*, but it had to be something major.

Fearing that someone had gotten hurt, god forbid a child, she opened the front door. Several reporters rushed toward her, shouting questions, and she was so confused she couldn't absorb or make sense of anything they were saying. Finally she heard something she understood: 'Deborah Berman.' *Deb*? This was seriously about *her*? Though Karen still couldn't process what any of this was about, hearing that name again irritated, making her think, *Will this ever stop*? *Are the Bermans going to make my life hell forever*?

'Deb Berman?' she asked. 'What about Deb Berman?'

'You didn't hear?' a reporter, a young guy with a beard, asked.

'Hear what?'

'She's missing.'

Karen absorbed this, but she still didn't get it, said, 'Missing? What do you mean, *missing*?'

A female reporter with short dark hair and thick glasses explained that Deb's car had been discovered in the parking lot at John Jay High School. Karen remembered how crazed, how irrational, Deb had been behaving yesterday at the country club and how Mark had said they were divorcing. Karen should have been upset, but her naturally empathetic nature took over and she wasn't angry with Deb at all anymore – she was just worried.

'Oh my god,' Karen said, thinking about Mark and the kids. Despite how inappropriate he'd been lately, he was still a friend, and he had to be worried sick right now. She had an urge to call him, give him her support.

But now the reporter with the beard was asking, 'Can you tell us about the fight you had with Deborah on Saturday?'

This was strange; why were they asking her about *that*?

'I don't understand,' Karen said.

'We understand she attacked you,' the woman with the thick glasses said.

Oh, okay, Karen got it now – well, thought she got it. Maybe they were trying to determine if Deb was unstable on Saturday or unstable in general.

'Her behavior was very odd, yes,' Karen said. 'I don't know what she was upset about exactly, but I was concerned about her when I left. I really hope she's okay.'

'Did you have another argument with her after you left

the club?' an older male reporter who hadn't said anything yet asked.

'No, I didn't,' Karen said. 'Why do you...' She stopped herself. She didn't get why they kept harping on this, but she feared that it wasn't appropriate to be answering these questions about Deb at all. After all, the most important thing right now was that Deb was safe and okay, not whether or not she was stable. So Karen added quickly, 'I have to go, I'm sorry, thank you,' and went inside and shut the door.

Well, so much for a routine, relaxing morning. Karen was aware of how tight and stressed out her whole body was. She thought she'd gotten through the worst of it and now something else had come along to knock her down.

She needed to relax, do more yoga, but she was running late now and was too scattered to focus. Somehow, within a few minutes, she showered and dressed and got the kids out the door. The reporters were still outside and had more questions about Deb and the incident at the club on Saturday. What was up with this? Why wouldn't they let up? The kids wanted to know what was going on, but Karen wanted to be careful; she didn't want to frighten them and make them think something bad had happened, but she didn't want to lie to them either.

In the car, turning off Savage Lane, Karen said, 'The police are looking for Deb, but she's going to be fine. She's probably just away, staying with a friend or something.'

'Why would the police be looking for her if she's at a friend's?' Elana asked.

'Because that's what the police do,' Karen said. 'They have to look for her and ask questions, even when nothing's wrong.'

'How come the people were asking you about a fight you had with her?' Matthew asked.

'Yeah,' Elana said. 'What was that all about?'

'Nothing,' Karen said, regretting she'd started this conversation. 'It doesn't matter. What matters is that Deb is going to be fine.'

'Why are you acting so weird?' Elana asked. 'Why won't you tell us what's going on?'

Glaring at Elana in the rearview, right at her daughter's eyes, Karen didn't say anything but got the message across.

No one said anything for the next maybe ten minutes.

At Elana's school, Karen pulled over where she usually pulled over, down the street from the school because Elana didn't want to be seen exiting a car that had her mom and brother in it, as if she wanted her friends to believe that she was a homeless orphan and had been magically teleported to school.

'Have a nice day,' Karen said.

Elana mumbled something that may have been, 'Thanks,' as she let the door slam.

Next, Karen dropped Matthew at his school. Matthew was young enough to not be snotty and said, 'Goodbye' and 'I love you' to Karen before he went into the building.

Finally on her way to work, Karen was exhausted, the way she usually felt at the end of the workday, not the beginning. She still couldn't figure out why the reporters had kept asking her about the fight with Deb. Had Deb said something to Mark about it? Was there something Karen didn't know? She knew they couldn't have been suggesting that Karen had something to do with Deb's disappearance. That couldn't be it; that would be absolutely insane.

Karen put on the speakerphone and said 'Mark,' and the call connected.

Mark picked up and in an excited tone said, 'Hey, how are you?'

217

Shit, Karen had assumed that Mark would be in a worried, grieving state, but he still had that *tone*, as if he thought he was in love with her. What would it take for him to get past his obsession with her?

Mark's behavior was annoying and pathetic but, focusing on the reason she'd called, she said, 'I heard the news. I'm so sorry, but I'm sure everything's going to be okay.'

'The police aren't sure,' Mark said. 'They seem seriously concerned.'

'Look, you have to stay positive right now. Just think good, positive thoughts.'

'I saw the reporters near your house,' Mark said. 'Did they ask you about Saturday at the country club?'

'Yes, and I don't understand why,' Karen said. 'The focus should be on finding Deb, not about some stupid thing that didn't mean anything.'

'I just want you to know.' Mark sounded serious, somber. 'I don't believe what they're saying.'

'Saying?' Karen asked. 'Saying about what?'

'About you,' Mark said. 'I mean, I know Deb was upset, and I got you in the middle of our bullshit, and I'm sorry for that, but I know you'd never do anything to hurt Deb.'

All the blood in Karen's body seemed to rush to her head.

'Excuse me,' she said. 'What? *What?*'

'That's what they're saying, what the reporters are saying, but I know that's just bullshit,' Mark said. 'I mean, I know that's not you, that's not who you are, despite your feelings for me.'

'They're saying that? How could they say that? How could... and *feelings* for you? What feelings for you? I've never had feelings for you. We're friends, just friends, that's all we are. I can't… I can't believe I'm even talking to you about this right now.'

Karen tasted salt on her lips and realized she was crying.

'It's okay,' Mark said. 'We don't have to discuss this right now.'

'This is so fucked up,' Karen said. 'This is fucking ridiculous.' She was losing control; she knew she should pull over, but she couldn't because she didn't want to be late for work. 'Okay, where the hell is Deb anyway? Where did she go?'

'I don't know,' Mark said.

There was something odd, tentative about Mark's tone. Karen wondered, *Was he hiding something*? If their marriage was falling apart, he could've snapped and…

No. She didn't want to even go there.

'Look, they'll find her,' she said. 'They'll find her and everything will be okay.'

She wished she believed this.

'Thank you for saying that,' Mark said, his voice cracking, getting emotional.

Karen couldn't help feeling bad for him. She asked, 'How are your kids doing?'

'They seem okay,' Mark said. 'Riley's having a hard time, though. She's very concerned. I took the day off work.'

'Just be strong for them. Did they go to school today?'

'They didn't want to, but I insisted. I wanted them to have a normal day.'

'That's good. That was smart.'

'I need you here, Karen.'

Shit, when he was he going to stop with this crap?

'Look, I'm sure everything's going to be okay,' she said. 'Just stay strong.'

'Can you come by later?' Mark asked. 'I mean if Deb doesn't come home by then.'

'She will come home.'

'But if she doesn't, can you come by? Maybe bring the kids? It would be good for the kids to have your kids here with them.'

Although she felt a little manipulated – Mark knew that pulling 'the kids card' always worked with her – Karen knew she couldn't blow off him and his kids when they were going through something so difficult and needed support.

'Okay, I'll be there later,' she said, 'but I really don't think it's going to be necessary. She'll come home any second now, you'll see.'

'Thank you,' Mark said.

'Text me if there's news,' she said. 'Goodbye.'

Karen arrived about five minutes late for school. When she rushed up to the principal's office for the morning staff meeting she noticed she was getting unusual looks from several of the other teachers and staff members. Her initial thought was that it was because of her lateness; she was usually prompt and maybe it had thrown people off. So she apologized, but as Lucy, the vice principal, was talking about a budget issue, Karen noticed that people, including Seth, the principal, were still looking at her weirdly. It almost seemed as if they were judging her and then, with a rush of shame, she realized this was because they *were* judging her. They must've heard the reports on the news, or one of them had heard and had told the others, but what exactly was the report on the news? Was it possible that that stupid incident at the country club was on the *news*? What did people think of her? What assumptions were they making? Did they think she was having an affair with a married man? Did they think she was crazy, had done something to hurt Deb? It had been bad enough that her kids had been affected by this, but if this was going to affect her work life, maybe even her career, that would be way too much.

The half hour meeting seemed to last half a day. Afterward, she wanted to avoid the phony conversations, people offering their support when they were probably actually suspicious. Lisa, a special ed teacher whom Karen was very close with, approached her in the hallway and said with a pseudo-concerned tone, 'Hey, Karen, what's going on with –' and before hearing anymore Karen cut her off with, 'Sorry, I have a student waiting,' and rushed away.

Even Jill, her best friend at school, wouldn't support her.

During a break, Karen went into Jill's office and said, 'I think people are talking about me behind my back,' and Jill said, 'Really? I haven't heard anything,' but Karen knew she was lying.

'Wait, don't tell me you really think I have anything to do with this,' Karen said.

'No, of course I don't,' Jill said. 'It's just... never mind.'

'It's just what?'

'Nothing.'

'Tell me.'

'It's nothing, it's just... Well, you talk about Mark a lot, so I mean...'

'What?' Karen said. 'What does it mean?'

'Nothing. It doesn't mean *anything*.'

'Do you think I'm involved with Mark?'

'No, of course not.' Jill wasn't making eye contact.

'Just because I talk about him, doesn't mean I'm involved with him,' Karen said.

'I'm not saying you are,' Jill said. 'But, I mean, I saw the way he was looking at you at the country club on Saturday.'

'That's *him*. That's not me.'

'I know. I know that.'

221

'And if it was true, if I was having an affair with him, why would I keep it a secret? Why wouldn't I tell you?'

'Well, I guess if you didn't want his wife to find out you wouldn't –'

'I can't believe this.' Karen hadn't expected this from Jill of all people. She felt as if she'd been punched in the gut.

'I'm not saying you *are*.'

'But you think it,' Karen said. 'You really think these things about me.'

'Of course I don't think you'd actually... You're misunderstanding me.'

'I thought we were friends.'

'We are friends.'

'Fuck you,' Karen said, leaving Jill's office.

Karen was so upset and hurt by what Jill thought of her, what *people* thought of her, that she was hyperventilating and actually thought she might faint. To get a hold of herself, she went into the bathroom and splashed her face with cold water. It didn't work and she left – still angry, still a mess. Her plan was to go on with her day, block out all of this bullshit the best she could, pretend it was a normal morning, because she knew if she accepted what was going on she was going to totally lose it.

Fortunately Karen's job was all-consuming. Working with autistic kids, trying to figure out the best ways to reach each child, as if each child's brain were a unique maze that needed its own solution, required intense concentration and focus, and she wanted that feeling of disappearing into a maze right now. It was truly a joy to work with such pure, unaffected souls, with children who needed her, and who had no interest in judging her. Her work, as difficult and frustrating as it was at times, was the perfect escape from the cruel, punishing world.

Her first student was William, an adorable, severely

autistic, seven-year-old who had serious medical issues, including diabetes and partial blindness. The boy's parents had four other children and weren't giving him proper medical care, or enough emotional attention, which upset Karen but also made her time with him even more precious. With many of the kids she worked with, especially the ones who were most severely impaired, she had the ability to connect with them on an intimate level, to understand their feelings that they were unable to express. In her last session with William, Karen had made a lot of progress, and had been very close to getting him to say his first words. If she could get him to say, even basic words, it would have an enormous effect on his life, so she was eager to get to work with him.

After practicing the sounds he'd made last time, she tried to get him to say the word 'ball.' He seemed eager and attentive today, and she sensed that he wanted to speak so badly, and he was trying as hard as he could to take the leap into language. But then an alarm went off somewhere outside the building, it sounded like a car alarm, and the noise upset William, maybe because he had been so locked in, and he kicked and flailed his arms and legs. Karen held him in her arms, trying to subdue him, but he was a big kid, weighed about one hundred pounds, and he broke free and swung one of his arms and slapped Karen hard in the face, over her mouth and part of her cheek. Her lower teeth tore into her gums, and she tasted blood.

Finally she was able to calm him down, but it took a while to get the bleeding to stop. As she pressed a wad of tissues over her mouth, she continued to act normal and playful around William because she didn't want to upset him, make him feel he'd done anything wrong. Although he could barely see, so he didn't know she was

223

bleeding, she knew he was incredibly perceptive and knew when something was wrong, even when he didn't have the physical ability to comprehend a situation. She was mainly concerned about William, but it was hard to completely distance herself from her own feelings. As she made fake smiley faces, and resumed trying to get him to speak, she was thinking, *What next*? After the weekend from hell, she'd woken up to find she was a possible suspect in the disappearance of a neighbor, and now a sweet, innocent child had hit her in the face. The onslaught of things going wrong in her life seemed relentless.

She saw a couple of other students after William, but it was hard to focus and get lost in her work. Then she went online on her phone, hoping there was news about Deb, a break in the case, but she was still missing. Worse, a couple of articles mentioned the fight Deb and Karen had at the country club, and there was even a video posted. Now Karen remembered seeing people with their phones out on Saturday during the scuffle with Deb – she'd blocked it out until now. With dread, she clicked PLAY and then watched a fifteen second-long video of herself, wrestling with Deb.

'Fuck me,' she said.

It was humiliating and surreal, like she was watching two crazy people on a daytime talk show, except one of those crazy people was *her*. She was overcome by embarrassment and shame. All she could think was, *Everyone is seeing this*. Her colleagues, her family, her friends, her neighbors, guys she'd dated, the parents of the kids she worked with. She knew how it must seem to people, taken out of context, and she was angry with herself for letting her guard down on Saturday and for letting Deb coax her into the ridiculous fight. But she had to make people understand that this wasn't how it seemed, and this wasn't who she was.

But panic set in when she realized how easily this could all blow up – she could be fired from her job, she could go to jail. She called her union rep and got emotional, and she explained what was going on and how terrified she was. The rep, Mary, calmed her down, and told her to go about her business for the rest of the day and just wait for the facts to come out.

'It's just a video on the internet and people talking,' Mary told her. 'You haven't been charged with any crime.'

Mary assured Karen that her job wasn't in jeopardy. Karen knew this could change if the rumors continued to spread, but she understood that panicking wasn't helping. She needed to remove herself from the situation, as much as she could anyway, and wait to see how things played out.

As noon approached, she was looking forward to having lunch alone in her office. She'd packed her usual lo-cal lunch – yogurt, an apple, and iced green tea in a thermos. She would eat, relax, and focus on the rest of the day at work. Then, when she got home later, she'd discover that the nightmare was over. Deb would be home, the reporters would be gone, and everything would be back to normal.

After eating, she did feel somewhat better, until she left her office to use the restroom and saw the slim dark-haired guy in a sport jacket approaching her in the hallway. The guy didn't have to say a word or show a badge – his whole vibe screamed, *Cop*.

Sure enough, he said, 'Karen Daily?' and she said, 'Yes,' and then he showed a badge, said a few sentences that included 'Detective Walsh' and 'police' and 'Can we talk?' A few teachers, including Stacey, the social studies teacher who'd been at the staff meeting earlier, and a few students, looked like fifth-graders, were eavesdropping, close enough to have overheard the entire exchange. Great, this was all Karen needed – *more* rumors going around school about her. Karen was mortified. It may have been the most humiliating moment of her life which, given what had happened to her over the past couple of days, was saying a lot.

'What's this about?' Karen asked quietly, practically whispering.

'It's about a neighbor of yours who's missing,' Detective Walsh said.

Stacey and the kids were still listening in. Karen glared at Stacey until she got the hint and said to the kids, 'Come on kids let's get to class now,' and they walked away down the hallway, the kids looking back over their shoulders and whispering to one another.

'Do you have any idea how humiliated I feel right now?' Karen asked. She suddenly felt weak, dizzy, and her whole face was burning up as if there were an interrogation lamp shining on it.

'I'm sorry about that, I didn't mean to make you uncomfortable,' Walsh said.

Yeah, right, like an arrogant cop really gave a shit whether he made her uncomfortable or not. She'd had it with people. She'd seriously had it.

'Is that your office?' Walsh asked.

She must've answered, 'Yes.'

'We can either talk here or you can come down to the station with me, whichever you prefer.'

Imagining the further humiliation of being led out of the school into a squad car, she heard herself say, 'Here's fine, I'll meet you back in a minute.'

She went to the teacher's bathroom, into a stall, where she lost it, balling hysterically. After a few minutes she managed to calm down, mopping up her tears with such thick wads of toilet paper that she stopped up the toilet.

When she returned to her office Walsh was standing near her desk.

'Look, I have no idea where Deb is,' she said. 'I have nothing to do with any of this. *Nothing.*'

'How did you know I was here about Deborah Berman?' he asked, trying to sound casual, but his accusing tone was obvious.

'Because there were fucking reporters in front of my house this morning, and there's video online, and I'm sick and tired of this bullshit fucking up my life!'

She knew she was losing it, but she didn't care. It felt too good to vent. Maybe, she thought, this was how William had felt when he'd lost control.

'I think you should sit down,' Walsh said.

'I don't want to sit,' she said.

'Fine, but I'm going to have to ask you some questions, okay?'

'I really can't take any more of this, I just fucking can't,' she said, letting loose with her anger, not caring anymore. Then she realized she was acting the way she had when she'd fought with Deb, losing control, and this wasn't a good idea in front of the detective. So in a much calmer, quieter voice she said, 'I really don't know where Deb is. I feel awful for her husband and her kids, and I hope to god she's okay. But people think I'm involved now and it's crazy, it's just crazy. I'm a schoolteacher, for god's sake. I have children who depend on me, who *need* me, and I have my own fucking problems. You have no idea what kind of problems I have, okay? You have no idea what my fucking life is like, what kind of shit I've been through lately. So then to have you come in here accusing me of something I have nothing to do with is ridiculous, it's just fucking ridiculous!'

So much for calmness.

Walsh waited during Karen's outburst. When she was through he took out a pad and pen and said, all cop-like, with no emotion, 'Let's start with Saturday. Tell me what happened at the country club.'

17

WHEN THE SCHOOL bus let Riley off, she sprinted up Savage Lane, wanting to get home as fast as possible to hopefully find out that her mother was home and everything was back to normal. But her panic got worse when she saw that there were news trucks, a police car, and lots of reporters and some neighbors near her house.

Okay, she told herself, *this doesn't mean something* bad *has happened. Maybe everybody's here because they found her.* This gave her some hope, but not much.

She went over to one of the people she knew: Rachel Fuller's mom. Rachel was a, like, seven-year-old girl who lived in a house down the road.

'Did they find her?' Riley asked. 'Did they find my mom?'

Rachel's mom shook her head, looking the way people at funerals looked, and said, 'Not yet, sweetie.'

'Oh no, oh my god, oh my god,' Riley said and then everything got confused, like somebody had whacked her over the head, and then it seemed like a second later she was in the house, in the kitchen, saying to her dad, 'Where is she? How come they haven't found her yet?'

Her father was with some old guy, probably another cop. They were sitting at the table.

'Everything's going to be okay,' her dad said.

'Something bad happened.' Riley realized she was shaking. 'Oh my god, I know something bad happened. She's dead. I know she's dead.'

'She's going to be fine,' her dad said, getting up and hugging her.

But she didn't want to be hugged – not by *him*. She'd been angry all day, hating him, knowing he had something to with this, that he wasn't telling her *something*. She stood with her arms at her sides, thinking about what people had been talking about at school, and on the bus, about how her mom disappearing might have something to do with Karen Daily, and that Karen and Riley's dad had been having an affair.

'It's all because of you,' Riley said.

'*What*?' Her dad stopped hugging and took a couple of steps away. He was looking over at the older guy, as if he were embarrassed.

'What they're saying about you and Karen,' Riley said.

'What who are saying?' her dad asked.

'Everybody! Kids at school, on the school bus. It's true, isn't it? Karen killed her, and you *know* she killed her.'

'Okay, you have to calm down right now.' He was looking at the man again, but now he seemed more terrified than embarrassed.

'It's true, it's true, I know it's true,' Riley said.

Her dad started to say something, but the man, standing now too, said to Riley, 'What makes you think it's true? I'm Detective Piretti, by the way.'

'Because they're always together,' Riley said to Piretti. 'It's been like that since she got divorced. It's so obvious. It was obvious to me, it was obvious to Mom, it was obvious to everybody.'

'We're just friends, that's all we are,' he said.

'I looked at your texts on your phone one time,' Riley said. 'I saw a bunch to her.'

'That's because we're *friends*.'

'Friends don't text that much, especially grown-ups who are friends. That's why Mom wanted a divorce, because she knew what was going on too, she wasn't a fucking idiot.'

'Riley, that's enough,' her dad said, raising his voice.

But Riley kept going, saying, 'It's true. That's why she'd been acting so weird lately.'

'How was she acting weird?' Piretti asked.

'She's very upset, she doesn't know what she's saying,' her dad said to Piretti.

'She was too acting weird,' Riley said. 'She was distracted all the time, and she was drinking like crazy. Sometimes I'd come home from school and smell the alcohol on her breath. Saturday morning, in the car on the way home from dance class, she was acting really weird.'

'That's enough Riley,' her dad said.

'Let her talk,' Piretti said. Then to Riley he said, 'Did you hear your mother specifically talk about any threat from Karen?'

'No,' Riley said.

'That's because there weren't any threats,' her dad said.

'Why are you defending her?' Riley said. 'I mean if she's just your friend, and there's nothing else going on with you two, then why are you afraid to admit that she's crazy and did something to Mom?'

'First of all, Mom's coming home,' her dad said. 'Second

of all, I know Karen, and I know she's a good person, she's not crazy. She wouldn't hurt anybody and she definitely wouldn't hurt Mom.'

'Were you having sex with her?' Riley asked.

'Excuse me,' Mark said.

Then Justin came into the kitchen, holding an XBox joystick, and asked, 'Is Mom home yet?'

'Is that why Mom wanted a divorce?' Riley said to her dad. 'Because you were going to leave her for Karen?'

Now Casey came into the kitchen and was barking.

'Shut up,' Mark said to her, and maybe to the dog too.

'If Mom and Dad are getting a divorce that means Mom's home, right?' Justin asked.

'No, Mommy's never coming home,' Riley said to Justin. 'Because dad's girlfriend killed her.'

Riley saw her dad's arm move, like he was about to hit her, but he stopped when Piretti said, 'Okay, okay, this isn't very productive right now. What I'd like to do is talk to your dad alone right now, and maybe I'll talk to you kids another time, if necessary. But just to be clear we are looking for your mother, and we're still hoping to find her very soon.'

'Look for her in heaven,' Riley said as she marched out and went upstairs.

In her room, she let the door slam as she collapsed on to her bed and lay face down crying hysterically into her pillow. Her mother was gone, forever, and her father was a liar. She'd never felt so alone. Today at school had been so awful, with all the rumors going around, and tomorrow would be worse. Tomorrow everybody would know. She'd be the girl whose dad's girlfriend killed her mother. Already she wasn't popular and she didn't have any boyfriends. Now she wouldn't have a mother or a boyfriend and she'd be a joke, a freak.

Her pillow was soaked. She was afraid that her face would break out from the tears so she went out to the bathroom and heard explosions coming from Justin's room. She went in and saw him playing XBox.

'What is wrong with you? How can you play games when Mom's missing?'

She grabbed the joystick from him, and then snatched the other one from near the TV.

'*Stop,*' Justin whined.

She hated his whine; it was so annoying and always cut through her, like fingernails on a blackboard.

'Don't you have a heart?' she screamed at him.

'Give 'em back,' he shouted, 'give 'em back!'

He tried to grab them from her but she took them into the bathroom with her, shoved him out of the way, and locked the door.

'Dad, Dad!' Justin said, running out of the room, then downstairs.

Riley hid the joysticks under towels on the top shelf of the closet, and then splashed her face with cold water. She felt empty inside, as if a giant vacuum had sucked all of the blood and bones and flesh out of her. She was never going to see her mother again, never hear her voice, never hug her, never smell her. What did her mother smell like? She already couldn't remember. She couldn't even remember the last time she'd told her mother she loved her. It was a fucking nightmare, worse than a nightmare because she wasn't going to wake up. It was going to go on and on forever – well, until she died. That was the only thing that would make this better, make the pain go away – death.

'Come back, Mom,' she said through the cold water. 'Come back, Mom. Please come back, please come back.'

She continued to splash her face until her skin was numb. Then she toweled dry and left the bathroom.

Justin was there, crying, saying, 'Where are they? Where did you put them?'

She went downstairs, hoping Detective Piretti was still here, and there was news, but she went into the living room and saw her dad on the couch, watching some stocks channel on TV.

'What the fuck?' she said. 'Justin's playing video games and you're watching the *stocks channel*? Don't you even care that Mom's gone?'

Looking at the TV, her dad said, 'You have no idea how angry I am at you right now.'

'*Me*? What did *I* do?' Riley asked. She really was clueless.

'Your behavior before was horrible.'

'I just told the detective the truth.'

'You have no idea what the truth is and isn't. You're sixteen years old, for god's sake. You don't know shit about anything.'

'Well, I know if you cared about Mom you wouldn't be sitting here watching TV.'

'I'm trying to hold it together,' he said. 'Do you want me to cry? Do you want me to yell? Do you think that'll accomplish anything?'

'You can look for her,' Riley said. 'You can get in the car, *we* could get in the car, and we can drive around, be proactive.'

'The police are looking for her,' he said. 'They know how to look better than we do, so we have to let them do their job. I called all of Mom's friends, they haven't heard anything. Hopefully Mom'll contact us soon, let us know she's okay. I've done everything I can.'

'You didn't do *everything*.'

Her dad was still staring at the TV. He waited, the way

he always did when he was trying not to get angry, then he said, 'What do you mean?'

'You can call your girlfriend,' Riley said, 'ask her where Mom is.'

On 'is' he lost it and flung the remote at the TV, smashing the screen, and screamed, 'Shut the fuck up!'

Riley had never heard her dad scream so loud at her, or his face get so red. She seriously thought he was going to have a stroke. She didn't care, though. He was so mean, such an asshole.

'I hate you so much!' she yelled, crying so hard she could barely breathe as she ran upstairs.

Justin had found the joysticks and was playing XBox again. What was wrong with her family? Why was everybody acting so cold and insane? Didn't they even *care*?

Whatever, she couldn't deal. In her room she was still crying when Elana FaceTimed her.

'Is she home yet?' Elana asked.

'No,' Riley said. 'Why do you think I look like *this*?'

'Did she call or text?'

'No, and can you stop asking questions?'

'Sorry,' Elana said. 'I'm freaking too and my mom's so upset. Why did you run off the bus?'

'What?' Riley asked, distracted, thinking about Karen. Yeah, right, she was upset. It was all just an act.

'Why didn't you walk home with me?' Elana asked.

'I don't know. I just wanted to get away from everybody.'

'I know, it was so bad, everybody reading about our moms on their phones, and now it's worse.'

'Worse?'

'Did you go on Facebook yet?

'No,' Riley said.

'Don't,' Elana said. 'People are such assholes. I'm

serious. I unfriended like ten people before. Okay, maybe not ten, but I unfriended people. They posted that video and they're laughing about it, making jokes. They said our moms should be, like, mud wrestlers. I unfriended Hannah Goldstein. She was so mean, saying that my mom and your dad were having an affair, and they were planning to elope together, and that my mom... I can't even say it. It's so horrible, I hate these people so much.'

Riley hated looking at Elana on FaceTime right now, because she reminded her of Karen. They had the same hair, the same shaped mouth.

'I think it's true,' Riley said.

'What's true?' Elana seemed confused.

'What everybody's saying,' Riley said.

'Saying about them having an affair?'

'No, what they're saying about *everything*. I think it's *all* true.'

Riley and Elana had known each other for years and, like a lot of best friends, knew each other's thoughts.

'Oh my god, I can't believe you think that,' Elana said.

'My mom's gone,' Riley said. 'If your mom didn't do something to her, then where is she?'

Crying, Elana said, 'Oh my god, you too? I can't... I can't take this anymore.'

'They had a fight at the club,' Riley said. 'Your mom threatened my mom. Everybody saw it, it's so obvious, it's on *video*. Stop crying, stop being such a baby, and go ask your mom what she did. Maybe my mom's still alive. Maybe the cops can still save her. Maybe –'

Elana cut off and the home screen appeared.

'Ask her!' Riley screamed at the phone. 'Fucking ask her!'

Then she tossed the phone away onto her Foof. Sobbing again, she hated Elana so much and didn't see how they could ever be friends again. She hated her father and her brother and all her friends – she hated everybody. She wanted to go online and take down her Facebook. Worse, she just wanted to crawl into a hole and disappear. Or not just disappear – die. She wanted to die.

'Where are you, Mom?' she said, her lips quivering so much it was hard to speak. 'Where *are* you?'

18

MARK KNEW WHAT he had to do next. He'd been kidding himself, in denial, hoping that Deb would show up after being missing for two full days, that there would be some miracle explanation for all of this besides the obvious one. He didn't want to believe it, but staying in denial was causing his family pain, hurting his relationship with his daughter, and he needed things to return to normal for his own sanity, if nothing else.

Karen had said she would stop by after school today, but she hadn't shown. Was she avoiding him for a reason? He needed to talk to her in person, to get some clarity.

'Going out for a few!' he called out near the staircase, but he didn't wait for a response from Riley or Justin. When he left the house, several reporters there asked him questions – 'Have you heard from your wife yet?' 'How are you and your family holding up?' There were others, but Mark blocked out the noise, waving the reporters off, waving his arms in front of his chest. Near Karen's house there were more reporters gathered, but he ignored them and approached the front door, noticing that her car was in the driveway. So she'd returned from school as he'd suspected, but hadn't contacted him or come over to his house.

Hmm.

Figuring she wouldn't answer if he rang the bell, he texted her: *I'm outside lemme in*. About a moment later the door opened just wide enough for him to slip inside.

Standing face to face with her, he was convinced she was hiding something.

'Have you heard from her?' she asked.

'No,' he said.

'Shit,' she said. 'I wish there was something I could do. I'm so, so sorry.'

This sounded sincere, but it could be an act.

'What're you sorry for?' He was examining her closely, looking for a sign of guilt. A 'tell' they called it in poker.

'That you have to go through all this,' she said. 'What else would I be sorry for? ... And why are you staring at me like that?'

'Nothing,' Mark said, noticing that she was blinking a lot. Was that the tell?

'How are you?' she asked. 'How are your children?'

'How do you think?' he said.

'It's so awful,' she said. 'And I'm so, so sorry.'

Was all of this a sort of confession? Was she showing remorse? Maybe it was a mistake to give her the benefit of the doubt before, telling her he believed she was innocent when there was so much obvious evidence against her.

'You don't look good,' she added. 'Come in, sit down.'

'I'm fine right here.'

'Are you mad at me?'

If she were guilty and asking this, she was a total psycho.

'Sorry I didn't come by before,' she said. 'I was planning to call you later. I just had such an awful, awful day. I couldn't deal with talking about it. People at work are thinking horrible things about me, and a detective came to talk to me at school. It was the most humiliating experience of my life.'

'Why?' Mark asked.

'Why?' Karen was pretending to be confused.

'Yeah, why?'

'Why what?' She was squinting. 'Are you sure you're okay? You're acting really weird. You're scaring me, Mark.'

He wanted to hate her. After all, this was the woman who may have killed his wife, his children's mother, who may have ruined his entire life. But it was hard to see her for what she was – a calculating, cold-blooded murderer – when he couldn't deny that she was still the most beautiful woman he'd ever seen.

'You killed her, didn't you?' He didn't mean to say this; it had slipped out.

Karen's eyes widened and now *she* was the one not blinking. 'Excuse me?'

'Please,' Mark said, 'just tell me why.'

She backed away a few steps and it occurred to Mark that she might try to kill him too. If she felt threatened, thought he was going to blow the whole thing for her, why wouldn't she try to take him out? It seemed crazy that she'd try something like that with her kids at home, but maybe that didn't matter to her.

'You,' she said softly. 'You really... believe this.'

'Well, I'm just telling you how it seems.'

'What about what you said before? About how you don't believe what people are saying? How you're on my side?'

'I see it differently now,' Mark said, looking at her face, but also watching her hands closely to make sure she didn't suddenly reach for a weapon. 'Come on, you can be honest with me. Everybody saw you at the country club, fighting with Deb, and they know what was going on with us. It's only a matter of time till the cops find out the truth about what happened.'

'I thought you were crazy before,' Karen said. 'I thought it was a midlife crisis or something, a delusion. But it's more than that, isn't it? You're officially out of your mind.'

'Why couldn't you wait?' Mark said. 'Deb and I were splitting up. You would've had me anyway. But instead you had to *kill* her?'

She didn't answer; he could tell her mind was churning. Was she going to confess? Say it was a crime of passion? Would she explain how she'd done it? Give all the gruesome details? Or maybe she'd kiss him, beg for forgiveness, finally admit how in love she was with him and how she'd killed Deb in a jealous rage. It was so Romeo and Juliet – even though Mark wasn't sure what the plot of Romeo and Juliet was, he knew it was like that. He wouldn't forgive her, of course, he *couldn't* now, she'd gone way too far, but he wouldn't mind being kissed by her. He'd been waiting so long, had so many fantasies, he just wanted to finally experience what it was like to kiss her, even if it was right before she went off to spend the rest of her life in jail for murdering his wife.

He may have even pursed his lips a little, waiting for her lean in for the big moment, and was actually surprised when he heard her saying, 'I really don't know why you're doing this and, honestly, I really don't care. If you want to live in fantasy land, live in fantasy land. Be my guest. But we both know that nothing was going on with us, *ever*, and you have to go outside right now and tell the reporters that and call the police and tell them too. Maybe I was a little too friendly with you, maybe some people got the wrong idea, but I didn't *do* anything. If you care about me at all, you'll call the police right now and tell them the truth and put an end to this fucking bullshit.'

Mark wished he could feel sorry for her. She was still playing the role, pretending to be innocent. She was so far gone, so deep in love, that she had totally lost touch with reality.

'I want you to be honest with me about something,' Mark said. 'Did your love for me drive you crazy? Is that why you were so cold and distant yesterday, because you felt guilty? Were you holding your love in, the way I've been holding it in for years, and it suddenly burst out? Not the love, the emotion, the violence. Is that why you did it? Is that why you killed her?'

Karen was shaking her head. 'You're horrible,' she said. 'You're a fucking monster.'

'Look who's talking,' Mark said.

'Get the fuck out of my house.'

Karen had opened the door and was pushing Mark outside onto the porch. As the door slammed, reporters swarmed him, shouting questions. He wasn't sure if he couldn't understand what they were saying, or he was just too overwhelmed. He heard the names 'Deborah' and 'Karen' but the rest sounded like noise. He couldn't believe this was actually happening, that it had come down to this, but it had.

He'd officially lost her.

19

*O*H MAN, OWEN thought. *Was this perfect or what?*

He'd been trying to figure out a way to get to Karen's house, to be there to support her and shit, when he got a call from Elana, going on in that annoying, whiny tone about how kids at school were giving her a hard time about her mom, and how this was the worst day of her life, and she was so upset and missed him so much. At first, when she was bitching, he was barely listening, but then it clicked that this was exactly what he needed. He'd never believed in god, but it sure as hell seemed as if *somebody* was looking out for him.

So he left the motel and headed over to the Dailys'. If things went well, maybe he could move his stuff over late tonight or tomorrow morning. He was glad because the motel was too stuffy and, besides, he was used to living in a house. When he and Karen got married the house would be half his. Owen Harrison, homeowner, who would've thought? Just a few days ago, his future had seemed so bleak. He was an eighteen-year-old high school dropout with a shit job and was living with his parents, but pretty soon he was going to have a sexy wife, step kids, and a house with a big back yard and a lawn to mow. Talk about turning his life around.

Shit, there were lots of people, reporters and camera people probably because there were news trucks too, in front of Karen's house. Owen should've expected this, but he hadn't. He was too excited about the future to pay much attention to anything else.

He rang the bell a couple of times then saw the blinds in the living room part for a second. He hoped Karen would answer the door but it was Elana who opened it just wide enough for him to slip inside, then she closed it and locked it again.

'Oh my god, it's so great to see you,' she said, hugging him tightly.

'Yeah,' Owen said, looking past her, toward the kitchen, hoping to see Karen there.

'Come on, let's go up to my room and hang,' she said.

'Where's your mom?' Owen asked.

'Why?'

'I just want to say "hi" to her, see how she's doing.'

'I don't think that's a good idea. My mom's really not handling this too well.' She whispered, 'She just had this big fight with Riley's dad.'

'Really?' Owen wanted to hear about this. 'What about?'

'Come up and I'll tell you.'

'Just tell me now.'

'I only heard some of it, I was upstairs, listening in,' Elana continued, whispering. 'It was really weird though. He was telling her to turn herself in to the cops, and my mother was like, "I didn't do anything, why should I turn myself in?" and Riley's dad was like, "But we're in love," and my mother was like, "That's crazy."'

'Wow,' Owen said, thinking this was great news. If Karen was really hooking up with an old guy like Mark Berman there was no way in hell she'd be able to resist a hot young stud like himself. After all, Deb had blown off Mark to be with him, so why wouldn't Karen do the same thing?

'I know, it's so fucked up,' Elana said. 'That's why I need you here. I love you so much.'

Shit, she didn't just say 'love' too, did she? Was everybody around here losing their minds?

'You don't mean that,' he said.

'That I need you here? Of course I need you, that's why I called you. Come on, let's go up and hang.'

He'd have to straighten her out later, or she'd just figure it out on her own. But right now he had one thing on his mind.

'Where's your mom?'

'In the den, I think, but –'

'Lemme talk to her,' Owen said. 'I'm really good at like, you know, consoling people. I ever tell you, when I was growing up I wanted to be a funeral director?'

'Really?' Elana asked.

Sticking with the bullshit, Owen went, 'Yeah, I was gonna go to school for it. I still might someday. I'm great with grief. In my family, whenever someone died or got sick or something bad happened, I was always the one who talked to whoever was hurting and made them feel better.'

How was he able to think of this shit so quickly? It was like a fucking gift.

'You're so amazing,' Elana said.

'Wait for me in bed, baby,' Owen said.

''Kay,' she said and finally went upstairs.

Okay, that was one problem out of the way, now down to business. Owen went to the other end of the house, past the living room, and then there was a room with the door closed. He could hear Karen talking, sounded like she was on the phone. He knocked softly, then opened the door a crack and poked his head in.

Standing, facing away, talking into her iPhone, Karen was saying, '... They're staying here with me and that's final!' Then she turned and saw Owen and seemed surprised, or maybe angry. She said into the phone, 'I have to go now. I said I'm hanging up.'

Then she ended the call and said to Owen, 'What are *you* doing here?'

Putting on his sexiest smile, Owen said, 'Elana called and wanted me to come by, and I wanted to check in on you.'

'Well, she shouldn't've called you, and you shouldn't be here now,' Karen said. 'You have to go home.'

'But I *want* to be here,' Owen said, coming fully into the room, and taking a couple of steps toward her and then stopping, maybe three feet away.

'You have to leave, right now,' she said.

'It's okay,' he said.

'No, it's *not* okay,' she said, crossing her arms in front of her chest. 'This is the last thing I need right now. I want you to leave.' She called out, 'Elana!'

Elana was all the way upstairs and they were at the other end of the house; Owen knew she couldn't hear.

'Please, just try to chill, look at things in perspective,' Owen said.

'Perspective?' she asked.

'Yes,' Owen said. 'I think it's horrible what they're saying about you, I think it sucks so bad. But they don't know who you really are. They're just talking, saying whatever

246

they want to say. But you know who you really are. Your family knows too.'

Shit, he was good.

'Thank you,' Karen said, 'but actually you don't get it.'

'Get what?'

'Nobody –'

'– Believes you didn't do it?' Owen said. 'Well, who gives a shit what everybody thinks? I believe you didn't do it, because I was there.'

'What do you mean you were there?'

Owen had to be careful. He said, 'At the country club. I was there when Deb Berman attacked you out of nowhere. You didn't do anything – it was all her. She was drunk and acting crazy. I saw her drunk at the country club all the time, acting crazy. You weren't doing anything wrong.'

'Tell the police that,' Karen said.

'I already did,' Owen lied. 'As soon as I heard what was going on I called the police and told them.'

'Thank you.' Karen wasn't crossing her arms anymore; her arms were at her sides. 'It was very nice of you to do that.'

'Of course I'd do that,' Owen said. 'I'd do anything to help you and your family.'

He saw a look in her eye – a green light. He'd seen the same look from Deb, about two years ago, right before it had all started. He wanted to hold Karen's hand again – fuck, he wanted to do a lot more than that – but they had their whole lives together; there was no rush.

'I'm sorry I flipped out when I saw you here,' Karen said. 'I've just been under an incredible amount of stress. You're welcome to stay for dinner.'

'Can I help cook?'

'Thank you, I don't think I'll be cooking much. Just fish cakes and vegetables and the fish cakes are already made.'

JASON STARR

'Then at least let me set the table, and I'll do the dishes too.'

'It's okay, I can do it,' Karen said. 'Why don't you go spend time with Elana? I'll call you down when dinner's ready.'

She smelled so good. He wanted to ask her what perfume she was wearing, but he knew he should probably keep his mouth shut.

'What perfume are you wearing?' he asked.

Shit, it had slipped out.

'Excuse me?' she asked.

'I mean I just noticed you smell good, and I think I've smelled it before. Maybe on Elana.'

'I'm not wearing any perfume,' Karen said.

'Oh,' Owen said. 'Then maybe it's just soap.'

Upstairs, Elana was waiting for him in her room, lying in bed, on her iPad, going, 'Facebook is like a total clusterfuck. You can't believe what people are saying about my mom. How was she? What's going on?'

'She's cool,' Owen said. 'I talked to her and helped her, I think. She invited me to stay for dinner.'

'Really? That's so awesome. I mean, my mom has been kind of strict about us, because you're older and everything, but it's awesome that she invited you to dinner.'

'Yeah, your mom's amazing,' Owen said. 'You're lucky to have her.'

'Come here,' Elana said, putting down the iPad.

Owen didn't want to get in bed with her, but he didn't see how he was going to avoid it. For right now, Elana was the thing that was keeping him close to Karen, so he had to make sure not to mess this up. Eventually he'd have to tell Elana the truth, that he was in love with her mother, or, actually, it would make sense if Karen had that talk with her. She was her mom after all. She would know the best way to break the news to her daughter.

Owen was kissing Elana, imagining that it was Karen. Karen had great lips – thick, but not too thick – and he bet she was a great kisser.

'I'm so happy you're here,' Elana said. 'I almost didn't call you.'

'Why not?' Owen asked, distracted, still thinking about Karen's lips.

"Cause the other night, I don't know... I didn't think you were into me anymore.'

'Sorry,' Owen said. 'I was just in a bad mood. It had nothing to do with you.'

'Yeah,' Elana said. 'That's what I thought.'

They kissed some more and Owen could tell Elana was getting into it. He let her go down on him, which was pretty amazing actually because he imagined it was Karen doing it.

He almost fucked everything up, though, when he said, 'Oh, shit, that feels so good, Kar...'

Elana stopped, went, 'What did you just say?'

'I said careful,' Owen said.

'Oh,' she said.

'Dinner time!' Karen called from downstairs.

Owen and Elana were still in bed, cuddling. Oh, man, Owen loved Karen's voice. He couldn't wait till he heard her screaming out his name when they were doing the teacher-student fantasy. He bet she'd be better at it than Deb.

He and Elana went down to the kitchen. Her little brother was already at the table. This was so cool – a built-in family, waiting for him. When Kyle was here, it would be even cooler. All they needed was a dad – and now they had one.

'Let me,' Owen said, going over to Karen at the stove, *smelling* her. 'Sit down, relax, I'll serve.'

'It's okay,' she said.

'No, I insist,' he said.

Karen sat and Owen brought over the fishcakes and broccoli and salad that she had prepared. Then he got apple juice for Matthew and seltzer for Karen and Elana and then finally he joined them. Karen seemed kind of out of it still so Owen took control of the conversation, asking Matthew what was going on at school and then talking about swimming. Although Matthew didn't swim, he knew Kyle from school and wherever, and Elana knew Kyle too.

When Matthew said, 'Mom, can I have ice cream now?' Owen cut in and said, 'You have to finish your broccoli first or you can't have dessert.' Owen liked this new tone in his voice, how fatherly he sounded, and he could tell Karen liked it too. She'd been alone, divorced for a while now, and she was probably sick of dating. She liked having a man in the house, somebody who could take charge and be a good role model for the kids.

'Okay,' Matthew said and stabbed a piece of broccoli with his fork and stuffed it into his mouth.

Owen saw Karen smile, just for a second, but he could tell inside she was happy.

'Where do you live, Owen?' Karen asked.

Owen, getting a flash of seeing all his stuff on the lawn in front of his mom's house, wasn't sure how to answer.

'What do you mean?'

'I know your mom, Linda, has told me where she lives, but I forget. Is it Katonah or Lewisboro?'

'Katonah,' Elana said.

Then, suddenly, Owen saw an opportunity.

'Actually I'm not living anywhere right now,' he said.

'What do you mean?' Karen asked, and Elana asked, 'Yeah, what do you mean?'

'My mom and stepdad… Well, they asked me to move out.' Owen wasn't sad, but he forced out a tear or two to make it look good.

'When did this happen?' Elana asked.

'Yesterday,' Owen said. 'I came home and my stuff was on the lawn.'

'Your mother put your stuff on the lawn?' Karen asked.

'Not my mother, my stepfather, but my mother lets him do whatever he wants so I guess it's the same thing. Raymond, my stepfather, he isn't the nicest guy in the world. We got into a fight, and he hit me.'

'Hit you?' Karen asked.

'Yeah, he hits me all the time… He molested me one time too.'

'Oh my god,' Karen said.

'What's molested?' Matthew asked.

'Never mind,' Karen said to Matthew.

'Oh my god, he really did that to you?' Elana asked Owen.

'It's okay, I'm all right,' Owen said. 'I'm just worried about my brother. He's only eleven years old, and I'm afraid with me out of the house Raymond will need somebody else to pick on. I don't want what happened to me to happen to him.'

'What's molested?' Matthew asked again.

'Shut up,' Elana said to him.

'We need to call Child Protection Services,' Karen said to Owen. 'I deal with this sort of thing all the time at work. I can help you and your brother.'

'Thank you,' Owen said. 'I think Kyle's okay for right now, but that's probably a good idea.'

'If you're not home now, where are you staying?' Karen asked.

'Some shitty motel off the Saw Mill,' Owen said.

'You didn't tell me that,' Elana said.

'Sorry, I was embarrassed,' Owen said.

'Don't you have any relatives you can stay with?' Karen asked.

'No, not really,' Owen said. 'I have a couple of cousins, but they're in Arizona and California.'

'Well, you're not going back to the motel tonight,' Karen said. 'You can stay in the guest room.'

'It's okay,' Owen said. 'You don't have to do that.'

'I want to do it,' Karen said, 'and we'll help you figure out a longer term plan. Don't worry, you're not alone.'

Karen reached out and held Owen's hand, just for a second, but she'd still held his hand, actually held it.

'You're the kindest woman I've ever met,' he told her.

For Karen, the day from hell was getting worse. It was starting to sink in that Deb might never turn up and that the horrible rumors that people were spreading about her would continue to spread. It had been so awful at school after that detective came, treating her like a murder suspect. Teachers and even kids were cold and distant and she hadn't gotten any support from the principal or vice principal. Then she came home to find the reporters still camped out in front of her house, shouting questions, and then Mark came over, trying to get her to confess. It was hard for Karen to believe that she'd once considered Mark to be her friend, maybe her best friend.

Karen's relatives were supporting her, though she could tell they had their doubts too. Her mother had left a worried voicemail while Karen was at school and during her drive home Karen called her and explained that the whole situation was a crazy misunderstanding and that she wasn't having an affair with Mark and had nothing to do with Deb's disappearance. Her mother said she believed her and told her how it was 'so horrible the way people talk,' but Karen picked up on a tone in her voice and knew she wanted to believe her daughter was telling the truth, but wasn't quite convinced. She got a similar vibe when her sister and aunt called and in texts from a couple of friends. A few friends had left voicemails, making sure she was okay, but she felt no real support. But the worst betrayal by far had come from her ex-husband, Joe.

Despite the differences that had led to their divorce, Karen still considered Joe to be a friend. After the tension subsided about the custody and financial stuff, their relationship stabilized and while most of their conversations were about the kids, they were comfortable talking to each other and asking for help when they needed something. They'd lost their relationship, but they hadn't lost their respect for each other. When Joe got laid off from his job last year as an ad exec at Smythe and O'Greeley, a top Madison Avenue ad agency, she'd helped him get through it, and now he had a better, higher paying job. When she had drama last year with her supervisor at work, Joe was there to talk to her and help her see the situation from a different perspective. They'd even gotten to the point where they could comfortably talk to each other about dating other people. When Joe went through a difficult break up with a girlfriend last year, Karen spoke to him a few times to counsel him and give him 'the woman's perspective,' and when Karen had drama with a guy, Joe was great with 'the guy's perspective.'

Today, while Karen was at work, Joe had texted her a couple of times to 'check in' and make sure she was okay.

Karen appreciated the contact from Joe, it made her feel like she had an ally when the whole world seemed to be ganging up on her, and she told him how awful the situation was and how betrayed she felt by people at work. Joe suggested they talk later so when she got home, after the ridiculous visit from Mark, she went into the den and called Joe, in need of a dose of sanity.

What she didn't expect was Joe to ask her, 'So is it true about you and Mark?'

'Excuse me?' she asked, hoping she'd misunderstood him.

'Did you and Mark... you know... have something going on?'

Karen was floored. Joe too?

'I can't believe you're asking me that,' Karen said. 'How can you say that to me?'

'Calm down,' Joe said. 'Relax.'

'Don't tell me to relax.'

She hated when he told her to relax. It reminded her of the frustration she'd had during their marriage, when she'd felt she couldn't express herself fully.

'Okay, then at least stop yelling.'

'Why shouldn't I yell when you're accusing me, like everyone else?'

'I'm not accusing you, I'm asking you, because it kind of makes sense.'

'Make sense? How does it make sense?'

'You and Mark have always been close, even during our marriage.'

Oh my god, he's just like them, she thought.

'We were good friends, that's it. And lately we haven't been good friends, or even friends.'

'I'm not trying to get you defensive,' Joe said. 'If you'd calm down you'd understand this. I don't think it's an unreasonable question I'm asking because it's something I've wondered about for years.'

'*Years?*' Karen couldn't believe this.

'Deb and I used to joke about it,' Joe said. 'At parties, at get-togethers, when we were over at Mark and Deb's or had them over at our place. Deb used to say that if she and I died you and Mark would probably wind up together, raising the kids, you know, that sort of thing. So all I'm saying is the idea that you and Mark had something going on now isn't completely one hundred percent out of left field.'

'The answer to the question is no,' Karen said. 'Nothing was ever going on with Mark and me. And I think it's disgusting, absolutely disgusting, that you of all people would say such a thing to me. You think I'd have an affair with a married man, someone I've known for years, who our kids know, whose kids are friends with our kids? Is that really the type of person you think I am?'

'I was just asking a question,' Joe said, 'and you answered it.'

'I have to go make dinner for the kids,' Karen said, wanting to get off the phone.

'I was thinking,' Joe said, 'maybe I should drive up tonight and take the kids back to the city for a while.'

'Why?' Karen asked, though she knew what he was getting at. 'What for?'

'It sounds chaotic up there now,' Joe said. 'I'll be up there in an hour and take them.'

'They might find Deb any second now,' Karen said. 'The chaos'll be over.'

'Still,' Joe said. 'I think it's for the best.'

'You don't trust me, do you?'

'I didn't say that.'

'You don't have to say it, I can hear it in your voice. You think I'm crazy, losing it.'

'No, I just want the kids to be safe.'

'Safe? Safe from *who*? What, you don't think I'm *competent* now? Mr Self Absorbed, Mr Checking Out Of Our Marriage, Mr Every Other Weekend.'

'I'm coming up there.'

'You come here, I'll call the cops. You want drama? I'll give you fucking drama, you bastard.'

'Karen, calm down.'

'Why, afraid I'm gonna snap? They're staying here with me and that's final!'

Then Karen heard a noise and she turned and saw Owen Harrison, Elana's friend.

'I have to go now,' Karen said to Joe.

'Come on, Karen, don't –'

'I said I'm hanging up.'

At first she was angry with Owen, maybe taking out her anger at Joe and the world on him. But then she felt bad for blasting him when he actually seemed to be the only person who seemed to believe she was innocent and understand she was actually a victim. She still thought there was something off about Owen, something she couldn't quite identify. It was confusing for her because she was normally so good at understanding people; it was a big part of what she did for a living, reaching into other people's minds. But while Owen was inappropriate with her and crossed boundaries – asking her what perfume she was wearing; what was up with that? – there was still an endearing innocence about him. Okay, he was socially awkward at times, but he was definitely non-threatening, harmless, and Elana obviously liked him, so Karen wanted to be supportive.

During dinner, Karen was out of it, ruminating about the day, especially the conversation with Joe – the betrayal from her ex, her children's father, still stung the most –

and she was glad that Owen seemed to enjoy holding court, taking charge. Then when he mentioned that he was living at a motel and had been molested by his stepfather, Karen was aware that he was overstepping boundaries again, but she felt he was being sincere and honest, and she couldn't resist the urge to try to fix the situation. It sounded like he'd been through hell – something she could certainly identify with – and it partially explained the clinginess she'd felt from him. With his life at home so awful, it made sense that he was reaching out to another family for support. She was definitely going to contact Child Protection Services tomorrow and make sure his brother was okay and, while she knew that having Owen staying in the guest room would only be a temporary fix, that it wouldn't be practical for him to stay for more than a couple of days, it still made her feel good to be proactive, to be doing *something*.

Owen offered to help her with the dishes – he was such a nice kid – but she insisted that he go upstairs and spend some time with Elana. Karen knew they were probably fooling around, but Elana was going on seventeen, and Karen had to let go of her rigidness on this. From now on, she'd be okay with a don't-ask, don't-tell policy about sex, and as long as she and Owen didn't sleep in the same bed she'd be cool with it.

Karen was hoping, *praying* that some good news would arrive. If Deb would just return home unharmed, maybe things could be salvaged. It would take some work, but eventually she could forgive her friends, colleagues, and relatives for rushing to judgment about her. She knew that she and Joe could eventually get past it too; after all, they'd gotten through so much together, had so many ups and downs, they could survive this too. But in order for healing to take place there needed to be a break in the case and that didn't seem to be happening. The reporters were still outside in full-force, and she was getting more texts and emails from friends and family, and all of the messages seemed to have an underlying, accusatory tone. She could only imagine what the guys she'd dated lately must think. Even Steven, Mr Crabs, probably thought he'd dodged a bullet. She got an email from Richard Gross, the dentist she was supposed to go out with, cancelling their date. Big surprise there, eyes rolling. He, like everyone else, probably assumed that there had to be 'some truth' to what he was hearing on the news.

At around eight o'clock she got a call on her home phone from a local 'restricted' number. Hoping it was good news, maybe someone a neighbor or acquaintance calling to let her know that Deb was okay, that the nightmare was over, she picked up in the kitchen and said eagerly, 'Yes?'

But it was a man, shouting, 'Go to hell, slut!'

Shocked, Karen ended the call. People were so cruel and awful; she hated everyone.

'Who was it?' Owen had entered the kitchen.

Standing facing away from him, so he couldn't see that she was crying, he said, 'No one. Wrong number.'

She remained, waiting for him to leave, go back upstairs, but hoping he wouldn't. She felt so alone.

'Do you want to talk about it?' he asked.

She did want to talk about it, and he was the only one who seemed to understand her, so why not?

So she turned toward him, letting him see her tears and said, 'It's so hard to explain, I'm not sure you can relate.'

'I'm good at relating,' he said, smiling. He had warm blue eyes and cute dimples; no wonder Elana liked him so much.

'Where's Elana?' Karen asked.

'Upstairs, doing some homework or something,' Owen said.

'Good, I'm glad she's able to focus on something else.'

'So who was that on the phone?'

'That was actually a prank call, some man called me a slut.'

'Shit, I'm really sorry,' Owen said, taking a couple of steps toward her.

He was a bit too close, violating her space, but she let him.

'He's probably somebody I know,' Karen said. 'Maybe a dad from school, or somebody from the country club. Probably somebody I've been to parties with, somebody I've laughed with, somebody I like. But then a story got around, he made assumptions, and turned on me. It makes me wonder, how can I trust anything anymore? How do I know what's real and what isn't?'

'It must be so hard,' Owen said, even closer now.

'You have no idea,' Karen said, needing to vent. 'Being a divorced woman in the suburbs, in a small community, is like a curse. People need to talk about something, so what're they going to talk about? They talk about what's different, what doesn't fit. Then they start with their assumptions, they think they know me, but they don't, they don't. I've sensed it since Joe and I separated – the undercurrents. People say things but they're really saying something else, I always know what they're *really* saying. Then something like this happens and it proves that not only was I right all along, but the reality is even worse than I thought. Suddenly I'm not just a slutty divorcee, I'm an adulteress, and a killer too. It's not just a suspicion anymore; it's what they actually think. I've been through so many changes in my life the past few years – the divorce, adjusting to life on my own, being single again, dating, meeting new people. I never expected to be where I am now, this isn't the way I've planned it. I've grown a lot, don't get me wrong, but I've also been through so much disappointment, so much pain, so much struggling. I know I'm rambling, but it's how I feel, I can't help it. What I'm trying to say is trust has been hard for me, it's been my biggest struggle of all – to learn how to trust people, trust situations. People sometimes tell me that I put walls up. Joe, my ex, used to say it all the time, and other people have complained about it too. But I don't do it to hurt anyone, I do it to protect myself, and today people's reactions have confirmed what I've been trying not to believe. I'm sorry, I know I'm not making any sense, and I shouldn't be telling you this. You should go upstairs with Elana. Please, just go.'

But Owen didn't go. Instead he moved closer, they were maybe six inches apart now, and he said in a warm, kind voice, 'You can trust me.'

It was weird, but she *did* trust him, more than she'd trusted anyone else lately anyway. After all, who was this guy, this *kid*? She'd only spoken to him a couple of times, but she couldn't deny how she felt. He was the only one she was able to let her guard down with, even if it was just a little bit.

'I'm glad I can trust you,' she said. 'Actually, you're part of my alibi. Can you believe that? I need an alibi.'

'What do you mean?'

'When the detective came to talk to me at school, he asked me where I was Saturday night and I said I was home and you and Elana saw me here.'

'Oh,' Owen said.

'Don't worry, I won't drag you into anything, I promise,' Karen said. 'But, I have to say, it's nice to have somebody to talk to about all this stuff. I feel like I've been going through this alone.'

'Yeah, I know how that is.'

'What do you mean?'

'I walk around feeling alone inside all the time,' Owen said. 'I mean, 'cause of everything I've been through with my family and shit. It sucks.'

Feeling connected to Owen with their shared pain, Karen said, 'Well, you have us now,' and reached out to Owen and held his upper arm for a moment then, feeling a little weird about it, let go.

'I've been thinking about this whole thing with Debbie,' Owen said. 'I think that people got it wrong.'

'Do you know Deb?' Karen asked.

Karen saw a flash of something – concern or maybe just awkwardness – in Owen's expression.

Then he said, 'No, I mean just from around. I've seen her at the country club a lot, and I know she's Riley Berman's mom.'

'Oh,' Karen said, 'because the way you called her Debbie, it sounded like you knew her. So what were you saying, about how people have it wrong?'

'Yeah, I mean, I don't understand why they're talking about you when they should be talking about her husband, Mark. How do you know Mark didn't kill her?'

'First of all, Deb isn't dead,' Karen said. 'She's just missing.'

'You know what I mean,' Owen said. 'Usually when a wife goes missing the cops blame the husband and usually they're right. But this time they're talking about you just because of one stupid argument that wasn't even your fault. I think it's bullshit.'

'You know you make a really great point,' Karen said. 'Why *isn't* Mark more of the focus?'

'Because it's bullshit, that's why.'

'Mark has been acting so weird lately,' Karen said, 'but I couldn't imagine him actually *hurting* anyone. Then again, you never know about people, do you?'

'Nope, you never do,' Owen said.

All day Karen had been so concerned with what people were saying about her and so hopeful that Deb would return home at some point unharmed, she hadn't really thought about other possibilities. Maybe Mark snapped, killed Deb in a fit of passion and rage, and maybe that's why he'd come over before, trying to get her to confess. After all, if he felt the police were on the verge of discovering the truth, he'd get desperate and desperate people will do anything to avoid getting caught, including trying to coerce other people into a confession.

Karen had already lost faith in Mark, and felt betrayed by him, but this clinched it; she officially hated him.

'We should tell the cops to leave you alone, go talk to Mark Berman,' Owen said. 'He's the one who knows where his wife is.'

'I think you're right,' Karen said. 'I hate to admit it, but I think you're right.'

Owen was hugging her. At first she was so absorbed, thinking about Mark, that she didn't realize what was going on. Then she was aware of it, but she didn't say anything because she'd felt so alone all day that it was nice to get support from somebody, to have an ally.

'Owen?' Elana had entered the kitchen? '*Mom*?'

Karen immediately ended the embrace and pushed Owen back a little, which probably made it look much worse.

'Elana,' Karen said.

'What's going on?' Elana asked.

'Uh...' Karen couldn't think clearly, feeling weirdly guilty.

Owen cut in with, 'Nothing. Your mom was just upset and I was soothing her.'

Karen didn't like that word, *soothing*, so she explained, 'I was just having a moment, and Owen was nice enough to help me through it. Thank you, Owen, I really appreciate it. Why don't you two go upstairs and watch TV or something? I have some things I need to take care of.'

'Okay,' Elana said, giving Karen a look that said, *What the hell*? and Karen gazed back as if saying, *Oh, stop it, it was nothing*.

They left and Karen was aware of how much more empowered she felt. All day she'd been the victim, but now anger was taking over. Usually she went out of her way to avoid anger – it was how she'd survived her divorce – but now she needed to motivate herself, to get in control. *It's all Mark's fault*. This had to be her mantra, whenever she felt like the victim, she had to remind herself that Mark had caused this, that he was to blame, not her.

She peeked through the blinds and saw the reporters were still camped in front of the house. She checked online and nothing had changed there either – as of the latest news report, in the Westchester Gazette eleven minutes ago, Deb was still missing. There were more articles about the argument in the country club and one even called Karen 'a person of interest.'

'Are they fucking kidding me?' Karen said, then she shut her eyes and told herself, 'It's all Mark's fault, it's all Mark's fault.'

A little calmer, she decided to be proactive and called the cell number on the card Detective Walsh had given her earlier.

'Detective Walsh, Bedford Police.'

'Detective Walsh, it's Karen, Karen Daily.'

'Oh, yes.' He sounded surprised to hear from her.

'Have you found Deb Berman yet?'

'No, in fact, we haven't.'

Because she's dead, Karen thought.

Then she said, 'I feel strange bringing this up because he's been a friend for a long time and I don't want to cause more trouble for his family, but I'm concerned about Mark Berman.'

'Concerned how?'

'He's been acting weird for a few days now,' Karen said. 'It started at a party in Bedford Hills on Friday night. He held my hand and Deb saw it, that's why she was upset at the country club. I don't know why I didn't think of telling you about this at school today, I think I was too upset. Anyway, Deb had the wrong idea about us because of Mark. I think he's been having a midlife crisis or something. He thinks he's in love with me, and I have no idea how he got this idea into his head, but he obviously has issues. I think he… I don't want to even imagine the scenarios, but maybe he was afraid of going through a divorce, maybe he was worried about money or custody or who knows what, so maybe he… Maybe it was for the life insurance money. I'm just thinking of this right now, but it makes sense. He's the husband, in these cases it's always the husband, and I'm just saying he's the one you should be investigating not me. He's the crazy one, not me.'

When she finished her rant, she was out of breath, and she realized how manic she must have sounded, and wondered if this call was helping, or hurting, her cause.

'I understand your concerns,' Walsh said. 'Rest assured, despite what you might be hearing in the media we haven't reached any conclusions in this case. We're exploring every possibility and actively searching for Deborah.'

'But what about Mark? Have you questioned him the way you questioned me?'

'Like I said, we're actively exploring –'

'I'm telling you, he's hiding something. Look, I'd be shocked if he actually... if he actually *hurt* Deb, but people are always shocked about people. Don't you see that all the time?'

'Ms. Daily, as I said, we're talking to everybody, not just you.'

Christ, he was talking to her as if she were a child, or if she were crazy, she didn't know which was worse.

'Just talk to him,' she pleaded. 'Stop wasting your time and talk to him.'

About twenty minutes later, Karen was in her room, regretting her call to Detective Walsh. She didn't regret trying to get him to focus more on Mark, but she wished she had come across calmer, more in control.

Though it wasn't nine o'clock yet, she got ready for bed – well, splashing her face with cold water and putting on sweats and a T-shirt. The way her mind was churning she had no idea how she'd sleep knowing that as bad as today had been, tomorrow could be much worse.

Then someone was knocking hard on the bedroom door.

'Yes?' she asked.

'Lemme in.' It was Owen.

Karen, remembering the awkward scene in the kitchen, didn't bother going over to the door and called out from near the bathroom, 'This isn't a good time, I'm kind of busy.'

'I need to talk.' The doorknob was rattling. 'Right now.'

It sounded urgent. Had Deb come home? Was there going to be a happy ending after all?

When Karen unlocked the door, Owen opened it. She saw his intense expression, heard him say, 'We need to leave.'

His eyes were so wide she could see white all around the irises.

'What?' She was confused, had no idea what he was talking about.

'We have to go.' He grabbed her hand with a grip that was so firm it startled her. 'Right now.'

20

'WHAT'S YOUR TAKE on Karen Daily?' Nick asked Larry.

They were at the Bedford police station – both standing outside Larry's office. Larry had just come back from interviewing Karen at Meadow Pond Elementary School.

'I don't believe she's involved,' Larry said.

'But *could* she be involved?' Nick asked. 'There's a difference.'

Instead of letting Nick's belittling tone get to him, Larry threw it back at his superior, going, 'Do you mean does she have an alibi? Not really. She dropped her son at a sleepover at around seven on Saturday evening and she said she returned home afterward. There's no reason to believe she's lying about this, but she says that no one saw her at home until her daughter and her daughter's boyfriend arrived at approximately eleven-fifteen on Saturday evening. So is it possible she met Deborah sometime during that time? Yes, it's possible. Do I think she did? No, I do not.'

'And what's this based on?' Nick asked. 'I mean, except your gut feeling.'

'That's all it is, a gut feeling,' Larry said.

'Fuck gut feelings,' Nick said. 'If I was going on gut feelings, I'd be pulling Mark Berman in here and booking him for murder before we found any evidence or any body. My gut was screaming at me that this guy's hiding something, his own daughter thinks he's guilty, for fuck's sake. Oh, and hearsay, I've got lots of hearsay too. I interviewed four witnesses so far who saw the incident at the country club and they all told me that it's common knowledge that Mark and Karen Daily are having an affair. Are they actually having an affair? Did it get out of control? Who knows?'

'You got nothing from Deborah's car, huh?' Larry asked.

'*Nada* so far,' Nick said. 'But right now it looks like she went to that parking lot to meet somebody and got into the other person's car.'

'Doesn't it seem unlikely that that person was Karen Daily?' Larry asked. 'I mean, if there was bad blood between them after the argument at the country club, why would Deb get into Karen's car?'

'I'm with you on that,' Nick said. 'But an altercation could have taken place outside and maybe the rain washed the evidence away. Unfortunately there are no security cameras in that area, so no help there either.'

'And no witnesses,' Larry said. 'That's surprising, I think, on a Saturday night.'

'The rain probably kept kids away,' Nick said. 'We did find a couple of kids who said they were there that night and they thought they saw another car, but they couldn't remember. They might've just seen Deborah's.'

'What about credit card and cell phone info?'

'We have most of Deborah's, no red flags,' Nick said. 'The credit cards going back three months look pretty normal. No trips, no hotels, no restaurants. Her cell looks normal too. Her most recent calls were to family members. Her last call was to Scott Greenberg, a divorce lawyer, which jibes with what the daughter told you, about her wanting a divorce.'

'What about Mark and Karen?'

'Not much there either. Mark certainly texted with Karen frequently and there's phone calls too, but nothing to prove one way or another that an affair was taking place. Most of the texts came from Mark, and it definitely seems like Mark has some kind of obsession going on with her. It could just be a bored married guy looking for some action on the side. But what does that tell us about what happened to Deborah?'

'Okay, I have another theory for you,' Larry said. 'What if it was all a setup? Deborah's unhappy in her marriage, suffering from depression maybe, so she decides to disappear and ditches her car in a place where she knows there are no security cameras.'

'Okay,' Nick said, 'then where'd she go?'

'Maybe she ran away, left the country,' Larry said. 'She could've gotten into another car, or taken a cab somewhere.'

'Then why was she looking up divorce lawyers?'

'Part of the setup, to throw us off? Okay, I admit there are holes but, okay, what if it's something else? What if it's part of a suicide plan?'

'A little elaborate for suicide, don't you think? What's wrong with the ol' slitting your wrists in the bathtub or OD'ing on pills?'

'If she was pissed off at her husband, maybe she hoped he'd be blamed,' Larry said. 'Or, okay, maybe it was about her kids, she didn't want to put them through the trauma of finding her body.'

'Interesting,' Nick said, 'but before we start checking the borders, I think we have to focus on the idea that she was meeting somebody at that parking lot. There are no cameras there, and she probably knew that, so why do people meet at a spot where there are no cameras?'

'Maybe Deborah was the one having the affair, not Mark,' Larry said. 'Maybe that's why she left Saturday night without saying where she was going, and maybe that's why she was the one looking up divorce lawyers. Maybe she met her lover at that parking lot and an altercation took place or they went somewhere.'

'I don't know,' Nick said. 'Don't you think it's a little weird that a woman in her forties would meet her lover in the parking lot of a high school?'

'No weirder than her meeting Karen Daily there,' Larry said.

'The problem is we haven't found anybody who's even suggested Deborah was fucking somebody. All I hear about is Mark and Karen. And there was nothing on Deb's phone to suggest that.'

'People who cheat get disposable phones,' Larry said.

'Yeah, so?'

'Can we take a closer look at the call histories on their phones? See if any numbers are called frequently from month to month.'

'What'll that get us if we don't know whose numbers they are?'

'We can recheck the credit card info,' Larry said, 'see if anybody bought a disposable phone and charged it. I worked on a case a few years ago where a guy thought he was being clever, using a disposable, but he bought it on his AmEx. Once we had the phone number we were able to pull up his texts and calls from the carrier.'

'Sounds like a long shot, but we'll check it out,' Nick said. 'I still think our priority now has to be Mark and Karen, trying to find holes in their alibis.'

'Speaking of alibis, there was one thing that struck me as a little odd in my talk with Karen Daily today,' Larry said. 'I'm really not sure what to make of it.'

'Okay…' Nick seemed intrigued.

'Well, she told me her daughter's boyfriend saw her at home Saturday night. I asked her what her boyfriend's name is and she said, "Owen Harrison."'

'So?'

'So I knew that name sounded familiar and I asked her if it's the Owen Harrison whose mother is Linda Harrison and she said, 'Yes, it is.' I didn't question her further about it, because I didn't think it necessarily meant anything, but it's still nagging at me.'

'You lost me,' Nick said.

'About three years ago Owen Harrison's ex-babysitter disappeared,' Larry said. 'Her name was Melanie Foster.'

'Right, right, I was working Narcotics, but I remember that case,' Nick said. 'Melanie Foster. College kid, going to Oneonta. But she was a runaway, right?'

'That's what her parents thought, and still think. She'd threatened to run away before and, even though her life seemed stable at the time, it seemed like the most likely scenario. There was nothing to indicate otherwise, anyway, but it's been three years and no one's heard a word about her.'

'So what does this have to do with Owen Harrison?' Nick asked. 'Was he a suspect?'

'No, not really,' Larry said. 'He was home with his mother at the time Melanie was last seen, that was his alibi, but I remember a feeling I got when I interviewed him, a feeling that something was off. He was, I don't know, too slick, too cool for somebody his age. I thought he may have had a relationship with Melanie. People had seen them together, and some of Melanie's friends suspected something was going on, but I couldn't prove they'd had an actual relationship. Then, today, I thought it was odd when his name popped up again.'

'Okay, so his name popped up,' Nick said. 'What does that mean? So he's dating Karen Daily's daughter. What does that have to do with Deborah Berman?'

'Nothing, I guess.'

'Exactly, that's why...' Nick looked like he was having a brainstorm. 'Hold up a sec.' He opened his pad, said, 'Yeah, I thought that sounded familiar. Owen Harrison's name popped up at one of my interviews today too.' Nick was looking at a page in the pad. 'At the country club today, I was doing a follow up with Jenna Frisco, the bartender at the club, and I asked her what other club employees witnessed the fight and one of the names she mentioned was Owen Harrison.'

'I think it's worth looking into,' Larry said. 'If Owen works at the country club he could've met Deborah there. And if he was involved with Melanie there's a chance he was involved with Deborah.'

'That's a lot of could'ves and chances,' Nick said.

'True, but I'm telling you, there's something off about this kid,' Larry said. 'He's a smooth operator. Deborah could've been lonely in her marriage, felt adventurous. Maybe he's the one she went to meet at the high school parking lot. If we check Owen's phone records we might find something.'

'Hey, I love the Patriot Act as much as the next cop,' Nick said, 'but we can't go around checking phone records based on hunches.'

Larry knew Nick was right, but said, 'There's always a way to get a warrant. If we can prove he's a suspect.'

'A suspect based on what? We have nothing on him.'

'Yet,' Larry said.

'Look,' Nick said, 'if you want to check out Owen because he witnessed the fight at the club and may give us some info we don't have, go for it. But right now it's just a theory, like all the other theories, and we still have to focus on Karen and Mark, and to see if we can find a witness at that parking lot. I have to go take a leak.'

Nick walked away, down the hall.

Larry went into his office, sat at his desk, when his cell vibrated. As always, he was happy when he saw 'Stu' on the display, but he didn't have time to get into a conversation right now.

'Hey, how are you?'

'Okay,' Stu said.

'Sorry, I'm swamped right now, bro, can we talk later?'

'Actually, we can't.'

'Everything okay, man?'

'No, not really.'

Larry went over, shut his office door, and said, 'Where are you?'

'Driving.'

The line was silent. Now Larry was seriously concerned; this wasn't like Stu at all. 'Are you sure you're okay? Where are you driving to?'

'Nowhere. Just driving. I told Janet I was going out for milk.'

'What's going on? Talk to me, man.'

Long silence.

'Stu, you –'

'Yeah, yeah, I'm okay... It's just...'

Stu was normally talkative, very direct.

'You're scaring me, bro,' Larry said.

'Sorry. It's just… well, Janet's suspicious. She knows I've been out a lot, and she seemed to believe my excuses, but now she's suddenly asking lots of questions. I don't know, maybe because of what's going on with Mark and Karen in the news. Maybe it put ideas in her head or some shit.'

'Fuck,' Larry said, though he was thinking, *Maybe this is a good thing. Maybe they needed openness, transparency. Maybe they needed to get this all out in the open and put an end to the sneaking around bullshit.*

'It's bad, man, it's bad,' Stu said. 'She asked me point blank if I'm cheating on her. I said no, of course, but I'm a shitty liar. I can't keep up a lie, not for a long time anyway. I'm afraid she'll start checking up on me now, and I'm afraid the kids'll find out and… I can't deal with that kind of drama in my life, I just can't.'

'Maybe it's –' Larry was going to say 'for the best.'

But Stu cut him off. 'She said she's been suspecting something for a while. What's the word she used? Aloof. Yeah, she said I've been acting aloof. See, I told you I'm a shitty liar.'

'I'm sorry,' Larry said, but he was more relieved than sorry. He was glad that the secret was getting out, that a door was finally opening to a future with Stu.

'I'm sorry too, man,' Stu said. 'You know I didn't want it to end this way.'

It was happening – Stu was talking about ending his marriage. The moment Larry had been fantasizing about for months was finally here. He could stop living in fear that he would lose the love of his life, and they could start building a future together. They could wake up every day in the same bed, plan trips, do the things that all couples do and take for granted. Except they'd never take anything for granted. They'd always cherish their time together.

'Don't worry, I'll be there for you, bro,' Larry said. 'I'll help you through it.'

'*Through* it?' Stu asked. 'What do you mean, *through* it?'

'Your break up with Janet,' Larry said. 'I know it'll be rough, but I'll be there for you.'

'Whoa, I'm not talking about leaving my *marriage*,' Stu said. 'Are you fuckin' high? I told you I'd never do that.'

Stu had never told Larry this, that was bullshit, a total lie, but Larry was too shocked and confused to get upset.

'Wait,' Larry said. 'What... w-hat're you –'

'I'm sorry man, it's for the best,' Stu said. 'We can't see each other anymore, and you can't call me or text me either. I need a clean break now, no contact.'

'What?' Larry had heard Stu, but he couldn't fully comprehend the meaning of the words. This wasn't right – this wasn't right at all. How had this gone from fantasizing about a life together to no contact, from life to death, in just a few seconds?

'Sorry, man,' Stu said. 'I really like you, you know that, but I have a family, I have kids. You knew this from the beginning.'

'You really like me?' Larry said. 'You really *like* me? What do you mean, you really *like* me? You fucking love me, man.'

'I can't have this conversation,' Stu said.

'You can't do this,' Larry said. 'You... you don't want this. How can you do something you don't *want*? How could you do that to me? How could you do that to *yourself*?'

'Goodbye, bro.'

'Wait, Stu. Stu? Stu, you there? Stu?'

Had he seriously *hung up* on him? That was it, 'Goodbye, bro,' and the most meaningful relationship of Larry's life had ended, forever?

Larry called Stu back, but voicemail answered – the son of a bitch had turned off his phone.

'Shit!' Larry shouted. 'Damn it!'

He knew he wasn't thinking logically right now; he had to resist impulsivity. He wanted to go over to see Stu, talk to him in person. He knew if they were together, could see and touch each other that there was no way he would be able to leave him. Or if Stu was stubborn, or being a chickenshit, and didn't want to tell his wife the truth, that he was gay and in love with a man, then maybe Larry should do it for him. Yeah, Stu would be upset, blame Larry for hurting his wife, and causing drama, but someday Stu would thank him, for helping him get out of his marriage, for ending the huge lie he'd been living for years.

But Larry didn't want to do something stupid, something he might regret big time. Fortunately, focusing on the Deborah Berman case was the perfect distraction.

Larry remembered where the Harrisons lived and figured it would be better to show up in person, unexpected, rather than give Owen a heads up. It seemed like seconds later he was driving, replaying snippets of the conversation with Stu, *I'm sorry it's for the best... I really like you.*

It still didn't seem real. It seemed like something he'd imagined.

His cell rang, but hope fizzled when he saw it was Karen Daily calling and not Stu.

He took the call on speaker. Karen was upset, like she'd been at the school earlier, and was insisting that Mark should be the focus of the investigation, and not her. Larry assured her that they were exploring all possibilities, which was true; he just hoped this trip to Owen Harrison's house wasn't taking the investigation way off course.

Larry parked in front of the Harrison's house, noticing

two cars in the drive. Some lights were on in the house, so he hoped he'd at least have someone to speak to and the trip wouldn't be a total waste.

He rang the bell, heard footsteps inside, and then the peephole cover shifted. Several seconds passed, long enough for Larry to consider ringing the bell again, and then Owen's stepfather opened the door. Larry couldn't recall his name but remembered speaking to him during the Melanie Foster investigation. He was gruff, middle-aged, had seemed like an asshole.

'Detective Walsh, Bedford police.' He showed his badge.

'I know who you are,' the man said.

Larry was waiting for him to go on, but he didn't.

'I'm sorry, I forgot,' Larry said. 'Your name is...'

'Raymond.'

'Right, Raymond. Is Owen at home?'

'Owen doesn't live here.'

'Really?' Maybe showing up unexpected had been a waste of time after all. 'Where is he living now?'

'No idea.'

Okay, this was odd. A stepfather doesn't know where his stepson is living?

'Well you must have some idea.'

'It's not my problem anymore.'

Still an asshole.

'When did he move out?' Larry asked.

'Yesterday,' Raymond said.

This piqued Larry's interest. Maybe there were no facts yet, but the coincidences were adding up. Owen just happened to move out the day after Deborah Berman disappeared?

'Do you mind if I come in for a few minutes?' Larry asked.

Raymond did seem to mind, but he moved aside anyway.

In the house, Larry glanced around. There was a putrid odor, as if someone had been farting.

'What's this about?' Raymond asked. 'Owen in some kind of trouble?'

'Not necessarily,' Larry said.

'Well, he was nothin' but trouble when he was living here,' Raymond said. 'Didn't do any chores, was only out for himself. He had to get on in the world so I did him a favor.'

'Favor?' Larry asked, realizing that Raymond's breath reeked of beer and that he was probably drunk.

'I told him that it was time to get out, fend for himself.'

'Oh, so you *kicked* him out?'

'Damn right. Kid's eighteen years old and he was living here like a child, eating free food, waiting for meals to be cooked for him. What kind of man does that?'

'Do you know if Owen was involved at all with a woman named Deborah Berman?'

'You mean the one I heard about on the news?'

'Yeah, her.'

Raymond laughed.

'What's funny?'

'Just the idea of Owen with a woman. I can't picture that at all. If you want to know the truth, I think the kid's a faggot.'

Larry wanted to punch this drunk asshole in his gut, follow with a big uppercut to his jaw that would snap his head back and splatter blood.

But, calmly, Larry said, 'If you can avoid the slurs, I'd appreciate it.'

'Slurs? What slurs?'

'Faggot,' Larry said.

'Since when is a faggot a slur? Is that some new political correct bullshit that's goin' around?'

'Hello?' a woman said.

Larry looked over toward the entrance to the kitchen, saw Owen's mother, Linda Harrison, along with a young boy. That's right, Owen had a little brother.

'Larry Walsh, Bedford police.'

'Yes, I remember meeting you before. Is there some sort of problem?'

'I'm handling it,' Raymond said. 'Go back to the table.'

'No, stay,' Larry said, not letting this homophobic prick usurp him. He said to Linda, 'Do you know how I can get in touch with Owen?'

Her eyes shifted, maybe nervously. 'No... no, I don't.'

'Is there a number where he can be reached?'

'Yes,' Linda said and gave Larry Owen's cell number. Then she asked, 'Is Owen okay?'

'Yes, as far as I know,' Larry said. 'I just need to ask him some questions. Do you know anything about a relationship he's been having?'

Raymond said, 'I already tol –' and Larry shouted, 'I told you to shut your fuckin' mouth, okay?'

That felt good. Linda seemed to like it too.

'No,' she said. 'No, I don't.'

'I do,' the boy said.

'What's your name?' Larry asked him.

'Kyle.'

'What did he tell you, Kyle?'

'He didn't tell me, but I heard him talking about stuff with Elana.'

'Elana Daily, right?'

'Owen doesn't have a girlfriend,' Raymond said. 'He wouldn't know what to do with a girlfriend.'

'Hey,' Larry said. 'I'm telling you for the last time.'

'I'm sorry, but I'm confused,' Linda said to Larry. 'Why are you looking for Owen? What does this have to do with Elana Daily?'

'It has nothing to do with Elana,' Larry said. 'You've probably heard on the news about Deborah Berman, though. I'm just trying to find out if Owen had any involvement with her.'

'Involvement? What kind of involvement?'

'Perhaps some sort of relationship?'

'Oh, really?' Now Linda was upset. 'Just like the last time when you harassed us with that ridiculousness about Owen and Melanie when there was no evidence at all that Owen had anything to do with anything?'

'That's right,' Larry said. 'And you were his alibi.'

'That's right,' Linda said.

'Are you protecting your son again?'

'Hey, what the fuck?' Raymond said.

'Are you?' Larry persisted.

'No,' Linda said.

Larry looked at Linda for a few extra seconds, getting a vibe she was lying about something, then said, 'Do you know where he was Saturday night from seven to ten p.m.?'

Linda's eyes widened. 'This is harassment,' she said.

'My wife's right,' Raymond said. 'This is fuckin' bullshit.'

'If you know anything,' Larry said, 'you have to let us know.'

'Yeah, we'll let you know,' Raymond said, 'with our fuckin' lawyer we'll let you know.'

'It could save a woman's life,' Larry said to Linda, 'and you know what your son's capable of.'

'I'm gonna sue your ass,' Raymond said. 'Watch me.'

Larry didn't see the point in staying any longer.

'Well, thanks for all your help,' he said sarcastically.

Then, as he was heading toward the door, Kyle said, 'I saw them together once.'

Larry stopped, turned, said, 'Saw who together?'

'Owen and Justin Berman's mom.'

'What're you talking about?' Linda asked him.

'Go on,' Larry said to Kyle, 'Where'd you see them?'

'At swim practice once, like last month,' Kyle said. 'I followed Owen up to a classroom, wondering where he was going… and then I looked in and saw him and Justin's mom, and they were doing all this weird stuff.'

'What kind of weird stuff?' Larry asked.

'Really weird stuff… They had their clothes off.'

Now Larry was bending down, to talk to Kyle at eye level.

'This is very important,' he said. 'Do you know where your brother is now?'

'He's just a dumb kid,' Raymond said, 'what's he know?'

'Shut the fuck up!' Larry screamed at Raymond. Then to Kyle, calmly, 'Do you know where your brother is?'

'No.' Kyle looked and sounded scared. 'I'm not gonna get him in trouble, am I?'

Larry rushed out of the house, calling Nick, telling him that Owen was probably their guy.

'I'll get the word out immediately,' Nick said, 'and we'll try to track down the GPS. What's Owen's number?'

Larry gave it to him.

In the car, Larry called Owen, figuring maybe he'd just pick up. He was surprised when he did.

'Hello.'

'Owen?'

'Yeah.'

Larry went for a relaxed tone. 'This is Detective Larry Walsh with the Bedford Police.'

Pause, then Owen said, 'Okay,' sounding suspicious.

Larry didn't want to tip him off that they were onto him. Calmly, he said, 'I'm calling about Karen Daily. I understand you were at the country club when Deborah

Berman and Karen were fighting the other day, and I just wanted to meet with you, to ask you a few questions about –'

The call disconnected.

Larry called back, but got voicemail. He'd probably turned his phone off – so much for tracking his GPS.

'Shit, goddamn it!'

Larry knew he'd made a mistake; calling Owen had been impulsive, stupid. Now Owen might try to run or, worse, he might go to his girlfriend, Elana Daily's house, if he wasn't there already.

He called Karen, to try to warn her, but the call went right to voicemail as well. Did Owen turn her phone off?

It was all Stu's fault. Larry was usually level-headed, rational, but tonight he had too much on his mind, wasn't thinking straight, and now a suspect who may have killed two women, might get away, or might kill again.

'Fuck you too, Stu!' Larry shouted as he sped toward Karen Daily's house on Savage Lane.

21

FOR MARK, IT WAS all hitting home. For the past couple of days he'd been so absorbed with being angry at Deb for causing a drunken scene in the country club, and asking for a divorce, that he hadn't really considered the possibility that she could be dead. But after he returned from Karen's, trying to get her to confess – he'd recorded their conversation on his phone just in case – he was overwhelmed by everything that had happened and broke down crying. He didn't want the kids, especially Justin, to see him so upset, so he went into the bathroom and sat on the closed toilet seat, sobbing so uncontrollably that he used up almost an entire roll of toilet paper to soak up his runny nose and tears. His thoughts were jumbled, but mostly he kept flashing back to the good times with Deb, when they'd first met in the city at that bar on Amsterdam Avenue. She was with friends and he was with friends and his first words to her were, 'Do I know you?' They joked about that for years, because it had sounded like such a shitty, corny pickup line, but the truth was he really did think he knew her. There was something familiar about her, she was like an old friend. When they were dating, those first few years, they were best friends, went everywhere together – Europe, Mexico, to a share in the Hamptons in summers – and he couldn't imagine that things would ever change. But now, as he was crying, and thought, *Do I know you*? It had a different meaning, because somehow, after getting married, kids, a house in Westchester, she had become a total stranger. He had no idea how things had changed so drastically, gotten so fucked up. All those things should have brought them closer together, not farther apart, but look what had happened. He didn't know how they'd gotten from point A to point B, from the smiling, happy kids at that Upper West Side bar, to *this*. They weren't even the same people. They'd become characters in a movie, strangers.

Now Mark was thinking about Jimmy Stewart in *It's a Wonderful Life*. Like Stewart, Mark just wanted one more chance to do it over, do it right. Although everything had gone to hell lately, he still loved Deb, and he still needed her, and the kids loved her and needed her too. If he could just rewind a few years, no five years, okay five years, to when things were still good he wouldn't let things unravel, he wouldn't. He'd go to counseling, go on date nights, go on more trips, have more sex, read more books, go to more fuckin' period movies, do whatever he had to do to keep his head in the marriage. If he could do it again, he'd stay away from Karen Daily, know that she was his Kryptonite, that she could bring him down. He couldn't see it then, but he'd fucked up like a lot of married men do, had fallen for the hot divorced chick next door. He was weak, okay? Shoot him. But next time he'd see it coming, when that train came barreling down the tracks right toward him, he wouldn't just stand there like an idiot with a big dumb smile on his face and let it run him over. He'd jump off the track way before the train ever got there.

Riley was right about Karen. She'd been trying to suck Mark in for years and maybe she panicked after the Lerners' party, after Mark had held her hand and let go too soon, and she was afraid she wouldn't get what she wanted, that he'd never leave Deb, so she did it herself, met Deb somewhere and killed her. Yes, killed her, Mark wasn't in denial anymore; he was ready to accept the truth. The more he thought about it, the more sense it made. That was why Karen had made out like she was upset that Mark had held her hand, because she was trying to twist everything around, make out like she was the victim. Trying to make Mark believe that he was imagining their connection – yeah, right. She was in love with him; she was probably obsessed. That was why she had been texting with him all the time since her marriage ended, and why she was dating all those guys – to make Mark jealous. It was so obvious to Mark now, how twisted Karen was. During her divorce Karen used to complain to Mark about how her ex Joe's lawyers had accused Karen of being 'unstable.' See? It all made sense now, every piece to the puzzle fit. Mark had taken Karen's side, been her 'shoulder to lean on,' because he was getting sucked in, because he was in a bad marriage, but now the Kool-Aid drinking was over, and he understood what had been going on, he finally got it: Karen was an obsessed psycho who'd sucked him in to her sticky web and killed his wife. He didn't know how he'd ever forgive himself.

When Justin knocked on the bathroom door, asking Mark if he was okay, he said, 'Yes, fine, I'm just going to the bathroom.'

'You've been in there a long time.' Justin sounded upset.

'Give Daddy some privacy, okay, Justin?'

'I'm scared.'

Now Justin was crying. Shit, Mark wanted to be strong for his son, but he looked like a mess himself. He rinsed his face with cold water, toweled dry, then left the bathroom. Justin was standing there, crying, shaking. He wasn't a tall kid, he was one of the shortest kids in class; he looked particularly small right now.

Mark picked him up, holding him, unable to hold back tears himself, and said, 'I'm scared too, kiddo. We're all scared.'

Remembering saying, *Do I know you?* to Deb, Mark sobbed harder. But then he fought harder to stop crying, to be strong for his son.

'Is Mommy coming home?' Justin asked.

Mark didn't want to lie. He was done with lying, with game playing. It was time to grow up, be a fucking man.

'I don't know,' he said. 'I hope so.'

Crying, Justin said, 'I want Mommy back, I just want Mommy back.'

'We all want her back,' Mark said, proud that he was no longer crying. 'You're going to be a man soon. Men have to be strong.'

Then Mark was suddenly aware of the warm dampness on Justin's backside and realized he'd wet his pants again. He wasn't angry, though. He just wanted to take care of his son, make him feel better.

'Let's go upstairs and get you out of these clothes, okay?' Mark said.

Justin was light enough for Mark to pick up, but too heavy to carry up the stairs. So he put him down and walked his son up to his room, holding his hand. Mark noticed the door to Riley's room was shut. He knew that regaining his daughter's trust would be a much bigger challenge.

He laid out some new clothes for Justin and then got a call from a number he didn't recognize.

'Mark?'

It was a guy, voice was kind of familiar. He sounded rushed, frantic.

'Yeah.'

'Larry Walsh, Bedford Police.'

'Did you find Deb?' Mark asked with no hope. He was ready for the worst, to hear that she'd been raped and her naked, mangled body had been found.

Riley came into Justin's room, asking, 'Did they find her? What's going on?'

'No.' Walsh still sounded harried, out of breath. 'Do you know if Karen's home now?'

'I'm not sure… I think so. Why?'

'She could be in danger.'

'What? Why?'

'Does she have a landline?'

'Yes, but –'

'Just give me the number.'

Mark gave it to him, said, 'What the hell is going on?'

'I believe your wife was having a relationship with a guy named Owen Harrison and that Owen could be at Karen's house now.'

'Owen *who*?' Mark asked.

'Who're you talking to?' Riley asked.

'Owen Harrison,' Walsh said. 'He's eighteen years old, and he could be dangerous. If Karen contacts you tell her to lock herself in a room and that help is on the way.'

'I don't understand,' Mark said. 'What does this have to do with my wife? And what do you mean, *relationship*?'

Walsh had ended the call.

'Jesus Christ.' Mark cocked his arm, ready to toss the phone against the wall, but stopped himself.

'What's going on?' Riley asked.

'Nothing,' Mark said. 'Just a weird call from the police.'

'Weird how?'

'It's okay, I'll handle it,' Mark said.

Riley glared at him, then went into her room and slammed the door.

Mark was angry and confused. Karen could be in danger and Deb and an eighteen-year-old were having a relationship? This didn't make any sense at all. There was no way some guy, especially an eighteen-year-old, would have any interest in Deb and it was even more ridiculous that Deb would be able to keep something like that a secret. After all, Mark wasn't one of those guys who's so lost in his own world that he can't see what's going on right in front of him. He was sharp, he was tuned in. If his wife were cheating on him he'd sure as hell know about it. Why were the police wasting time with their ridiculous theories when they should be investigating Karen?

He went down to his office and went online, searching for PI's. Fuck the police, Mark was going to solve this case on his own. He was sick of sitting back, being the victim, waiting for things to *happen*. It was time for Mark Berman to take charge.

'Dad, I need to talk to you.' Riley had an angry, bitchy tone.

'Look, we need to stop this right now,' Mark said, feeling good taking charge. 'Listen to me, actually listen. I was not, was *not* having an affair with Karen. We were good friends, that's it. *Were*, past tense.'

'Whatever,' Riley said. 'I just got a weird text from Elana that her boyfriend's there saying he's going to kill her and Matthew and her mom. She sounded really scared.'

'Elana's boyfriend?' Mark was trying to process this. 'Who's Elana's boyfriend?'

'His name's Owen, and he's really weird, and Elana sounded serious.'

.'Owen *Harrison*?' Mark asked.

What the fuck?

'Yes,' Riley said.

'Who's Owen Harrison?'

'He used to go to my school. He works at the country club.'

Wait, Mark thought he knew Owen, the tall, doofy kid who did landscaping?

'Why is he threatening the Dailys?' Mark asked.

'She didn't say. Dad, I'm really scared.'

An idea was coming to Mark.

'You sure he's Elana's boyfriend, not Karen's?'

'What?' Riley asked.

Yeah, okay, this made sense. The police had it wrong, of course they did, because they've had it wrong all along. *Karen* was having an affair with Owen, not Deb. After all, Karen was sleeping around, on all those dating sites, and everybody knew it, everybody talked about it, so why not an eighteen-year-old? Maybe she was experimenting, just wanted to see what it was like with a younger guy. Yes, yes, that's what was happening. But how did Deb figure into it? Mark's mind was racing now, dozens of ideas hitting him at once. The one he liked most was that Karen and Owen wanted money to run away, or buy something, so they figured they'd kidnap Deb and hold her hostage for ransom. Maybe they were holding Deb someplace, maybe even in Karen's house. It was Deb who was in danger, not Karen. Yes, yes, Mark was convinced this was all happening, that he'd solved the mystery.

'Wait here,' he said, heading toward the front door.

'Where are you going?' Riley asked.

'To bring your mother home.'

'*What*? Shouldn't you call the police?'

Mark left the house and he headed toward Karen's. He wanted a do-over, like Jimmy Stewart. He wanted to go back in the past to four years ago, or to whatever the point was when he felt unhappy in his marriage. There had to be a first time that he'd first thought, *I want out*, when he'd stopped focusing on Deb, and started fantasizing about Karen and he wanted to go back, make a better decision, tell himself to stop fantasizing. He'd tell himself, *You think you can handle it but you can't.* Fantasies seem great, but they're just gateway drugs. You need more and more and then, when reality kicks in, you're totally fucked.

Mark rang Karen's doorbell, remembering meeting Deb at the bar on the Upper West Side twenty-two years ago. That night he'd thought she was the most amazing woman in the world. For years he'd forgotten this feeling; it had been buried somewhere, under all the fantasies, all the bullshit, but now it was out, now he remembered. This was his chance to get his life back, and he wasn't going to blow it.

He kept ringing, but she wasn't coming to the door. Shit, what if time was running out?

He went around to the garage. She left a key under the mat there. Mark had warned her not to do it, that it was a security risk, but obviously Karen didn't give a shit about what he, or anybody else, thought. She was only thinking about herself.

He went in to the storage area, heard voices coming from upstairs in the kitchen. A boy, probably this Owen asshole, was yelling. Mark didn't want to go empty-handed. He needed something, a weapon. From a basket of sports stuff, he grabbed an aluminum baseball bat and crept up the stairs.

'Leave? What're you talking about?'

Karen didn't get why Owen seemed so upset. Then, remembering what he'd said about his stepfather, she thought, *Could it be that*?

'We'll take your car,' Owen said. 'Is there gas in your car?'

'Did you call home?' Karen asked.

'What?' Owen asked.

'Did something happen at home? Is your brother okay?'

'It has nothing to do with my brother, but you're right, we'll have to come back to get him, or send him money to come to us. You don't have time to get dressed. Just bring your pocketbook, your credit cards. You'll take a coat downstairs, buy clothes in Canada.'

'Canada? *What*?'

'That's where we're going.'

'Owen, you have to stop this, you're not making any sense.'

He grabbed her hand, like he had before. He was squeezing so hard it hurt.

Then her phone chimed. Owen rushed to it, on the bed, and shut it off.

'We don't have time to bullshit around,' Owen said. 'Your ex-husband's gonna have to take care of Elana and Matthew for a while.'

He was trying to pull her out of the bedroom. *What was happening*?

'Let go,' she said. 'Stop it!'

She managed to free herself, but he grabbed her by the shoulders, pushed her back up against the wall, and said, 'Shut up and listen to me, you stupid bitch!'

The rage in his eyes was terrifying. She was normally so intuitive, was able to read people so well. How had she missed this?

'Sorry.' He let go, trying to cover with a smile, but it was too late. 'I… I didn't mean to do that. It's just we have to get out of here, fast, and I can't explain everything now. But I will when we get there, I promise, okay?'

Doing her best to stay calm, and to calm *him*, Karen said, 'I don't know what's going on, but it's going to be okay, *you're* going to be okay.'

But he went into a rage again, grabbing her again, this time closer to her neck, and screamed, 'Nothing's okay! You're driving me out of here, you don't have a fucking choice!'

In her peripheral vision, Karen saw that Elana and Matthew had just entered the room, appearing shocked.

'*Owen*?' Elana said. 'What're you *doing*?'

'Let go of my mother,' Matthew said protectively.

'Call for help!' Karen shouted. 'Run!'

Elana grabbed Matthew and they ran out of the room.

'Shit!' Owen shouted and chased after them.

Karen followed, dashing out of the bedroom, hearing the bathroom door slam. Then in the hallway she saw Owen banging on the door, cursing – good, Elana and Matthew had locked themselves inside. She headed downstairs, stumbled to her knees, got up, and continued down. She wanted to call the police, then remembered the reporters right outside, but it was too late. She was on her way toward the front door when Owen grabbed her from behind, a hand over her mouth, muffling her scream. He dragged her back into the kitchen and when she was finally able to free herself enough to call out for help she saw that he was holding a knife, one of *her* knives, the big one she used to chop steak.

'Scream and I'll kill you,' he said, now with the blade against her throat. 'Understand?'

She nodded slightly, but it was enough to poke the

underside of her jaw with the tip of the blade. She was probably bleeding.

She heard the patter of Elana and Matthew's feet on the stairs. She wanted to yell out, 'Go back,' but when her mouth started to move she felt the blade again.

The kids entered the kitchen and Elana shrieked, like a girl in a horror movie.

Owen cut her off with, 'Shut the fuck up, or I'll cut her.'

Karen hoped Elana's scream was loud enough for someone outside to hear.

'Do that again, your mother gets cut,' Owen said. 'I'm not kidding around either.'

The phone in the kitchen, the landline, starting ringing.

'Did you call anybody?' Owen asked Elana.

'No,' Elana said, but Karen knew she was lying.

'You better not've,' Owen said.

Elana crying said, 'W-w-why… why are you doing this?'

Matthew was crying too, looking terrified.

'Let's leave the kids like you said,' Karen said. 'Just take me, I'll go wherever you want.'

'Yeah right, so the kids can run and call the cops? What, you think I'm an idiot, like one of those retarded kids you work with?'

The phone stopped ringing. Karen was afraid that Owen would kill her children. He seemed *that* crazy.

'No, they won't do that, I'll make them promise. We can just go out to the car in the garage, drive away, go to Canada. Isn't that where you said you wanted to go? Canada?'

'I need rope,' Owen said. Then to Matthew, 'You know where there's rope?'

Matthew looked at Karen.

'It's okay, tell him,' Karen said.

'There's some in the basement,' Matthew said, amazingly calm.

Karen was so proud of her son.

Please, God, give my boy a chance to grow up.

'Go get it and come back right away, or I'll kill your mother and sister, understand?'

'Yes, you stupid asshole,' Matthew said, and he headed down to the basement.

Elana, crying, said, 'Owen, please just stop this. Just let us all go and everything'll be okay, I promise.' She came toward him with her arms out. 'Please, Owen, just stop, please just stop.'

'Elana, get back,' Karen said.

But Elana continued toward Owen saying, 'Please, please…' and when she got a few feet away, he lashed out at her with the knife, and she collapsed onto the floor. Karen screamed, thinking Elana had been stabbed, but then saw that he hadn't stabbed her, he'd just backhanded her across the face. Elana's nose was bleeding.

Karen broke away from Owen, trying to get to Elana, to help her up, but Owen grabbed her again, had the knife back up to her throat. Then Matthew dashed back up into the room with the rope, stopping when he saw his sister holding her hands over her bloodied face.

'Give it to me,' Owen said to him.

Matthew remained, staring.

'Do what he says,' Karen said.

Matthew hesitated for a few seconds, then went over, and handed the rope to Owen and spit in his face at the same time.

Owen, not even bothering to wipe away the saliva, said, 'Sit in the chair' to Matthew.

Matthew didn't move.

'If you make me ask you again your mother and

bitch sister die,' Owen said.

'Sit,' Karen ordered Matthew.

Matthew reluctantly sat in a chair at the table.

Then Owen cut off some rope with the knife, gave it to Karen, then said, 'Tie him up.'

As Karen started to tie up Matthew, Owen went to Elana, grabbed her by the arm and said, 'Get up, come on, get up, you dumb spoiled brat,' and then pulled over toward the table and said, 'Sit.' Then he said to Karen, 'When you're through with him, do her, then we're leaving, okay?'

Karen was tying the knot around Matthew loosely, so it wouldn't be hard for him to escape, but Owen saw this, and said, 'It better be as tight as you can get it, or I'll kill them instead.'

Elana sobbed, saying, 'W-w-why... why...'

'Don't be afraid,' Karen whispered into Matthew's ear, 'Don't be afraid,' and she tied him tighter, telling herself that maybe this wouldn't be so bad. The reporters were right outside – the kids would be found. Let Owen take her. As long as the kids were okay, she didn't care what happened to her.

'See, this is how it could've been all the time around here,' Owen said. 'With a man around here, a *real* man in control. That's what you guys have been missing. Somebody who makes rules, knows how to discipline. But now we're gonna have to wait to have our happy family, but don't worry, it'll happen, it'll happen.'

Then Karen's empathy skills kicked in, and she felt what he was feeling. It was what she did every day at her job – she got into the heads of the autistic kids she worked with; she understood them.

'You're not angry at us,' Karen said.

'What?' Owen was confused.

'This isn't about us, it's about your stepfather, isn't it? He hurt you and you want to hurt us to make up for it. It's okay that you feel this way, it's natural. Anybody would feel the way you do right now, but that doesn't mean you have to act on it. You can be stronger. You can rise above it.'

Karen was straining for the right words to connect with Owen, but it was so much simpler to interact with non-verbal kids.

'I said we're leaving now.' He gave her more rope. 'Tie up the little bitch, *tight*, then we're outta here.'

While Karen tied Elana, she whispered, 'It's okay, sweetie, it's okay,' and she was thinking that when she left the house with Owen, or even when they were in the garage, she'd start screaming for help as loud as she could and someone would have to hear her. She didn't care what Owen did to her, she just wanted her kids to be okay, to not suffer anymore.

'Hurry up, and no fuckin' talking,' Owen said.

This switch in Owen had been sudden, something must have sparked it. Things had been so frantic since he came into her bedroom, saying they had to run away, that she hadn't been able to think it through, but wasn't it weird, very weird, that this was happening while the police were searching for Deb? There had to be some connection, some logic.

Then it hit.

'You called her Debbie,' Karen said.

'What?' Owen asked, but he'd obviously heard her.

'Before,' Karen said, 'when you said people had the wrong idea about the whole thing, you called her *Debbie*, like you know her. You do know her, don't you?'

'I don't know what the hell you're talking about,' Owen said.

Karen knew she was right. It explained why Owen was suddenly so desperate to get away, and why Mark had been so lost in his marriage, and maybe why Deb had been acting so paranoid.

'Are you close to her?' Karen asked Owen. 'Is she a friend?'

'Shut up,' he said.

She was on the right track; she could *feel* his thoughts, sense his panic. 'Do you know where she is? Do you know what happened to her?'

'Oh my god,' Elana said to Owen. 'It was *you*.'

'Shut the fuck up.' Owen, enraged, slapped Elana in the face.

'Leave her alone!' Matthew shouted.

Owen slapped Matthew too.

Karen shouted, 'Stop it! Stop it!'

Owen had his hand back, ready to hit her too, but he stopped before he did.

'Don't make me do it,' Owen said to her. Then, as if he was talking to himself, or maybe to a voice in his head, he held his hands over his ears and shouted, 'Will you shut up and stop it with the fucking giggling already?!'

The doorbell rang. Karen hoped the reporters had heard the screaming and were suspicious what was going on. Or maybe it was a cop.

'You can't get away,' Karen said. 'Just do the right thing and turn yourself in. You can get help. You can be happy.'

The bell rang again, a steadier ring.

'She doesn't like you,' Elana said, crying. '*Nobody* likes you. You're a fuckin' psycho.'

'That's not true,' Owen said to Karen. 'Tell her.' He put the knife back up to her throat and, with his face maybe an inch in front of hers, said, 'Tell her the truth. Tell her you love me, or I'll slit your throat right here in front of your kids. Say, "I love you, Owen." Come on, say it. I said, "Say it".'

His face was sweating. His eyes were wide, crazed.

'I-I...'

'Say it. *Say it.*'

'I-I love you, Owen.'

'Louder.'

'I love you, Owen.' Karen was sobbing.

'See?' Owen said to Elana.

Now Matthew was crying with Karen and Elana. The doorbell was still ringing.

'Will everybody just shut the fuck up?' Owen said with his hands over his ears. Then he said to Karen, 'Come with me, and make a sound, I'll slit your throat, understand?'

The bell was ringing repeatedly.

'Stay where you are,' Karen said to her kids. 'I love you both.'

Owen led Karen toward the front door. Karen was thinking about screaming for help. Maybe Owen would kill her, but then whoever was out there would know what was going on, and at least the kids would be saved.

But was this the right thing to do or would it get them all killed?

Karen was about to do it, she was about to scream, when Owen looked in the peephole and said, 'Are you fuckin' kidding me?'

Just an hour ago Owen was having dinner with his new family, starting to connect with his future sexy wife, and then he got that call from that cop, Detective Walsh, the same one who'd once given him a hard time about Melanie, and he knew they'd caught on about Deb. But that was okay – he was a cool-under-pressure kind of dude. When he'd gotten the call, he was smart about it. He didn't talk long, like maybe ten seconds, and then he shut the phone off, hopefully before they could trace it. Then he came up with the new plan – Canada – and it was looking good, he was actually seeing himself and Karen there, living a happy as hell life, but now Mark Berman was ringing the doorbell. Seriously? What the fuck did *he* want?

'Who is it?' Karen asked.

Owen still had the knife to her neck. He didn't want to kill her, he wanted to love her, but he'd wanted to love Melanie and Deb too, and look what had happened to them.

He brought her back to the kitchen and said, 'It's just Deb's idiot husband. Did somebody call him?'

Looking at Elana, he knew it was her. When she went into the bathroom before she'd had her phone with her.

'You little bitch,' he said, 'was that a nice thing to do to your future stepfather?'

He wished he had time to take off his belt and whip her, give her what she deserved.

She was crying again, like a fucking baby. Yeah, she was gonna cry a lot. Just wait.

Meanwhile, Mark was still ringing the doorbell.

Karen was saying shit like, 'It's over now, can't you see?' and 'People are out there, you'll never get away,' but he didn't want to hear any more of it.

'Do what I tell you to do or I'll give you all what you deserve,' he said. Then he heard the giggling, louder than ever, and he said to her, 'And *you* stop it too. I'm warning you, bitch.'

The bell wasn't ringing anymore. Good, Mark had given up; the plan was still on track. They'd leave the kids and go to Canada in Karen's car. Maybe the reporters out there would see the car leave but, whatever, they'd switch cars somewhere, make it over the border to Toronto. Wait, wasn't Niagara Falls up there? They'd go to Niagara Falls first, get married, check into a hotel. Yeah, he could see it clearly now, him and Karen, looking at the waterfall, holding hands.

Then he saw that Karen was looking past him, toward the other side of the kitchen, and he turned and saw dumbass Mark Berman standing there, holding a baseball bat.

'Where is she?' he asked.

Owen grabbed Karen, had the knife close to her throat, and said to Mark, 'Get out of here, you'll get us all killed.'

'I know you two have her someplace. Is she here?'

Karen said, 'Mark, what're you *doing*?'

'I just want my wife back,' he said, coming closer with the baseball bat. 'I know she's here.'

He thought Karen had Deb in here? Jeez, the guy had his head farther up his ass than Owen had ever thought.

'Take one more step, I'll do it,' Owen said. 'I swear to god I'll do it.'

'Mark, just leave,' Karen said.

'Shut up,' Mark said. 'I know what's going on, okay? I know you and this maniac here have been fucking.'

'*What*?' Karen said.

'Is that true?' Elana asked her.

'No, it's not true,' Karen said.

'Hey, don't lie to her,' Owen said, seeing Niagara Falls, hearing the water.

'Oh my god,' Elana said. 'Oh my god.'

'Mom, watch out!' Matthew yelled.

Idiot Mark was charging at them with the baseball bat. He tried to swing it at Owen, but Owen grabbed the barrel with one hand, and jabbed the knife into Mark's neck with the other. Owen wasn't surprised by how much blood there was, and how bright red it looked. He flashed back to his room, the day Melanie told him it was over for good and he'd jabbed those scissors into her throat to shut her up. His mother came in and saw him, with blood all over him, and he was happy because he'd wanted her to see what he'd done. He wished she were here now, to see this – Mark squirming on the floor in a puddle of blood, Karen and the kids screaming.

He thought he heard his mom's voice, or maybe it was Deb's, but it didn't matter because he couldn't understand what she was saying.

The blood puddle was growing.

Driving with the siren on, Larry made it to Savage Lane in about ten minutes, meaning he must have been going at least eighty on the narrow, windy roads. He'd tried Karen's cell a few more times, gotten voicemail, and she wasn't picking up her landline either. He was hoping Owen wasn't there, but unfortunately his instinct hadn't let him down so far.

'He's in the house,' a reporter, a young woman, said as he got out of his car.

'Who?' he asked.

'Mark Berman,' she said. 'He went in through the garage. We just heard screams inside.'

Shit, now what? What the hell was Berman doing in there, trying to play Superman?

Larry didn't want to risk waiting for backup.

'Get the reporters away from the house,' he instructed her. '*Now.*'

Larry called for backup, then, with his gun out, he approached and heard a kid, a girl, maybe a teenager, scream.

Larry couldn't get a view into the house through any of the front windows. He didn't want to break down the door, and wasn't sure he could even do it – well, not fast enough anyway.

Wait, she'd said Berman went in through the garage, right?

He went around the house, to the garage, and saw that the door to the house was open. There was more screaming now – he thought he heard Karen's voice.

Rushing in, up the stairs, with his gun aimed, Larry stopped when he saw Owen, holding a large knife with blood on it. Berman was down, wounded. The kids were tied up, and Karen was looking right at him.

Thinking about Stu, about how much he needed him, Larry aimed at Owen's chest.

'Drop it!' he shouted. 'I said drop it!'

Stu was with him, rooting him on, saying, *Be strong, buddy, be strong.*

Owen's arm, the one with the knife, moved toward Karen, and Larry fired, knowing he'd gotten him right in the heart, but he fired again in the same spot, just to make sure.

Owen was on the floor, Karen was hugging her kids, and Larry was kneeling next to Mark, telling him to 'hang on' and that he was going to be 'okay.' Sirens were getting louder and Larry was imagining Stu, hearing about the news, hearing that Larry was a hero, realizing how much he'd lost, and wanting to be with him forever.

He'd have to want me back now. He'd have to.

22

THE DAY AFTER THE night from hell Riley didn't believe what people were saying about her mom. Even though they'd found a bunch of disgusting texts on Owen's phone, she didn't believe that her mom had really been having an affair, an actual affair, with him, and she definitely didn't believe that he'd killed her.

After her dad got stabbed and Owen got shot to death by that detective, Walsh, there was so much crazy drama at her house with cops and reporters and neighbors coming over to make sure she and Justin were okay that it was a blur for Riley. All she really remembered was somebody, maybe a cop, telling her what had happened and her yelling, 'It's not true, you're lying! Karen did it! It was Karen!' At some point that night, she and Justin were brought to a neighbor's house – the Walkers who lived down the road. Her dad was at some hospital, in critical-but-stable condition. The doctors said her dad was 'lucky.' When Owen stabbed him it had just missed something in his neck and if it had been like a quarter of an inch in another direction he would've died. Riley was happy her father had survived, but she knew she'd never forgive him for having that stupid affair with Karen and ruining their lives.

The next day her grandma Fran and grandpa Allen – her mom's parents – came from Florida so Riley and Justin were able to move back home. Later, Detective Walsh, who they were calling a 'hero,' came to the house to ask Riley about her mother and Owen. He wanted to know if Riley had ever seen them together, or if she had mentioned anything about their affair to her.

'No,' Riley said, 'because she wasn't having an affair.'

They were in the living room. Her grandparents were maybe in the kitchen.

'I understand it's hard for you to accept,' Walsh said, 'but we have text messages –'

'I don't care,' Riley said. 'I know my mother, and I know there's no way she'd be having an affair, an actual *affair*, with the grossest guy on the planet. She'd think that was the biggest joke ever. She'd be laughing about it so hard right now.'

'You have to understand,' Walsh said, 'that people who are having affairs can be very clever. They take precautions, almost like the way spies take precautions. This was why your mom bought disposable phones.'

'How do you know? You can't prove that.'

'Actually we saw her old credit card bills, on the card she kept with her maiden name. Like I said, people who are cheating can be very clever.'

'Maybe she bought the phone for somebody else, for a friend of hers or something.'

'She purchased multiple phones, and the messages Owen received were clearly from your mother.'

'What about Karen and my father? How come you forgot all about them?'

'Because there's no evidence that your father and Karen were having an affair.'

'What're you talking about? It was so obvious to everybody.'

'Sometimes the truth isn't what's obvious.'

'Yeah,' Riley said, 'and what makes you such an expert about all this?'

Walsh stared at her. He crossed his legs, then uncrossed them again, and said, 'Well, it's my job.'

'No, your job is to find out the truth,' Riley said, 'and the truth is that Karen killed my mother, not Owen Harrison.'

Her grandmother rushed into the room and said, 'Everything okay in here?'

'Everything's fine, Grandma.'

Riley waited for her to leave then said to Walsh, 'I know why you're doing this. Because you like being famous, that's why.'

'Excuse me?'

'Your name's in the news, people are talking about you, like you're this big hero. And Owen's dead now, so nobody can prove anything, but you're going around acting like you have all the answers. Meanwhile, you know nothing.'

'Look, you're right.' Walsh's eyes were bloodshot, the lids were puffy; maybe he was tired, but it looked like he'd been crying too. 'We don't have all the answers yet, and that's why I'm here talking to you. Your mother's officially missing, but based on evidence and witness accounts, and information we have about Owen's past –'

'His past?' Riley said. 'You mean his *babysitter*? You can't prove that he killed her either. I read all about that online. Even her parents think she ran away.'

'That's true too,' Walsh said, 'but right now, based

on what we know, and what occurred last night, we're presuming that Owen was responsible for your mother's disappearance.'

'Well, I'm *presuming* that Karen's responsible,' Riley said. 'So what makes you more right than me?'

Finally Walsh gave up and left.

Riley was exhausted. She was up crying all night, missing her mom and hating Karen, and hadn't slept at all. Her grandparents were worried about her and insisted that she keep talking to this grief counselor guy, Dr Adler, who'd been talking to Justin too. Justin had been crying a lot and had peed his pants a couple of times. Riley didn't trust Dr Adler, though, because even though he was acting like her friend, and saying he understood why it was so hard for her to accept the truth, she knew he was just playing mind games, and he actually thought there was something wrong with *her*, that she had a problem, because she didn't want to believe the lies that everybody else was believing. It turned out she was right. He must've said something about her to her grandparents because the next day a shrink arrived to talk to her, and the shrink gave her some kind of drugs to take. Drugs, like she was insane, just because she wanted the police to punish her mother's killer.

On Friday, Riley's grandparents made her and Justin go back to school. It was weird how all the kids were suddenly acting nice to her, even the people who'd posted all that shit on her Facebook just a few days ago. The story was all over the news – not just in Westchester, so the whole country knew about it – and everyone felt sorry for her because of everything she'd been through. Elana wasn't in school, supposedly because she was still recovering from trauma, but Riley knew that Karen was just keeping her home from school, to keep the whole act going. She wanted everyone to believe that her family were victims and were suffering, while she was actually responsible for everything.

Then, when Riley got home from school, her grandparents were in the living room, staring at the TV with the cracked screen. They were both crying.

'What's going on?' Riley asked, hoping that the truth had come out, and Karen had been arrested.

'They found your mother's body,' her grandfather said.

He explained that the police had found her body at the country club, in the woods, not far from where Owen had worked.

Her grandmother came over to Riley, sobbing, and hugged her and said, 'You have to let go now, sweetie. You have to let her rest in peace.'

'Why should I?' Riley asked, not crying at all.

'Because they know what happened now,' her grandfather said. 'They know Owen killed her.'

'How do they know that?' Riley asked. 'Maybe Karen buried the body there to make it look like Owen did it.'

'Please,' her grandmother hugged her tighter. 'You have to stop this craziness.'

Riley wriggled out of the hug, went up to her room, and slammed the door. She spent the rest of the afternoon and evening online, reading the latest news about her mother. They said that she'd been strangled and that skin under her fingernails had Owen's DNA on it, but Riley knew these were just more lies so Detective Walsh could go on playing Mr Hero. Karen had probably found out that Owen's old babysitter had disappeared and knew that Owen would be blamed for the murder. Karen had probably been having an affair with Owen and when she broke up, he got jealous and went to her house to confront her, but that was part of her plan too.

Riley called Detective Walsh a bunch of times, but kept getting his voicemail. She had a feeling he was screening calls. Finally she left a message: 'Hi, this is Riley Berman, and I'm begging you to arrest Karen Daily. She killed my mother, and she'll kill somebody else if you don't stop her. Please, you have to listen to me. Somebody's life depends on this.'

He didn't call her back.

In the morning, her grandfather went to pick up her dad at the hospital. Riley was in her room, writing another email to Walsh. During the night she'd already sent him about ten emails, and she planned to keep sending them until he arrested Karen.

Then she got an IM from Elana: **we're moving to Manhattan today just wanted to say bye**

Okay, this was really weird. She hadn't heard anything from Elana in days, and now she writes, not to say, sorry about your mom, but to tell her she's moving? What the fuck? And why were they suddenly *moving* anyway?

Then it hit Riley. Holy shit, if this wasn't evidence that Karen was the real killer, what was? Yeah, Karen was running away from the police, trying to escape to Manhattan. She thought if she went there, people in Westchester would forget all about her. Or, even worse, maybe she had some secret plan with Riley's dad. She would move to the city first then, eventually, he would want to sell the house and move to the city too. Maybe they were even planning to get married. The idea of Karen, a psycho killer, becoming Riley's stepmother scared the hell out of her. How could her father do this to her? And what about the stupid police? Were they just going to let Karen run away and get away with it?

When her dad came home, Riley barely recognized him. Although he'd been in the hospital less than a week, he looked like he'd aged five years. His face was very thin, and he looked exhausted. After he hugged her grandmother and Justin, he limped over to Riley and hugged her as tight as he could, but Riley's arms remained by her sides.

'I'm telling you right now, that crazy woman isn't going to be my stepmother,' Riley said. 'I'll run away from home, I'll kill myself before I let that happen.'

Her dad looked confused. 'What are you talking about?' His voice was soft and scratchy; it was hard to hear him.

'Yeah, like you really don't know,' Riley said. 'Is that part of your plan too?'

'Riley, stop it, right now,' her grandmother said.

'Plan?' her dad said. 'What plan?'

'They're moving to New York today, then you'll want us to move in with them.'

Now her dad seemed terrified, but Riley didn't get why.

'I don't wanna go to New York,' Justin said.

Mark had opened the front door and was walking as fast as he could.

'Hey, the doctor said you need rest,' her grandfather said.

'Stay back,' Mark said, waving his arms.

'Mark, please!' her grandmother yelled.

'Back, back, back.'

Justin was crying, piss soaking through his pants.

Watching her father limping along Savage Lane, flailing his arms, Riley decided that this must be part of the act too. Detective Walsh had been right about people who have affairs: they always thought they were so clever.

At the hospital, after Mark had heard about the text messages from Deb on Owen's phone, the last thing he cared about was himself. It didn't matter to him if he had to live in pain for his entire life as long as he had a chance to talk to Karen, to apologize to her for the horrible mistake he'd made and to do whatever it took to make things right.

He wished he'd handled the situation differently from the beginning. Now, after being through it all, what he should've done was so clear to him. Pining for the days when he'd met Deb and things were good was ridiculous. Those good times had died out years ago, and he should've been strong enough to admit this to himself. When things had started going wrong in his marriage, he shouldn't have been such a wimp; he should've manned up and divorced Deb. Instead, he'd spent all that time fantasizing about Karen and thinking he was doing the right thing by repressing his feelings and staying in his shitty, hopeless marriage. Meanwhile, Deb had been screwing a teenager, a *teenager*. Worse, Deb had made him feel bad for holding Karen's hand at the Lerners' dinner party. What was up with that? Holding hands was wrong, but fucking a teenager was okay? Mark felt he'd been duped by Deb, his whole marriage had been a big lie. This was what happens when you don't confront a problem head on, when you stay in a relationship past its expiration date, when you let things simmer – the pain for everybody involved gets so much worse.

From the hospital, Mark called and texted Karen, but she wouldn't answer. He didn't blame her for being upset with him for accusing her of kidnapping and killing Deb. But it wasn't all his fault – everybody thought she'd done it, everybody had gotten it wrong. So, okay, he'd messed up, but he'd redeemed himself by saving her life, hadn't he? If he hadn't come into the house with the baseball bat and tried to fight off Owen, Owen might've killed Karen and her kids. Karen had to realize that, she had to understand that, and she had to forgive him for the things he'd said to her. Isn't there a saying that when there's true love there's always forgiveness? Well, if there was ever an example of true love, *enduring* love, it was him and Karen. She had to feel what he felt, she had to.

It was nice to have Deb's parents and Justin visit at the hospital. For some reason, Riley didn't want to come; it was probably too traumatic for her. Several friends stopped by – his boss and his wife, and some people from the country club, including Stu and his wife, Janet. As far as Mark was concerned, Stu and Janet were the model couple. They'd been married as long as Mark and Deb, but at the hospital they were holding hands the whole time and couldn't stop looking at each other.

When Mark heard the news that Deb's body had been discovered, near where Owen worked at the club, he was angry and sad, naturally, but he felt even more foolish for blaming Karen. The idea that she could've killed Deb, or anybody, now seemed ridiculous, absurd. She was a schoolteacher, a *mom*, for god's sake. She was kind and sincere, the opposite of that troubled maniac who'd killed Deb.

The next day, Deb's father drove him home from the hospital, telling him about the memorial plans for Deb, but it was hard for Mark to focus on anything he was saying. At home, he was planning to shower and change into some nicer clothes before he went over to Karen's, but then Riley, acting crazy, told him that Karen and the kids were moving to the city. Mark went outside and saw Karen's car pulling out of her driveway. He limped along Savage Lane, waving his arms, trying to get her attention. He knew he had to just get her to see him. If she just saw him, she'd understand how much he loved her, how much he needed her.

He was trying to scream her name, but his voice was too

weak and he could only say, 'Karen, don't leave me, don't leave me,' in a faint, hoarse tone.

Just look at me, baby, he thought. *Just look at me.*

Karen made the decision to leave Westchester as she watched Owen bleed out on her kitchen floor. She decided there was no way to come back from this, at least not here in Westchester. Too much damage had been done, too much trust had been lost. How could she stay here, in this fish bowl, knowing the way her friends and coworkers had betrayed her, made such horrible assumptions about her? And how could she ever go back to the country club where people had treated her even worse knowing now that, under their warm smiles and polite conversation, they were actually thinking horrible thoughts about her? Maybe time heals some things, but it can't restore trust. When trust is gone, it's gone forever.

On Tuesday morning, after a long night of police interviews and statements to the press and the treatment she and the kids got for trauma, she called the school and gave her notice to her principal, Seth. He seemed surprised and apologized profusely for any inappropriate behavior from himself and other teachers at the school, but Karen maintained a flat, professional tone and thanked him for the opportunity to work on his staff and told him that he would receive a formal resignation letter from her shortly. When she hung up she rattled off the letter, and cc'd it to all of the appropriate people, and then she called a real estate agent to make an appointment to get her house appraised.

That evening, she called the kids down to the living room, sat them down, and announced, 'We're moving to Manhattan.'

If she'd hit them with this a few days ago, they would've

flipped. Elana would've had a huge fit about having to leave all her friends, and having to switch high schools before senior year, and Matthew was very social as well, and his friends were extremely important to him. But now the kids seemed relieved, even excited. Like Karen, they were probably eager for a fresh start, as they'd also lost trust in their friends who'd rushed to judgment and tormented them.

'Manhattan will be awesome, I can go shopping any time I want,' Elana said.

'Yeah, and I can go to Knicks and Rangers games and be closer to Dad,' Matthew said.

Karen still had a lot of resentment toward her ex, for turning on her, and she doubted she'd ever be able to forgive him fully. But since the breakup, she'd never said a harsh word about him in front of the kids, and she wasn't going to start now.

'I'm sure your father would love that too,' she said.

Elana and Matthew hugged her.

'I love you so much, Mom,' Elana said.

'Me too,' Matthew said.

After everything they'd been through, all the trauma, it was nice to see the kids happy, with something to look forward to. She hugged them, squeezing them close, not taking this moment for granted, knowing that as bad as things had been lately, she could still hug her children. Deb Berman would never have another chance to do this.

'I feel like the luckiest mom in the world,' she said.

A couple of days later, an appraiser came and Karen put the house on the market, priced to sell at fifty thousand dollars below the appraised value of $875,000. Karen got right to work packing up and browsing online for apartments in the city. Searching for an apartment on the internet was so much more enjoyable than searching for a man.

She was getting seriously excited about the idea of a new life in Manhattan, of starting over. She didn't know where she'd work, but she was burned out of working at a school setting, and liked the idea of trying to find work at a hospital. Even if she couldn't find a job right away, and things were tight financially, it would be a relief to be in the city, where she could walk for miles all day long without seeing a single familiar face. Ah, to blend in, to be anonymous; the city was going to be such bliss.

Later, Elana, came into her room, got into bed with her, and snuggled close. She hadn't done this in years, since she was a tween, but Karen wasn't surprised because she'd been extremely needy and clingy the past few days.

'I wish we could go tonight,' Elana said sadly. Her face was still bruised from where Owen had hit her.

Karen sensed that Elana was upset about something in particular.

'What's wrong?' she asked. 'Did you read something on Facebook?'

'It's just hard,' Elana said, struggling not to cry. 'People were so mean to me, I can't forgive them. And Riley's been acting like such a total bitch, I hate her so much.'

'I understand, sweetie,' Karen said. 'But this has been a hard time for Riley too. Everybody has their own way of dealing with grief.'

'I know,' Elana said, 'but it's just like so much has happened, you know? And I know, I know it's not her fault. It was Owen's fault, just Owen's fault, but things can never be the same and I... I hate it. I just hate it so much.'

Karen held her daughter, trying to console her, squeezing

her own eyes shut so she wouldn't start crying herself.

'Don't worry, we'll be in the city soon,' she said. 'We'll all have new lives in the city soon.'

The next day they found Deb's body. Karen watched some of the news reports – scenes from the country club, a teary interview with Linda Harrison who swore her son was innocent – but she couldn't take any more of it. She wanted the whole thing to disappear, to be forgotten, but now the reporters were calling again, ringing her bell, wanting quotes from her. She refused to talk to anyone, but they kept harassing her.

Later, lying in bed unable to sleep even with Ambien, Karen thought, *What're we waiting for?* They were miserable here, and the house was starting to feel like a prison. They'd been avoiding the kitchen, so they didn't have to confront their memories of what had happened in there, and they'd been ordering in food for most of their meals or going out to eat. Why wait to move to New York? Why not leave tomorrow?

She didn't give it any more thought. Convinced she was making the right decision for her family, she went back online and booked a hotel in midtown Manhattan, close to Grand Central, and she was so excited that she spent most of the rest of the night packing a few suitcases with clothing, valuables and other essentials, leaving space for the kids to add their stuff in the morning. There was less than a month left in the school year, and she'd work out a way for the kids to complete their requirements at their schools, or maybe register them for summer classes at new schools in Manhattan. It could be difficult to coordinate, but she'd do the best she could. They would move into a permanent apartment as soon as possible and then, when the house was sold, she'd hire movers to pack up everything and move the stuff to the new place. Her hope was that, after tomorrow, she'd never have to set foot in the house again.

Karen finally got back into bed at about five am, but she only slept an hour or two and she was out of bed by seven, feeling fully awake. Besides being excited about telling the kids the news, and getting on with their lives, she was also eager to leave, if possible, before Mark came home.

In the past few days, Karen had been trying to block Mark out. She'd heard on a couple of news reports that he was expected to recover, and she didn't want to know anything else. She just wanted to forget about him and all the misery he'd caused her. He'd been texting her from the hospital and calling, leaving voicemails, and even emailing her and sending her messages on Facebook before she blocked him. She had no idea what he was writing her about; she just wanted him to leave her alone, and ignoring him seemed like the way to go.

While Karen felt awful for Mark's kids, she refused to feel any sympathy for him. The emotional torment he'd put her through had been bad enough, but stupidly trying to play hero and almost getting them all killed had taken things to another level. Deb obviously had had her issues, but Karen understood why she'd had an affair. Being Mark's wife must have been so difficult, so repressive. Yeah, Mark seemed like a great guy on the surface, but he wasn't actually the normal, funny, hardworking guy he seemed to be. He was actually selfish, immature, delusional, and had serious emotional problems. Deb had probably felt trapped, disconnected, helpless in her marriage, and then she'd met Owen, who must've seemed like the perfect escape. This was understandable too; Owen had been a charismatic kid and, admittedly, Karen had felt an attraction to him herself. Karen wished that after her divorce she hadn't hung out with Mark so often, and had become better friends with Deb. If she'd had a chance to talk to Deb, as a friend, she could've advised her to deal with her unhappiness differently. She would've told her to stop acting out, to leave her marriage, and get a divorce. If she'd listened, things could have been so different for everyone.

By noon, Karen had the car packed and the kids in the backseat. Elana was on her iPhone, and Matthew was on his DS. They both seemed giddy, as if they were leaving on a family trip, but Karen knew they were feeling more relieved than excited.

There was no sadness about leaving the house they'd lived in for seventeen years, no final goodbyes. Then, as she pulled away, she glanced in the rearview, and couldn't believe it. Mark was back there, looking like hell, limping along the road, waving his arms. Jesus, would he ever stop?

She focused straight ahead. She knew the memories of the past couple of weeks would never go away, but she hoped that eventually they'd at least fade, and that she'd never have to see Mark's stupid face again.

After she turned the bend, she checked the rearview and couldn't see him anymore. She already felt freer, happier, stronger. With the windows open and the cool air rushing into the car the tension in her body lifted and she was finally able to breathe.

THE END

Acknowledgements

I have immense gratitude to my German publisher, Diogenes Verlag, and my UK publisher, No Exit Press, for their steadfast support throughout my entire career. Margaux De Weck at Diogenes was a major champion of *Savage Lane* from the onset, read each draft of the book, and offered keen editorial insight. My parents have always been my biggest fans and were particularly encouraging while I was writing this novel. My daughter always helps me work through the trickiest plot points, and Jana Rosen and Stan Yarmolowitz were my go-to sources for details of Northern Westchester. And big-time thanks to Jason Pinter at Polis Books, for making the publishing experience so easy and enjoyable, and for giving *Savage Lane* its perfect home in the US and Canada.

About Us

In addition to No Exit Press, Oldcastle Books has a number of other imprints, including Kamera Books, Creative Essentials, Pulp! The Classics, Pocket Essentials and High Stakes Publishing > oldcastlebooks.co.uk

For more information about Crime Books go to > crimetime. co.uk

Check out the kamera film salon for independent, arthouse and world cinema > kamera.co.uk

For more information, media enquiries and review copies please contact Clare > cqoldcastle@gmail.com